STRIPING KAYLA

The woman was perhaps the same age as Charlotte and was entirely bare apart from the thick belt. Her breasts, oiled and heavy, swayed as she paced across the space. Charlotte passed the crop back to Imogen, slipped off both gloves and took the little key from her mouth.

'Your punishment will serve as an example,' she said as she stepped forwards to grip the little padlock, the saliva-coated key easily slipping in, the lock unfastening the belt with a click which made the woman gasp. 'Take it off, face your friends and bend over,' Charlotte ordered.

STRIPING KAYLA

Yvonne Marshall

This book is a work of fiction.
In real life, make sure you practise safe, sane and
consensual sex.

First published in 2004 by
Nexus
Thames Wharf Studios
Rainville Road
London W6 9HA

Penguin Random House is committed to a sustainable future for
our business, our readers and our planet. This book is made from
Forest Stewardship Council® certified paper.

Printed and bound in Great Britain by Clays Ltd, St Ives plc

ISBN 0 352 33881 4

MIX
Paper | Supporting
responsible forestry
FSC® C018179

You'll notice that we have introduced a set of symbols onto our book jackets, so that you can tell at a glance what fetishes each of our brand new novels contains. Here's the key – enjoy!

cp (traditional)

cp (modern)

spanking

restraint/bondage

rope bondage/hojojutsu

latex/rubber/leather/enclosure

fem dom

willing captivity

medical

period setting

uniforms

sex rituals

Prologue

She did not know his name, and was no longer curious. It didn't matter.

He stood at the window, scanning the busy junction far below his apartment, the cigarette issuing a long thin plume of blue-tinged smoke as she admired the necklace he had brought. The pearls were undoubtedly real, although she wouldn't have the first idea how to confirm as much.

The passport, however, was not real. That much she did know. Her own name had vanished, but no great loss – she'd never clapped eyes on her father and her mother was long dead. No blame, and no harm done. She was alive, and nothing else mattered.

'You know you must never come back here,' he said, still staring from the window. She turned to see his reflection in the window, clear against the ultramarine Prague sky. There was no sadness in his voice, but neither was there any hint of threat or warning. He was simply imparting another piece of information, ensuring that she was as fully prepared as possible.

'I will not,' she said quietly, raising the necklace to her chest, bringing the delicate platinum chain behind her head but leaving it unfastened. It was not so much a gift as another accessory, one more accoutrement to add to the various uniforms she'd been issued with, and she would know the proper time and place for its use when it arose. Not now.

He crossed the room slowly, eyes fixed on the ashtray on the old-fashioned triple-mirrored dressing table. She watched him warily as she lowered the necklace carefully into the slender silk-lined presentation box. He stubbed the butt in the shallow glass bowl, burying it among the other identically folded stubs.

'They will be ready now.'

She stood, smoothing the black calf-length dress over her breasts, lingering at the slight bulge of her belly, tugging the material to cling to her hips. The dark eye make-up could not be improved further and her scalp registered the tightening of her hair as the gel hardened. It was the simplest of the uniforms, and, in her experience so far, the most effective. The underwear was light and comfortable and black, the heels high and tight and well broken in. She felt good and knew she looked fantastic. She couldn't wait.

'I'm ready,' she said matter-of-factly, her voice calm and steady.

He slipped the short black silk jacket from the hanger and held it up for her. She took a deep breath, watching her chest rise, the valley of her cleavage shallowing as she turned slightly, admiring the neat flanging cut of the jacket where it hugged her bottom.

The broad-brimmed black hat was the finishing touch, and the dense netting veil provided the anonymity he insisted upon. He waited as she adjusted it, securing it in place with a couple of slender steel pins. For once he didn't interrupt, didn't make some alteration, although she could see him frown as he scanned her up and down, clearly worried.

Eighteen months of preparation in virtual seclusion, utterly dependent on him for survival, were coming to an end and she knew he knew it. She was ready, as ready as she could be, and it was time for him to let her go. Only this final seal of approval to secure.

He led, she followed.

The streets were busy, but they hadn't far to walk. It was another new route for her, still that mild feeling of unease as she mounted the worn stone steps leading into the narrow close, as if the caretaker might suddenly appear and shoo her away, back to the street where she belonged.

The ancient elevator brought them noisily to the sixth floor, but there was no reception committee, no fanfare. He allowed her to exit the antique contraption before slamming both concertina doors firmly shut. The cubicle sat, creaking, awaiting the call of another passenger as she followed him up the flight of shallow steps. The elevator clunked back into life and started its descent as they wound their way upwards, but as they neared the head of the flight he stepped aside, his hand extended to accept hers. She took it gently, felt the firmness of his grip and held his gaze for the few seconds it took for the door to be opened. He looked no sadder or happier than usual. She had always known there would be no long goodbyes with him.

The battered plain-panelled door was fully ajar, but there was barely enough room for it to open fully. She was aware of his footsteps descending quickly, the rhythmic echo reverberating in the tiny vestibule as she pushed open the inner door and squinted to adjust her eyes to the dimness within. Her hands rose to the veil but stopped – difficult as it was to see where she was going, she knew it would be more effective left in place for now. Her former guardian's footsteps were indistinct now, little more than a dull shifting way below. She was alone now. It was up to her.

She allowed the door to creak its way shut behind her, but, as directed, made sure it did not click fully closed. The dimness thickened, and for the first time she was aware of her trepidation. No matter – the bolstering adrenalin was easily manageable, familiar, and she'd learned how to channel it.

The hallway stretched long and thin before her, devoid of any furniture, and of the six available doors, only one showed any signs of life, a dull red band illuminating the dark carpet. She advanced slowly, aware of her reflection in the erratically spaced mirrors along both of the corridor's long walls. The scent was strengthening – cheap perfume, certainly, but another richer aroma, that of good fresh cigar smoke. She took in a deep breath, momentarily closing her eyes, drawing herself up to her full height – all that had passed was dirt and ashes, this was her renaissance.

She pushed the door and advanced, and kept pushing even as the bodies came into view.

The dark-haired woman was on all fours and the smaller brunette was working the strap-on in and out of her from behind. He was sitting on the edge of the bed less than six feet from them, the half-smoked cigar between his teeth as he grinned broadly by way of welcome. He raised the thick tumbler along with his eyebrows as he surveyed her, his lips manipulating the cigar from one side of his mouth to the other. He looked different, thinner than he seemed on the television, but when he spoke the familiarity of his voice was suddenly disconcerting, wildly out of place.

'At last. We got rather fed up waiting. I hope you don't mind that we started without you.'

His accent was stronger in real life, perhaps because he was relaxed, half-pissed. It didn't matter. He wouldn't be getting many more opportunities to speak.

The girl being fucked looked up, drawing her long hair away from her face to get a better view, but her colleague concentrated on what she was doing, her palms gripping the bigger woman's buttocks as she worked the thick pink tool between them.

'Won't you make yourself more comfortable?' he said, the smile wavering now, her silence already having the desired effect. He was getting scared.

She placed a hand high on the door, but remained facing him as she slammed it shut. The girl wearing the strap-on jerked back in alarm, the tool slipping from her friend as she sat back on her calves, hands rising protectively to her small breasts. The tool, gleaming red-veined in the soft crimson light, appeared to waver slightly, as if assessing this new development, as the man stood, the cigar traversing his mouth once more as the smile disappeared.

'I dislike cigar smoke,' she lied, hands clasped behind her back as she mentally checked her posture, the positioning of her feet, the tone of her voice. He would be pouncing on those few words in an effort to ascertain her origin, perhaps hoping to pin her down to a particular region or town. No chance. She was Czech, that much he would know. But no more than that.

She turned her shoulders slightly so that she was squarely facing him. He removed the cigar from between his teeth, looked down at it as if seeing it for the first time, then pressed it into the clear liquid in his glass as his smile made a hesitant, stuttering return.

'I did not mean to offend, it was–' he said.

'Sit down and say nothing more,' she ordered before his apology was complete. He complied instantly, eyes now widened and wary as she stepped nearer the uncoupled brunettes.

The squatting female, her breasts still concealed by her palms, was fearful – perhaps in her mid-twenties (it was hard to tell because of the thick, clumsily applied make-up), she appeared genuinely shocked, unsure what to do. Lowering her hand, she cupped the girl's cheek, eased the loose wisps of hair, gently aligned them with those bunched into the rough ponytail. The girl's eyes remained locked on hers, although the tension was evident in her neck and shoulders. She clearly hadn't been told what to expect.

The older woman was still peering up, had made no effort to conceal her open sex. The tool had left her wide, and the gentle spasming of her buttocks suggested that she was more than ready to resume the subservient role.

'Get up,' she ordered, and the woman did so languidly, breathing deeply as she rose, the defiant eye contact maintained throughout.

She was tall, her hair hanging thick and loose over her shoulders and heavy breasts. Maybe mid-thirties, but she was not beautiful – the eyes were cynical and challenging, as if daring the newcomer to show her something new. But she clearly looked after herself, and her physique was impressive – the long thighs were well tanned and powerful, her breasts lightly oiled, nipples peaked and dark.

The assessment was swift and instinctive – the older woman presented the clearest danger of dissent, so the hard back-handed slap across her face was crucial, decisive. The taller woman glared angrily, her mouth open. The man shifted uneasily, both hands now working about the broad glass, his fingers knitting together.

Carefully, slowly, she raised the veil and folded it back over the hat, her eyes never leaving those of the taller brunette.

'I am Kayla,' she said then, for the first time. She'd practised in private, alone at night, mouthing the words to shadows on the ceiling, convincing herself with every repetition that the identity was hers and hers by right. Now, as the older, undoubtedly stronger woman visibly wilted, she felt the surge of relief overcome by unbridled euphoria – she'd always hoped for the moment to come, for the chance to assert herself in her new role, her new life, but she'd never imagined it would be so utterly thrilling.

The vague sense of dislocation gradually dissipated as she directed them, had them do her bidding without question. The man grimaced and groaned his frustration as Kayla had the smaller brunette stand. After gently stroking the still-damp tool she raised her hand to the older woman and had her sniff her own scent, lick the residue. Then it moved steadily, easily, as if previously choreographed.

The smaller, younger woman unbuckled the toy and Kayla waited patiently as the older woman donned it, adjusting the straps to fit her broader shape. Kayla had the younger woman properly tighten the harness before allowing her to lubricate the end with her mouth. The older woman seemed comfortable with the false cock, keen to use it, and Kayla had to restrain her as she crouched, eagerly gripping her smaller colleague's hips.

Kayla gripped the short thick dildo, only the realistically moulded head protruding from her grip as the older woman strained to contain the strength of her rapid thrusts.

'Steady,' Kayla directed, gripping tighter as the woman breathed deeply, one hand pressing down firmly on the small of the younger woman's back to force her to raise and widen her sex. The warm scent of the women was powerful, invigorating, and Kayla wanted to strip, remove the hat, ream the visible holes, suck on the pendulous breasts now so close. But the self-control had been hard earned, well tested, and she knew she would not succumb. There would be many other opportunities.

She moved the dildo circularly, allowing the woman's thrusts to bring the heavy rubber tool ever closer to the dampening pussy, but it was time to get him ready, cut him some slack before he lost it completely.

'You may remove your clothing, but don't touch yourself,' she said, and he did so swiftly, his expression a mixture of disbelief and utter desperation as he kicked the trousers off together with all of his undergarments in a rabid flurry of limbs.

He was supporting himself on the bed's edge, legs parted, his little penis bloated purple among the hairy mass of hair below his belly, his hips jerking pathetically, chest heaving.

The younger girl was starting to buck. Kayla kneeled, reached below, brushed over the hardened nipples, briefly squeezed the petite tits – she was panting now, groaning lightly as the thick dildo started to register inside her, a little more with each thrust. Kayla kept her eyes on the man as she opened her mouth and stuck her tongue out, the older woman's breast now gently swinging within range of her mouth.

Kayla waited until the man's stare moved from the juncture of dildo and pussy to meet her eyes. She maintained the contact as she engulfed the goose-

8

pimpled breast-flesh between her painted lips, her hand rising away from the thick strap-on, freeing the woman to sink the tool into her whimpering friend.

The impact was immediate and noisy as the vacuum created by the removal of Kayla's hand was filled with the collision of the opposing mounds of flesh, the dildo disappearing fully as the women slammed into one another, the smaller bucking as hard as the elder fucked, and Kayla dropped her hand to the cleft of the older woman, fingers searching for her anus as the strong thighs pistoned the strap-on into the already full pussy.

The man had thrust his head back, was making noises of his own, his arm muscles now showing through his considerable layer of fat as he gripped the bedcovers, knuckles pale and shuddering. Kayla rose, stepped over the older woman's calves, and positioned herself directly in front of him. He opened his eyes, seemed alarmed to see her so close – she did not take her eyes off him as she reached down and swiftly located his testes, bunching them close together before squeezing hard, releasing him for only a split second before squeezing again, the pumping action in perfect synchronisation with the heightening shrieks of the girl being fucked behind her. The man looked down at Kayla's hand, then beyond her to the frantically fucking women, and Kayla stuck out her tongue-tip, drawing it to complete a circle about his parted lips as he grunted and came over her forearm and jacket sleeve, her hand still pumping his balls.

Kayla released his testicles while gently pushing his chest with her other hand. He flopped back onto the high bed, cock still twitching and dribbling as she stood.

It had taken only minutes, but as she watched him close his eyes, face flushed, the girls still noisily pumping one another behind her, she allowed the giddiness to wash over her. Her skin felt strangely taut, ultrasensitive, and her own need to find release, satisfaction was beginning to surface, as if perhaps this new body, this new persona would be the vehicle to take her to experiences previously only imagined.

But for now, her business was done and she'd taken the first tottering steps as Kayla. The mentor would get his feedback, further instructions would follow. And then?

It didn't matter. She would go wherever she was sent, do whatever she was told, no matter how irksome or distasteful the task – she had earned the right to adopt the name and mantle of Kayla and she would never allow anyone to take the title from her. Never.

One

Charlotte clicked her heels impatiently as the security guard neared the doors.

Great fat berries of rain slapped onto the pavement as the guard squinted through the thick tinted glass. Another London summer evening. She smiled, he didn't. But there was a click and a dull hum and the right-hand panel parted from its neighbour to allow her access.

The air conditioning inside the arcade was refreshingly cool on her bare legs – the August humidity had been intensifying for almost a week, and even now, at almost ten in the evening, the capital sweltered stickily with no breeze for relief.

She could feel the guard's eyes scanning her from toe to top as she advanced towards the escalator. He knew full well who she was, and he should have had that door open for her. She'd have to have a word with Blair. But that could wait. For now, best to concentrate on one thing at a time.

The arcade was, of course, completely deserted. Even on the busiest shopping days it was something of an oasis as the security chaps were ever so vigilant about barring entry to those who appeared unlikely to be customers of the top-rated jeweller's and couture outlets the mall had been designed to house

11

and protect. There would be cleaners around the place, but none were in evidence as she passed the gleaming shop-fronts loaded with fantastic silverware, artfully placed sparkling mirrors compounding the impression that every facade led to an Aladdin's cave of opulence.

The echo of her heels on tile reverberated up and down the broad, gently curving passageway. Although she'd been a frequent customer since the place had opened, it was always unsettling, rather sinister to experience the atmosphere at night – the sooner she got it over and done with the better. She stopped, suddenly wary. The ground seemed to tremble beneath her toes, vibrations, barely perceptible but definite enough. The faint juddering slowed and ceased – just a Tube train passing deep below.

But then, again, a sound. A person. Was if from further along the passage, or should she retrace her steps, scan the store-fronts again for evidence of an open door? She decided to advance. Realising her heels were too noisy she slipped them off, holding both shoes in one hand as the high, muffled cry came again – definitely nearer now.

The phone call flicked back into her mind, still tormenting her, and she had to struggle to dismiss it again, straining now to concentrate on the task in hand. The light overcoat was still zipped, so she slowly, carefully lowered and released it to flap open. It might be too noisy later. Another welcome wash of processed air across her belly and chest where the thin cotton was not clinging to her. Having forsaken a bra the brush of the rather rough material was pleasantly abrasive against her nipples, but she would much rather remove the clothes entirely. The chance would come soon.

She slipped off the raincoat and folded it over her forearm, her shoes dangling, swinging gently from her fingers as she looked up to the vaulted glass ceiling. As her eyes closed and she suspended her breathing, the sound came again, now guttural, male. She enjoyed the hunt, the anticipation, but she didn't have too much time to waste on preliminaries this evening. It would have to be as short and sweet as reasonable given the circumstances.

A dull electronic whirr brought her eyes open to focus on the tiny camera that was turning to find her. That bloated guard, sitting at his little desk with his bank of monitors, playing with his little joystick. She moved on silently towards the carpet of soft blue light spilling across the concourse, and as the boutique came into view she couldn't help smiling – a bridal outfitter's.

The shutters had not been drawn down over the two huge windows, but the door was slightly ajar. No doubt the security guard would be watching her even now, as he had surely watched the others enter earlier, and how keen must the wretch now be to see just what was happening inside. The cries were clear now, intermittent, with some evidence of restraint, but she could already picture roughly what was going on. Time to find out for sure.

The door opened easily, soundlessly, and she was inside, her bare toes registering the coolness of the marble flooring as she crouched, using the broad high pay-point to conceal her entry.

She placed the light raincoat on a shelf beneath the unit and steadied herself with one hand as she slipped the heels back on. As soon as she walked they would know she'd arrived, if they didn't already.

Now, with time to assess the man's sounds at closer quarters, it was clear he was near, somewhere down on the left of the room. She peeked out – the navy-blue carpeting in the recess of the boutique was banded with lighter strips where the spotlighting was mixing, morphing the cool bands, and the effect was rather maritime, vaguely hypnotic.

A gleam caught her eye, and there, close to the wall which served to separate the changing area from the reception, white satin shoes gleamed pearly blue in the shifting light. Only the lower calves were visible, probably stockinged although she couldn't yet be sure, but the tensing of the muscles, the pointing of the toes within the beautiful low-heeled slip-ons told Charlotte that the wearer was desperate to get busier, to part those feet and advance on what she being required to attend to so patiently. He was so fucking predictable. They all were.

Charlotte stood, arched her shoulders back, felt several of her smaller neck muscles unsnap their tension. Perhaps it would do her some good anyway – a chance, however brief, to let off steam.

The instant she stepped from behind the high desk and her heel clicked dully against the floor, the legs at the partition tensed, toes drawn beneath as if ready to stand, but even as Charlotte approached, tugging lightly at the blouse to bring it away from her perspiring flesh, she saw his hand on her piled, curled hair, and sure enough she was sucking him as he reclined in the armchair. He kept his eyes shut as Charlotte passed the partition, her balance adjusting to the deep carpet as the heels were silenced. And he knew.

Of course he knew. His ignorance was immediately infuriating, precisely the sort of inexcusable bad manners he'd never quite managed to control. And the girl knew now too, but with his hand so firmly in her hair, working her head around his exposed cock, she was in no position to acknowledge Charlotte's arrival.

14

'What did I tell you before?' Charlotte asked quietly, but her words smashed the silence. The girl sat bolt upright, the man's fat cock still firmly in her grip, shimmering with saliva, and she even continued to stroke him, the red fingernails firmly encircling him. He turned his face to Charlotte and allowed a deep satisfied groan to emerge as he scanned her standing there in her little black skirt and loose top. He lingered at the sight of her nipples, and she watched him study one, then the other, the smile slipping from his face as the girl suddenly squeezed him hard, her nails sinking into the reddened flesh about his cock-base.

'I asked you a question,' Charlotte said as she advanced; one, two steps more. He was less than six feet away, and there was defiance in his stare, as if he was weighing up his chances in the event of a full-blown argument. Perhaps he'd had too much champagne, was entertaining macho notions. Then again, he wasn't entirely stupid and had to be perfectly well aware of what she was capable of doing to him.

He glanced down at the girl. The wedding dress was simple enough, a classic A-line silk and chiffon layered calf-length job, and the cute little corset-top had been lowered to expose her plump breasts. Her hair looked good like that, all twisted and sculpted, but his fingers had already untidied it and her appearance was bordering on the sluttish given that much of her lipstick was now smeared across her cheeks and nose where his cock had been pulled from her mouth.

'We're not doing any harm,' he said then, and although he was slurring slightly it could have been plain lust which made him appear almost drunk.

'This isn't the first time you've been caught fucking the staff after-hours. You've been warned about it before,' Charlotte said slowly, menacingly, and the man straightened a little in the seat as she neared yet again, now easily within striking distance.

He appeared to have sobered a little, but his eyes were flicking back to Charlotte's nipples. She folded her arms, felt her hardened buds press into her forearms as she continued.

'The last time it was a written warning, and you know you only get one of them. You are sacked.'

He slumped back, face raised to the ceiling, arms outstretched. His cock appeared to wilt in the girl's hand as she looked to Charlotte, barely able to conceal the smile.

'Come on, please, come on,' he pleaded, and the girl got up, straightening her skirt as she turned from him. He sat forward, stuffing his shirt and genitals back inside his trousers as he begged.

'It'll never ever happen again. I promise,' he said, earnest and the very picture of sobriety now that Charlotte was hovering over him.

Charlotte frowned and raised a forefinger to her chin as she adopted the tone of a blonde bimbo.

'Let me see. Now, where have I heard that before? When was it? Oh, yes. I remember now.'

She reached forward and grabbed a fistful of hair. He yelped pathetically but she tightened her grip and twisted the trapped locks so that he knew which way she wanted him to turn. When he opened his eyes they were only a foot from hers.

'Yes, I went into the office that evening and there you were with that temp over the desk and your dick up her behind. How could I have forgotten?'

'Please, I didn't, I don't want to –'

'I won't even consider overlooking this unless you fuck her as I watch, and if you're good enough I might even let you try fucking me. If you make the grade, you can stay. If not, you'll be scanning the situations vacant tomorrow morning. Understood?'

Then she left him, his hair standing up like an exclamation mark of alarm as she retreated. The girl in the wedding dress stood, hands on hips, breasts still bared, waiting as he stood up. He moved slowly at first, cautiously as Charlotte stood with hands clasped behind her back, legs parted as far as the knee-high skirt allowed, her expression stern and impatient.

'What do you want me to –' he started.

'Just get on with it!' Charlotte yelled, and he visibly jerked with fright.

He reached out for the girl's breasts, face already lowering, mouth opening to take her reddened nipples, but Charlotte stepped forwards again, bringing the back of her hand hard into his chest.

'Give me your belt,' she said, staring hard up into his eyes.

He unbuckled the trouser-belt and started feeding it through the loops, but Charlotte grabbed the buckle and hauled at it, bringing it away from his waist in one swift motion during which she doubled the strap and brought it gently slapping into her open left palm.

'Get them off,' she commanded then, and he followed the order quickly, one eye on the heavy leather strap Charlotte was now flexing and smoothing.

The belt felt familiar, warm and pliant. She snapped it open to its full length, raised it to her face and closed her eyes as she ran it an inch below her nostrils, savouring its age and scent from one end to the other. When she opened her eyes, lowering and doubling the strap once more, he had stepped out of the crumpled trousers.

The white shirt hung over his crotch, bearing no impression now from his deflated cock. His eyes flicked from her hands about the strap to her face, as if awaiting further instructions. She wanted to laugh aloud at his pathetic little-boy-lost routine. He was desperate for the punishment to start, nothing surer. He wanted to be spanked, cajoled, thrashed with the belt, and probably assumed that she would fulfil the selfish expectation. Pitiful. He'd never ever really appreciated what Charlotte was capable of – not entirely his fault of course – but perhaps it was time to show him a new trick, one he couldn't possibly be expecting.

'Lift the shirt,' she said as she assessed the size of the belt-buckle – a little on the small side perhaps, but it would do. He raised the white flaps covering his cock, and Charlotte was aware of the woman smiling at the sight of the shrivelled specimen still retreating into its thickly haired protective sac.

Charlotte stepped forwards and brought the strap gently across the back of his thigh.

'Part them,' she said, and he did so, the stocky lightly tanned thighs shifting apart as he repositioned himself, slightly lowering his six-foot frame. Charlotte gripped the end of the belt, allowing the buckle to swing low behind him, gently tracing a parabola which brought the heavy brass loop up between his legs. She caught the buckle with her left hand and pulled the strap up so that it barely touched the juncture of thigh and buttock. He tensed, arse-cheeks clenching against the broad leather. A quick glance at the girl confirmed that she knew what was expected next, even if he didn't, and then the girl was on her knees before him, her hands teasing and tugging at his deflated manhood, her pinching finger and thumb firmly pulling his glans up and away from his balls.

The girl squeezed at the thin shaft, filling it as she maintained a steady grip on the loosely hanging scrotum – Charlotte looped the belt over his helmet to fully encircle his slowly swelling cock.

'You clearly want some direction,' Charlotte whispered, 'and I'm more than happy to oblige on that score.'

The girl secured the thick brass curve hard against the base of him as she resumed sucking his cock-head. Charlotte moved behind him, winding the loose end of the strap about her palm to secure a good grip. He hauled the shirt off, one button catching Charlotte's eye as it sparkled its trajectory through the shifting pale-blue light before bouncing silently across the carpet.

'On your knees,' Charlotte said, holding the strap tightly as he lowered himself, his trembling thighs sending vibrations through the belt as she resisted his descent. The belt eased between his buttocks as he assumed the position, but Charlotte maintained the pressure as it took more of his weight. The girl lowered herself in tandem, his pained gasps overriding the slight slurping of her tongue and lips about his swelling cock.

He raised a hand to his arse, presumably to ease the discomfort, but Charlotte slapped it away.

'You'd better get her ready,' she said then, and the girl dropped to the floor, turning to face upwards. Her face came into Charlotte's view then, the smudged make-up, the light curls at her fringe now matted to her forehead, eyes closed as she licked his tightening scrotum, her fingers lubing the edge of the belt as she pressed it harder into his crevice.

He pulled the layered silk and chiffon layers up the girl's legs, her hold-up cream stockings now exposed. As expected, her sex was uncovered, already pink and distended, the velvety flesh glistening shaven in the shifting light as his visibly trembling hands palmed across the fullness of her tensing, parting thighs.

Charlotte started tugging at the belt as he lowered his face into the girl's sex, and the high muffled cry from him signalled his distress – the girl opened her eyes, her fingers signalling that Charlotte should relieve the pressure. As she did so, lowering the strap a few inches, the girl quickly located the trapped testicles and brought them either side of the belt – they were bloated, unnaturally high between his cheeks as Charlotte carefully drew the belt up once more. The thick buckle glinted darkly among his bunched flesh and hair as his cock was drawn further down towards the girl's mouth, and Charlotte held him firm, careful not to draw him too far lest the buckle pull him entirely away from her. In any case, his shaft was now so swollen that the buckle was digging deep into his shaft, the entrapment of his erection virtually assured.

The girl wanked him slowly, forcing as much blood as possible into his helmet – if he tried to slip free of the belt now it would be painful, perhaps even damaging. She licked at the engorged head, fingers flicking at his balls while others pressed hard against the belt-protected anus, and when she opened her mouth fully, gaping to take the fleshy fullness, he jerked desperately, anxious to sink himself inside her. Charlotte stepped across his legs and switched the belt to the other hand – her arm was already aching – and resumed the pressure, holding him clear as his strong torso began to work inexorably towards his goal. The girl was grimacing as the cock filled her mouth sporadically, Charlotte dictating the rate at which he would be allowed to enjoy the oral attention, and when she did deign to give him more freedom he used it eagerly, plunging his cock as far between the scarlet-rimmed lips as was allowed. The girl pulled away only once, turning her face away as the slender string of pre-come traced across her cheek, silverish-blue. She wiped it into the perspiration already coating her face, swallowed hard and gaped again, eyes closed in anticipation, but Charlotte held the cock clear of the girl's face.

He had used the time before her arrival well, and Charlotte could see now that he'd brought the girl's clitoris to its fullest prominence, the little bud standing proud of her lips, hairless and slowly jerking the air below his tongue-tip as his fingers eased her apart. She was already ripe for fucking.

'You want in there don't you?' Charlotte said, lowering herself towards him as she increased the pressure, pulling the strap harder as his hips and thighs juddered, his shoulder and back muscles also spasming into prominence beneath the fine coat of sweat as he strained to maintain his own body weight.

'You want to sink your cock in there, don't you?' she asked again, and he was nodding, grunting agreement as he started to suck on the smooth pussy flesh.

Charlotte slackened the belt again and the girl released a deep throaty grunt as the engorged dick sank into her mouth, her hands now appearing at his buttocks, fingers kneading deep into the tense muscles as she pulled him deeper. He raised his face, coated with her fluid and his own saliva, eyes shut, the telltale abandon of impending orgasm now evident as he paled, frowning, his hips easing into the steady deep-throating rhythm the girl was dictating.

The cry which came from him when Charlotte yanked on the belt was laden with anger and frustration, and she heard the dull plop of his cock being released by the girl's throat as she drew him away from her face completely, forcing him to move down, away from the girl's distended sex, his fingers reluctantly coming away from her parted lips as Charlotte dragged him, arse ludicrously raised, his feet moving quickly to secure some grip on the carpet, away from the panting girl.

'No such luck, sonny,' Charlotte snapped. 'Even you aren't stupid enough to confuse pain and pleasure so completely. What punishment would it be to let you fuck her now?'

He hyperventilated as Charlotte calmly paced away from the girl, the strap stretched, his beleaguered buttocks still clamping about the leather band as if in a futile attempt to ease the pressure on the dick which now pointed out behind him like some obscene and hairless tail. Charlotte's intermittent release of the constriction had allowed his cock to fill beyond its normal capacity, and it bloated crimson, the buckle now barely visible, so strained was the hard flesh filling it. It would be starting to hurt him now.

'Your time is running out,' Charlotte said as she yanked the strap high and hard. He dropped his head to the floor, his groan loaded with rage. Letting the belt fall across his sweat-coated back, she stepped before him, parted her feet, placed her hands on her hips and nodded to the girl before he looked up. The girl seemed energised, eager to comply, perhaps now sensing Charlotte's urgency.

'Use your tongue only,' she ordered as she drew the skirt up over her thighs to reveal her naked, lightly haired pussy.

He raised himself, his grotesquely swollen cock-head bobbing up to point at Charlotte, the belt hanging from the shaft. He glanced down sharply, as if double-checking that the inordinately thickened

22

member really was his, but any sense of impending relief he may have been experiencing was surely shattered when the girl took up the end Charlotte had released and resumed the painful tugging, drawing the leather length back into the arse-cleft it had just slipped from.

Charlotte looked down at her sex as his face neared, tongue already pointing, straining as he laid his trembling hands gently on her thighs, perhaps afraid of rebuke. She leaned back, allowing her weight to rest against the wall as he started to lap madly at her, tongue forcing a damp path through her hair, seeking her lips. The girl maintained a steady tugging on the strap, his cock bobbing in and out of view as Charlotte raised her face and thrust her hips forward just a little bit more, then she drew the skirt up to form a tight black band about her waist. Misogynist pig and self-obsessed he may have been, but he'd always been good at this, and she was determined to enjoy it. His strong tongue-tip found her clit, rapidly teasing the height of the bud, and she closed her eyes, struggling not to display her mounting lust – if he thought he was taking control then he could, and would, assert himself quickly, attempt to dictate the scenario.

'Not quite good enough,' she said, her voice now deep and stronger to disguise any evidence that she was succumbing to the attention, 'You'll have to do a bit better.'

His groan seemed to pulse through her flesh as the tongue was briefly drawn down to trace the contours of her lips, parting the smooth access, and then her hands were in his short dark hair, pulling him closer as he started to probe more deeply, his nose now pressing insistently upon her throbbing clitoris. She wanted to raise her legs and close her thighs about

23

him, lock his head in place until she got what she wanted, but she knew she would come too quickly. She opened her eyes and found that the girl was smiling now as she tugged rhythmically on the belt, the thick band being drawn over her own pussy as she used the free hand to cup and massage her breasts. Soon. Very soon.

'Perhaps I'll let you put it in, but you've still to finish what you started with her,' Charlotte said, drawing herself away from his face. He panted, cheeks reddened, lips wet and puffed, sweat dripping from chin and eyebrows as he gulped for air.

She stepped away from him as he dropped his arms to the floor, chest heaving. The girl dropped the belt again, leaving it to snake from beneath him.

'Better get that thing off now,' Charlotte ordered, and he raised himself, still kneeling, staring at his solid cock as it rose before him.

He squeezed hard at his shaft, desperate to deflate the thing, ease the pressure so that the loop might be released. The girl came to Charlotte as directed, raising her breasts to be licked as he strained to free himself. Charlotte took the nipple between her teeth, staring at him as she rolled it gently. He released a snarl, screwing his eyes shut as he compressed his shaft in his fist, forearm muscles twitching as he increased the pressure. The girl moaned loud and high, deliberately tormenting him as she exaggerated her response to Charlotte's fingers brushing over her sex, but he was nothing if not determined – his fingers worked quickly, hand gathering his balls and scrotum as the other eased the buckle along the temporarily shrunken shaft. The brass loop would not pass beyond his glans, and he had to compress the helmet before yanking the belt away. He stared down at his distressed penis, and there was a split second where

24

Charlotte fancied he might wind the strap about his hand and use it to exact revenge, but his eyes moved to Charlotte's fingers, now kneading the girl's opening sex, and he dropped the belt, crawling towards the women.

'That's far enough,' Charlotte snapped as he started to quicken, his eyes now fiery with anger and peaking frustration, face smeared with her moisture. 'You may stand.'

He did so. Charlotte made him wait as she unbuttoned her blouse and pulled it open. The girl's mouth and hands were instantly upon her breasts, gently squeezing as her lips engulfed the right nipple, sucking, fingers smoothing her pubic hair, assessing the opening he had helped create. He was wanking himself slowly, powerfully as he watched, the dick now regaining some of the stature it had lost during the painful removal of the belt-buckle.

'Hold on to your ankles dear,' Charlotte said to the girl, and she did so in one elegant move as she turned, her posterior now raised and open and fully on view to him as he gawped, quickening the pace of his self-stroking. Charlotte smoothed her palm over the pale broad buttocks before slipping her joined fingers into the peachy crevice. The girl kept her legs firmly together, limiting the exposure of her pussy, and Charlotte's fingers registered the slackening flesh about her backside, the involuntary jerking of the girl's behind as the fingers passed over it suggesting that she was more than ready to receive there. He'd clearly noticed too, and his eyes were firmly fixed on Charlotte's fingers, as if urging them to attend to the higher orifice.

'Come on, then,' Charlotte said as she started to probe and ream the gently bucking arse. 'Let's see what you're made of.'

He needed no second bidding, and advanced quickly, his hand guiding his swollen cock-end towards Charlotte's finger. Charlotte brought her other hand swiftly to his shaft, gripping it tightly while simultaneously sinking her finger into the girl's behind.

'Ever so sorry dear, that's occupied,' she said as she lowered the thick cock and yanked it towards the tightly closed pussy. He raised his face as if about to scream his rage, but his expression mellowed as Charlotte directed his lunge and he slid with surprising ease into the girl – her yelp indicated the depth he'd achieved – and Charlotte could feel the solid breadth of him through the girl's behind, the prominent glans-ridge making its impression felt through the fleshy wall dividing her passages as he started to fuck her.

Charlotte plunged her finger fully into the girl's rear hole, and he reacted to the move, clearly sensing the pressure of her digit against his shaft as he quickened, his breathing quickening as he neared his climax. Charlotte tensed her thighs, forcing them to stay apart as she brought her own fingers down to ease the building tension in her own sex, her exposed pussy now cool and eager for attention. Better that it end for now. There would be time later, with him out of the way.

'Oh dear, I don't think we're going to manage two today are we,' Charlotte teased as he grabbed the girl's hips, hauling her against him as the orgasm gripped him and he started to empty into her. He withdrew, his cock spitting his thin milky fluid over the girl's buttocks as he endeavoured to finish off into her behind, but Charlotte maintained her finger's presence, denying him access, and she watched with some satisfaction as he wilted, his eyes shut, the sounds coming from him now drunken and weak as he slumped away from them, his expression pained and draining of colour.

Charlotte withdrew her finger, the girl's clamping backside protesting the departure.

'We have to be off now, dear,' Charlotte said chirpily as she beckoned the girl to get up, 'so maybe next time.'

He dropped to the floor, smiling, the sweat coursing along his shoulders, down his back.

'One of these times, surely, one of these times I'll do it,' he said, shaking his head as the droplets dripped from his forehead.

Charlotte adjusted Seona's skirt as her friend hitched up the silky corset and consoled her husband.

'Practice makes perfect, darling,' Seona said.

'And happy birthday,' Charlotte added as they left poor old Blair to recover.

'Please don't make me wait any longer,' Seona gasped, only briefly allowing Charlotte's nipple to escape her mouth as she whispered the request.

Charlotte slid back a little in the seat. The car accelerated onto the carriageway. Only a fifteen-minute drive back home at this time of night, but Seona was getting frantic, her dress hitched up again, her fingers urging Charlotte's to rub her. The little birthday 'surprise' for Seona's husband of five years had been too quick, hadn't allowed time for either of the women to find full satisfaction after his premature come.

'Seona, darling, you're not listening, please, you have to –'

Charlotte gasped aloud as Seona gently bit her left nipple, the teeth trapping the sensitive flesh as her fingers worked between Charlotte's and she started to finger herself.

'I need it right now,' Seona snarled into Charlotte's face, her make-up still messily smeared, the scent of Blair's sex still hovering on her breath as she panted, eyelids semi-shut.

The driver could see them. No matter. Charlotte stared at the reflection of his eyes in the rear-view mirror and he glanced up briefly, his expression impassive. He had seen them making love many times before, had never expressed any interest whatever. It was merely a part of the job, and his only concern was Charlotte's safety. He knew she was safe with Seona.

Charlotte opened her lips, accepted Seona's kiss. It had been a while. Months. Their various business and social activities had been unusually out of synch of late, opportunities had been few and far between. If Seona's uncharacteristically rabid behaviour suggested that she'd been suffering rather more than Charlotte, the increasing dampness now seeping across her fingers proved it.

Her best friend's tongue stabbed at hers, lapped at her lips as her fingers drew Charlotte's into her, the conjoined digits forming a thick multiheaded shaft against which she worked herself insistently, greedily. Charlotte yielded, helping Seona towards the peak she needed before any sensible conversation would be possible.

'We're going to be busy again,' Charlotte panted, but Seona was lost in her lust, leg rising to accommodate their joined fingers as Charlotte cupped the lace-bound thigh, supporting her as she jerked harder.

'Yes,' Seona panted as the come overwhelmed her, 'Yes, yes –'

'We have to prepare,' Charlotte insisted, gripping Seona's hair in a vain attempt to get through to her.

'Anything, yes, anything,' Seona gasped, her thighs twitching close about their hands, the pressure now painfully trapping them. Charlotte drew her fingers away from Seona's and pushed her open palm hard against her friend's sex – Seona released a long high shriek as the orgasm peaked, her mouth once again seeking Charlotte's breasts as the wave broke and she slipped slowly off the seat, fingers soothing herself.

Minutes passed as Charlotte scanned the dark sky, the mesmeric passage of motorway lamplight as the car overtook sinister nocturnal trucks.

It made no sense. Charlotte had renounced the position of Kayla, had made it crystal clear that she rejected the 'honour' and all it entailed. Her voluntary retirement had, of course, been unprecedented, and she'd been left in no doubt that such behaviour was not only unacceptable, but may well have serious repercussions. Well, she'd told them what to do with their charade, had dared them to do their worst, and had been all too ready to take the bastards on at their own game.

But it hadn't come to that. They had melted overnight, disappeared from England entirely, their assets and personnel untraceable. Although it seemed a lifetime ago, only five years had passed, and at no time had there been even the slightest suggestion that they had tried to re-establish contact. So why now?

The sudden jolt as the driver braked to prevent collision with a wayward boy-racer jolted Charlotte from the reverie. Seona groaned and buried her head deeper into Charlotte's lap, close to sleep. Her house would be busy already, there would be time to freshen up and have a couple of drinks before Blair returned. The party would undoubtedly be as eventful and depraved as all the others, but Charlotte knew she wouldn't stay. Perhaps sensing her concern, Seona stirred as if from a dream, her demeanour almost embarrassed as she got back on the seat beside Charlotte and made a token effort to fix her hair.

'I'm sorry,' she said, 'you were trying to tell me something.'

Charlotte raised her arm and cuddled Seona close as the driver slowed for the exit.

'There was a call. Today. They're trying to pull us back in. I don't know who, don't know why. They'll send someone soon.'

'But surely –'

Seona's head lowered, as if the mere thought was too weighty for her mind. Charlotte pulled her nearer. Despite the warmth of the evening, despite the proximity of her nearest and dearest friend, Charlotte felt the chill crawl across her skin – something, somewhere, was terribly wrong.

Two

'May I?' asked Charlotte, as she snatched up his cigarette case.

Three years since she'd had a smoke. Three full years, and yet this bastard had her reaching for one after fifteen minutes.

Charlotte inhaled deeply and turned from Leo, dear old Leo, funny old Leo who'd always liked the booze just a little too much.

Sunita's arrival with another pitcher of ice provided a welcome distraction throughout the silence, but the atmosphere was evident even to the maid, who swiftly fetched a few plates from the half-dozen tables as quickly as she could before retreating to the safety of Charlotte's busy home.

Blair's birthday party had been surprisingly quiet, and the unusually high humidity had literally put a damper on proceedings. But the post-party bash – a tradition the closest of her friends had established among themselves since they settled into relatively normal lives – had been altogether more interesting and pleasant, probably because most of those attending were so hung over that they were content to lounge in the garden, enjoying the blessedly cool breeze. It was a fine day, with fine company. Everything was OK.

Or it had been. Until Leo, erstwhile family friend, hit her with this completely flummoxing request as soon as he had a chance to speak to her alone once the garden-party formality started to disperse. She'd been anticipating the approach, but not from such close quarters, and certainly not from him.

Charlotte took another long drag of the cigarette and purposely kept the smoke inside, savouring it, dropping the butt into the grass as she reached for her glass and bid Leo sit. He appeared genuinely grateful to do so, juddering back the white metal-framed chair from the table as he squinted upwards, trying to decide what-position would best protect him from the mid-afternoon English August sun. With his straw boater and fitted blazer, an artfully dangling scarlet handkerchief fluttering from the breast pocket, he looked every inch the buffoon she'd always known he was meant to be.

As if telepathically confirming her suspicions, he glanced at her briefly before withdrawing the cloth square and opening it fully across his open shuffling palms, then sinking his face into it. She felt a shiver of disgust – the cloth had clearly been used already, and he was merely wiping old sweat into the new.

She picked up the sheet he had just shown her. It was a monochrome scan of a newspaper article. An Eastern European language, not Charlotte's forte, so she was reliant on Leo's mangled, half-forgotten account of the translation given to him by a mysterious man in the rest room of Leo's brother's favoured club. Something odd about the typesetting, strangely old-fashioned, but the piece was dated 9 July, only a month ago.

Of course, it could quite easily be a fake. Nowadays, even Charlotte, at a mere 35, had some modicum of experience with the newer technologies and, more importantly, she remembered the tales of those who had sought to deceive the world. Many great frauds and counterfeiters had only ever been caught because they wanted people to know how great they were, leaving avoidable clues here and there in the hope that someone would click and scream the knowledge from the rooftops – you're great, yes, but I'm as great, we are more than one. It would end a torment of rare sort, to know that one's insight was shared, that no one really is smarter than all of those souls comprising the herd. But the greatest dupers and forgers, of course, remained at large, never to be brought to account for their crimes because they left no trace of wrongdoing wherever they went. They hurt no one, they took no one's property or wife or child. They provided no reason for revenge.

'I'm ever so sorry to be the messenger,' he said huffily through the thin and dampened silk.

Charlotte perched herself on the edge of the chair and leaned on the circular wrought-iron table, rolling the champagne flute between index finger and thumb so firmly that the remaining drink was sloshing about the glass as she rotated it. When he finally emerged from the lurid patch of damp redness he jerked in alarm at seeing her seated and so close to him.

'Leo, let me explain this simply. That way, it'll be easier for you to remember. You come down here, ostensibly to see me and wish Blair a belated happy birthday.'

He glanced up at her angrily, clearly offended, but she was not going to allow him to interject and he knew it.

'You turn up, complete with beautiful new wife, a reasonably good Dali sketch by way of a gift, and then you hit me with some spoofy spy scenario and expect me to fall for it?'

33

She hadn't experienced the fear for years. Fear of disclosure, discovery. Nothing she had done in her own personal life was remotely scandalous, at least not according to county averages. (One divorce under the belt by one's mid-thirties was becoming practically *de rigueur*.) But the very fact Leo had been chosen to impart such a communication was deeply worrying.

'My dear, dear Charlotte,' he gushed, jowls reddened and swollen and adding a full decade to his 55 years, 'I've told you what I was told to tell you. There is no debriefing of any kind. I assume that the fact of me delivering it may be of some importance, but that's purely guesswork on my part.'

'So where did it come from?' Charlotte asked, now more curious than angry. He was telling the truth. Leo always told the truth. He was good at embellishing stories, adding little touches of his own to heighten the drama, increase the tension, make that punchline funnier when it finally did arrive. That's why everyone knew Leo, and that's precisely why Daddy had always kept him very close. But he was always truthful, if wickedly so – gossip would be conveyed through Leo in the knowledge that any original acts or words of bitchiness would be magnified tenfold in the retelling, guaranteeing further conflict and tattle when the grapevine had done its job and tempers had duly festered.

'The chap shows me this newspaper article, maybe a magazine, not too sure. According to him, it says that this girl, yes, the one in the picture, she's causing all sorts of trouble over there in Prague. Turns out she agreed to speak to this journalist about something, but nobody knows what it was. The local intelligence boys picked him up, but she went to the journalist's workplace, effectively barricaded herself into the editor's office, along with the wretched editor

I should add. The press portrayed it as a kidnap, but I'm assured that was just a cover.'

'Is this the best image they have of her?' Charlotte asked, tapping the sheet as he nodded, both of them now scanning the small arrangement of arms and heavy dark blanket under which the eyes of an angry and pale woman stared maniacally through tinted spectacles. The few visible wisps of hair were straight and light, perhaps blonde.

Leo paled as he sat back, sobriety sparking in his eyes – he'd been throwing champagne down his neck since his arrival three hours earlier, but he seemed to swiftly whiten now, as if perhaps seeing something Charlotte couldn't. And his voice had that tone, the voice the men always used when they were together and the women were safely out of ear and reach. He even attempted to jut his chin beneath the solid layers of blubber that concealed it, causing his neck-fat to wobble in a manner that suggested he was attempting to swallow a walnut. If she hadn't been so fond of him she could quite easily have been sick.

'Charlotte. I've known you since you were a tiny little thing, your parents have been marvellous friends. I don't know what you're doing, and I don't know why. But I will tell you this my dear, I will tell you only this.'

Charlotte couldn't take her eyes off Leo – she'd never seen him so serious, so puffed-up, so pathetically macho.

'I was sent pictures of what that woman was doing. Well, I don't know for sure it's the same woman, there's no way of telling from that picture, no way at all, but I got this stuff through, they came as e-mail messages, single images, and they were all of her. She was involved in the most beastly acts you can imagine, or I should say, that I can imagine.'

Charlotte raised her glass and drained it, keeping her eyes solidly on his as he puffed before continuing.

'Not that I imagine that type of thing. You know what I mean.'

She nearly leaned across to cuddle him then, but was aware that she'd also had a few glasses, more than she should have had, and she was supple, pliant to the forces of nostalgia and pity. But she'd just been delivered a challenge, and in the most uncivilised circumstances imaginable – her own garden had been soiled, invaded. Systems had always been in place when Charlotte was active as Kayla. So many systems, so many secrets and precautions. They had worked. And of course, those systems were bound to change. She had been away for five years, she couldn't be expected to know exactly how they worked these days, but surely, surely to God it couldn't be that people were so easily used?

Leo was a sad man heading for his sixties and a very early death due to utter hedonism, and he did not, and could not, recognise the boundaries which Charlotte had long ago set for herself, but whoever had sent him was serious. They had used him like a donkey which always goes home, and she had duly taken delivery of the message.

'Leo,' Charlotte said, reaching for the bottle on the neighbouring table, 'tell me what this woman did. I want you to tell me what you saw.'

The music blared loud and brash from the open lounge doors, accompanied by a series of high shrieks before it was turned down. They were getting their second wind, would soon be partying hard again, and the evening guests would be arriving within the hour. It would be a long night.

Leo started to jerk back the metal seat. It stuttered in the grass as he strove to raise his weight, free his

36

legs from beneath the table, and Charlotte knew what he wanted – she rose and crossed to the long table bearing the bottles, grabbed the vermouth and a semi-full pitcher of lemonade and dumped both directly in front of him. He wouldn't be shifting for a while, not until she'd gleaned as much from him as possible about this female who threatened to disrupt her pleasantly quiet life. Charlotte had been Kayla, but she had effectively laid the mythical creature to rest. The imposter – for how could she be anything else? – now threatened Charlotte, her family and her friends. Whatever Leo knew, unwitting or otherwise, he was going to divulge here and now, and as she flicked the cap off the bottle, slopping the clear spirit into his glass, she resolved that he would rue the day he ever got involved.

He gulped recklessly, chin dripping, his eyes casting about for something to focus on other than Charlotte.

'I don't know where to, I don't know how to start –' he stammered. Charlotte diluted the remnants of her wine with some soda water and quickly checked that no one was within earshot.

'Start at the start, Leo,' she said firmly.

Leo sporadically closed his eyes, shaking his head as if denying the awfulness of what was coming from his mouth as he related what detail he knew, and Charlotte sat, transfixed, for the next hour, as he described a series of images which at once appalled and aroused her. The strange couplings and rituals he spoke of were as familiar and irresistible as favoured but long-forgotten scents, and long before he'd completed his lurid testimony, Charlotte knew there was no option but to pack her bags and meet the challenge, wherever it might be. She also had no doubt that she would be expected. If this new Kayla was even remotely deserving of the title then she would, even now, be waiting for

Charlotte to come looking for her.

The images Leo had imparted in the garden tumbled in her mind, overlapping and morphing, the people and scenarios he had described in lascivious detail forming a running tableau which she couldn't help confusing with her own experience as Kayla.

She closed the bathroom door gently, didn't lock it. Seona would be up soon. The party was in full swing, the evening guests had arrived and there was no further need for her to hover about the front gardens, meeting and greeting. They wouldn't miss her for half an hour.

And it wouldn't even take as long as that. She needed to be licked, fucked, and she needed it right now. It hadn't been necessary to tell Seona what she wanted. They'd been lovers long enough for a two-second look to act as a signal, and the discreet code they'd long ago perfected, whereby the simple raising of an eyebrow was sufficient to signal interest, had once again proved invaluable. Seona needed it too – Blair was already quite spectacularly drunk and would not be capable of satisfying her in the near future.

She crossed the black-and-white tiled floor and pushed the window further open. The heat was building again since the wind had dropped, and raising herself on tiptoe to view the rear gardens, she could make out the sorry figure of Leo, slumped, head resting on folded arms as he snoozed at the table.

And even poor old Leo, so prone to exaggeration and embellishment, even he could not have imagined the pictures he'd painted for her less than an hour ago. Those photographs and video clips he'd been sent were undoubtedly real. The petite blonde woman, full breasted, athletically built, and sexually adventurous to a degree that had clearly astonished him. Yes, it smacked of the truth. But why? And who? Most importantly of all, why choose Leo as the contact?

She closed her eyes, savoured the fresh scent of mown grass wafting gently through the window. She dropped a hand to her breast, merely brushing her palm across her thickening nipple through the white cotton, then further to press the heel of her hand lightly against her pantie-shielded mound.

Something about Leo's rather childish outrage had aroused her beyond comprehension. As far as she'd heard, this new Kayla had done nothing that Charlotte, Seona and the long-lost Imogen hadn't done many times before, but to hear the practices described with such genuine shock made her reappraise her own experiences. He'd been particularly taken by a woman who'd appeared with the mysterious blonde in several of the images, a tall black girl who he described in almost reverential terms as the most beautiful woman he had ever seen. He'd been appalled at the way Kayla treated the woman, how she used different tools on her, pushing things into her, gagging her, even thrashing her with paddles and canes. It was a ghastly business altogether.

How right he was. She cupped her left breast, the image of the black woman hovering before her as she pressed again into her crotch, leaning forwards to rest her head against the high window-ledge as she resisted the urge to masturbate herself right there and then.

As if on cue, the door creaked lightly, and she turned to see it open slowly, Seona's hand appearing briefly before being withdrawn.

The girl who entered was not Seona, but the eldest daughter of the Duke of Halesome. Her recent 21st birthday party had been a splendid bash. Charlotte clasped her hands together, ready to apologise for leaving the door open, but something about the girl's colouring and wide eyes made her hesitate, and as she did Seona appeared close behind, closing and locking the door.

'Tara has been asking me about you for ages,' Seona said, clearly tipsy but still in giggly mode, 'so I said to her, didn't I dear, I said, you should talk to her yourself.'

Charlotte folded her arms and turned to face them.

'What did you want to ask me, dear?' she said, adopting the mildly schoolmarmish tone which suggested mild disapproval at being imposed upon. The girl blushed and fiddled with her short blonde hair, she seemed unable to take her eyes off the chessboard tiles.

'It was nothing really, well, it was just sort of, you know –'

'No,' Charlotte interrupted strongly, 'I don't know, and if you don't start speaking English then I'll never know. Some attempt at syntax would be appreciated, as would eye contact.'

The girl looked up. She was slightly shorter than Seona, but a smidgin taller than Charlotte. She had the kind of complexion Charlotte had always adored, a peaches-and-cream glow that owed nothing to make-up, everything to health and sexual arousal.

And she was aroused. No doubt about it. The eyes were wide and blue, her face slightly lowered, already signalling submission. Whatever Seona had told her, whatever she had hinted, the girl had seen a green light and decided to go for it. She was available – her bra-free nipples were pressing boldly against the pale-green, loose-fitting silk blouse, and her rather stocky, broad thighs were clamped tightly, one knee gently caressing the other as she joined her hands in front of her and knotted them nervously.

'I'm sorry, I'm just a little bit, you know –'

'Again,' Charlotte cut in, 'you assume that I know what you're thinking. A verbal mannerism, I know, just a casual figure of speech.'

Charlotte clasped her hands behind her back and stepped nearer the furiously blushing girl. This was fun. Just what the doctor ordered – good old Seona had accurately assessed the symptoms and known exactly how to address the ailment. The breaking-in of a celebrated virgin was as perfect a remedy as she could have wished for.

'But it's sloppy, my dear. The precise use of language is difficult, takes years to learn. You want to learn?'

The girl's gaze returned to the tiles, her eyes flicking from one to another as if trying to discern some pattern, perhaps formulate an exit. She was getting scared, was surely asking herself what the hell she was doing in a spacious bathroom with two older women and a locked door behind her.

'Yes,' she said, just a suggestion of a waver in her voice, 'I do want to learn.'

Charlotte stepped nearer. Her kitten heels clicked smartly against the tiles, the three paces signalling a final countdown for the girl – she would make her mind up in the next fractions of a second, decide whether or not to flee.

She decided to stay.

Charlotte raised her hand slowly, cupping the girl's face, savouring the peachy softness of her skin as she traced her fingers around and under the lowered chin. With index finger alone she drew the girl's face up, forcing her eyes to confront her own once again. So close now, so near she could smell the girl's sweet perspiration. She kept her finger at the chin, gently stroking the velvety underside, savouring the almost translucent flesh. She really was radiant, unspoiled.

'Tell me, then. Tell me what you want to learn.'

'I want to know –' the girl started, but her voice was quavering badly, her breath shallow as she closed her eyes, shoulders slumping. She appeared to be close to swooning, and Seona moved close behind, allowing the girl to lean back on her for support. Charlotte stepped nearer, both hands now raised and open, her palms gently circling the stiffening silk-covered nipples.

'You want to know what it's like with a woman?' Charlotte asked, barely able to conceal the glee in her voice, the raw excitement she was vicariously savouring now.

Tara nodded, arching her head further back, nuzzling against Seona as Charlotte started to unbutton the thin blouse, Seona's hands now rising to continue the gentle massage of the high plump tits as the girl released short audible breaths, her whole body trembling.

'What about your lovely boyfriend?' Charlotte asked quietly before gently kissing the girl's cheek. 'haven't you done it with him yet?'

Tara opened her eyes. Her cheeks were blazing, but the embarrassment had passed, and her complexion was now positively glowing, her lips already reddened and lightly puffed, her pearly teeth bared.

'No. I won't let him. He keeps on about it, but I won't.'

Charlotte released the final button and parted the blouse, aware that Tara was watching her as she looked down at the beautifully symmetrical tits, the pinkness on her upper chest matching the glow on her cheeks.

'So, what do you do?' Charlotte said as she thumbed Tara's nipples. The girl released a shuddering moan, her eyes closed again as Seona's hands cupped her tits, raising the flesh for Charlotte's mouth.

'I rub it for him sometimes, he uses his fingers on me, his fingers –' she panted, but speech was becoming difficult for her now, with Charlotte's tongue flicking at her breast-buds, Seona's hands establishing a harder, deeper massage as she tongued Tara's ear and neck.

'Have you ever sucked him?' Charlotte continued as she started to draw her fingers lightly over Tara's smooth, still-locked thighs while maintaining the oral attention, her tongue now rasping rather than flicking, a stronger movement which the girl clearly appreciated, her breathing now noisy and desperate.

'No, no.' She managed to gasp. Charlotte lowered both hands, gripped the hem of the miniskirt and hauled it up to form a thick rucked band about Tara's waist.

'You've never had a penis in your mouth?'

Tara moaned confirmation as Charlotte's hand closed over her moistening panties.

'Or in here?'

Again, Tara could only moan by way of reply.

Charlotte thumbed the pantie-line away from Tara's crotch and slipped her fingers down into the short-clipped hair. The pubes were fine and soft. She wanted to kneel and taste her right away, bring the girl off hard and fast, do to her what she wanted done to herself there and then. But there was no great hurry. She drew her hand away from the gently curled matt of pubic hair, the thin band of pantie-lace still looped over her thumb as she stretched it away from the girl's smooth hip. Quickly bringing her other hand to grip the material, Charlotte squeezed

43

tightly, and she had her mouth full of Tara's breast again as she tore the thin fabric. The soft rip signalled the parting of the pantie seam, bringing another gasp from Tara. Charlotte left the panties to hang, still trapped between the girl's thighs as the lightly moist material slowly peeled away from her sex to reveal the triangle of strawberry-blonde hair.

'But you've had a girl down there before, haven't you?' Charlotte said, fingers delicately assessing the contours of Tara's puffing lips.

Tara straightened her arms as Seona drew the blouse off her shoulders, allowing the lime-green garment to slip to the tiled floor.

'Yes,' Tara said, her voice stronger now, her tongue circling her own lips, wetting herself as she parted her legs slightly. Charlotte's fingers instantly took advantage of the space, further pressing down at her dampening sex. 'Yes, I've been licked before. I love it. I fucking love it.'

'So you won't mind doing it to us, will you?' Charlotte said, her middle finger now teasing the parting pussy lips.

'I'll do it, yeah,' Tara said, smiling now, 'I'll lick you both until you scream. Just let me, come on, please.'

Tara's plea was muffled by Seona as she turned the girl's face and started tonguing her lips, nibbling at her. The girl responded with violent enthusiasm, her fingers rising to wind through Seona's hair, pulling her closer, tonguing deeply as Charlotte slipped the loose cotton dress off her shoulders, leaving it to drop down her bare body.

'Believe me,' Charlotte said as she eased Tara's thighs further apart, the scent of her arousal now strong and unmistakable, 'you may have been licked before, but you've never had anything like this, and you won't ever get it again. So enjoy it, dear.'

Charlotte resumed tongue-lashing the solid nipples as she pressed her middle digit fully into Tara's pussy, holding it hard and firm, steady against the girl's gradually quickening thrusts.

'More, oh please, more,' Tara begged, her hand now at Charlotte's head, pulling her hard as she eagerly fed her reddened breasts to the lips and fingers of the older women. Charlotte withdrew her finger slowly, Tara's pussy seeming to clamp about it, reluctant to let it go. Bunching three fingers, firmly reaming the widening gap, the deliberate insertion of the compressed digits elicited a high loud groan from Tara, and Seona brought her palm across the girl's mouth to urge restraint.

Charlotte's thumb worked up and down at Tara's clit, now delightfully prominent, and the girl started to slump, her thighs shaking as the climax neared.

'Not yet, dear,' Charlotte warned, drawing her hand away from Tara's pussy, the relative coolness of the air enveloping her wet fingers as Seona supported the girl's descent to the floor.

Seona took over the oral assault on Tara's breasts as the girl lay, her legs already spreading, her sandals kicked off as she gyrated, her pussy fucking the air, awaiting Charlotte's tongue. Charlotte, now completely naked apart from her cute little suede shoes, positioned herself between Tara's legs, easing the strong, lightly tanned thighs further apart to view the perfect tightness of her. The panties were still in place, trapped by Tara's buttocks, but Charlotte drew the torn white band smartly away, ensuring that the moist cotton was drawn hard over the budding clitoris. The action seemed to spur Tara free of any vestigial inhibitions, and she released a low bestial growl of utter lust as she reached up eagerly to start kneading at Seona's behind, hauling her nearer.

Seona advanced, crawling towards Charlotte, eyes locked on Tara's sex, her own floral skirt now raised as she drew her tight top up, her breasts dropping freely. Tara's tongue eagerly lapped at Seona's chest as Charlotte got her hands behind the girl's knees and pushed the long legs back, drawing the reddening labia within easy tonguing distance of Seona.

And Seona did not waste any further time viewing the girl's body – she stuck her tongue out, briefly lapped at Charlotte's thickly haired pubis as if merely warming up, then lowered her face between the girl's legs, instantly plunging her stiffened tongue as far as she could, her head vibrating rapidly from side to side as Tara's arms enveloped Seona's behind, gripping onto them as she buried her face in the pussy above her to quell her shrieks.

Charlotte pushed Tara's legs higher as Seona started drawing the girl's pussy open, her lips tenderly cushioning the clitoris as her fingers parted the pulsing ridges of soft flesh. Lowering one of Tara's legs gently to the ground, Charlotte concentrated on using both hands to further elevate the other, so high now that the girl was forced to twist, the delicate brown tightness of her arse now bared and clearly visible as Seona's fingers drew the combined saliva and pussy-juice down to coat it. Charlotte rested the taut shaven calf against her chest and raised her face to lick at the girl's mother-of-pearly painted toenails, fingers caressing the slenderly boned ankle. She did not look down as fingers started to paw at her own pussy – she knew it was Seona, and she also knew it would be an unforgiving, speedy finger-fuck.

'Be careful with your teeth,' Seona warned, only briefly disengaging her mouth from Tara's sex as her face looked up, grimacing, eyes screwed shut. Charlotte cupped her friend's face and widened her knees a little further to let the fingers delve deeper.

'Suck her clit, Tara, she likes that,' suggested Charlotte, and it was clear from Seona's high sudden moan that the girl had instantly found the mark, was doing as ordered.

'I should've done a wee,' Charlotte said, and Seona looked up with a wicked wet smile, her lips and chin already glistening, 'but it would spoil the flow, wouldn't it?'

Seona shifted back a little as Charlotte moved forwards, forcing Tara's legs yet further back to bring her own pussy hovering over the girl's widening parting. With Seona now practically sitting on her face, Tara's climactic cries were effectively silenced as Charlotte thrust her hips forwards, her fingers now delicately, accurately framing her lips as she prepared to release the piss. Seona kept her head well back but used her fingers to part Tara's lips wide, her thumb flicking at the unusually prominent clitoris.

Tara seemed to convulse when the first strong jet of Charlotte's urine hit her sex, splashing wildly in a mushrooming series of arcs, like water hitting a spoon. Charlotte shifted a little, holding the next burst back as long as she was able before directing the next gush with pinpoint accuracy onto the point where Seona's fingers were now firmly teasing Tara's clit. The girl grunted, pulling her face away from Seona's sex only momentarily to draw in a huge and noisy gulp of air before once again plunging herself fully into the older woman's hole. Seona's face registered the resumption of Tara's attentions, her mouth now wide open as the girl's tongue explored new flesh, pushed new boundaries.

'Oh yeah, at my arse, yes, that's it, right there,' Seona gasped, her own climax nearing. With both of Tara's hands busy pulling at Seona's nipples, it was clear that the girl had decided to move her tongue higher, and Charlotte sensed that Seona's climax was now imminent. She plunged her thumb, wet with her own piss, into Seona's mouth as she directed the final stream of warm urine wildly, allowing the weakening jet to spray across Tara's thighs and belly as she concentrated on bringing herself off.

'Oh my God,' Seona cried, drawing her torso higher, the girl's hands still clamped about her breasts. Charlotte could only watch as Seona lowered her own hand to frig herself as the girl continued her anal exploration. Charlotte had to see what was happening, had to get some of it for herself – the slightest oral contact now would surely finish her off.

She got up, moving quickly. Seona remained crouching, and Charlotte could now see that the girl's long and stiffened tongue was indeed poking, stabbing at Seona's behind. Charlotte positioned herself directly behind Seona, knelt again, palmed her friend's buttocks fully apart to distend the hole the girl was aiming to occupy, and Tara moved swiftly, craning her neck to reach the brown hole. Seona's gaping pussy was virtually enveloping Tara's chin, her lips flanging the pale skin as she gently fucked the face, and Charlotte could resist no further, bringing her own sex behind Seona's, her palms still strongly parting her friend's arse-cheeks as she conjoined her own sex with Seona's to form a two-pussied, dual-arsed assault on Tara's face.

The girl's tongue did indeed come to Charlotte's sex, lapping at her piss-coated lips, moving away to resume her anal assault on Seona while her fingers busily pushed and teased Charlotte's lips.

'I'm nearly there,' Charlotte said, her eyes closing as she savoured the quickening fingers, the irreversible climb to the orgasm. 'Suck her, Seona, fuck her with your hand.'

Seona seemed unable to answer, her breathing now erratic, almost desperate, but Charlotte could tell from the shifting of her friend and the increasingly pained grunts from below her that Tara's pussy was now being filled, and probably licked simultaneously.

Charlotte's climax approached swiftly then, as she shifted slightly to see the strawberry-blonde pussy crammed with Seona's hand, the fingers fully embedded in her as she bucked madly against them, urging Seona to enter her fully.

The tongue was back at her clit, flicking wildly as two, maybe three fingers slipped into her, another digit pushing into her behind, and Charlotte was there, giddiness swamping her, the disorientation as delicious as it was utterly and instantly exhausting. She slipped away from the still-fucking women, gratefully finding the cool floor as the orgasmic waves receded. Pain tingled at her clit where Seona had been frantic, rough, and her backside was gently pulsing. The cries of Seona came next, and her climax was a slow, grinding one, perhaps prolonged by the enforced need to maintain a modicum of silence. And then Seona's heavy, throaty panting was overridden by the higher, girlier cries of Tara as Seona fist-fucked her to what surely was not her first come, fingers playing at her clitoris like some instrument, the hand now buried entirely within her as the girl writhed and thrashed beneath the older woman.

'Someone's coming,' Charlotte heard herself say, a familiar creak at the head of the stairs alerting her. Opening her eyes, it seemed that she had lost some time, perhaps momentarily passed out. Seona had slumped onto Tara, the girl's legs now concealing the older woman's face as they gently bucked against one another, their climaxes subsiding.

She had to move quickly. Her dress was crumpled beneath Tara's thighs, soiled with her own urine.

The gentle knock on the door was tentative, almost apologetic, as if the person perhaps knew what they were interrupting.

'Charlotte?' came the voice, male and low but surprisingly clear. She got to her feet, reaching for the towel rail, flinging one to the floor in front of Seona as she turned on the hand-basin tap and drew another larger towel to sling around her flushed torso as she neared the door.

The light rapping was repeated.

Seona pulled herself away from Tara, biting her lower lip to suppress the urge to groan as the younger woman's arms flopped to the floor. Tara's head was slowly swaying from side to side, eyes closed, a faint smile on her damp lips.

Charlotte unlocked the door and made sure her toes were braced against it as she opened it just a tad. It was Jerry, one of Leo's new wife's entourage.

'Charlotte, I'm so sorry, but you'd best come right away. It's Leo. I'm afraid, well, I think he's had a heart attack.'

Charlotte's eyes must have told him she recognised the urgency, for he turned quickly. She crossed to the window, still open, and raised herself to peer out down into the garden. Sure enough, the small crowd surrounding the table where Leo had been sitting dozing on his folded arms was dense enough to conceal a clear view of him, and from the attitude of the bodies it was clear that the old family friend was indeed in trouble. Someone was attending to him. There would be no shortage of expert help, but something about the messenger's tone and the anxious resignation of the spectators told Charlotte that the medics, even if they were already on the way, were already too late.

Leo was dead.

Three

He shifted in the seat, gripping the arching slender wooden arms to conceal the trembling of his fingers.

The girl was good. Very good. He'd seen four Kaylas at first hand, had the privilege of knowing two of them intimately. Of course, he'd once enjoyed access to all the files, knew what personal details existed regarding all the previous holders of the mythical title, but it had been a long time now since he'd been able to refresh his memories of them, and with the files now missing, presumed destroyed, he knew that his passing would take those details underground once and for all.

Quite possibly, she was the best he'd seen, although certainly not the most technically beautiful. Her body, although perfectly proportioned, was rather on the small side. She was probably shorter even than his favourite, the wonderful Charlotte. The manner of her leaving still disturbed him, and not a day passed when he did not rue the awful betrayal she'd suffered at the hands of erstwhile friend Imogen. Yes, he'd participated, assisted in the deception, and so had the Librarian, now senile and rotting in a sanatorium in Copenhagen, but they'd all been duped, laid low by a higher, mightier force that had required the total destruction of Kayla as revenge for indignities suffered at her hands.

He had fled Paris when they came for him and the Librarian, been forced to abandon her when she expressed doubt that anyone would dare assault them in such an overt way. What they'd done to her he couldn't begin to guess, but the experience unhinged her, and in a few short months she had lost her looks as well as her mind. He'd only dared ever visit the once, but she had no idea who he was – the name Kayla still registered with her, but only served to make her cry. He'd left her that rainy day determined that Kayla would be resurrected.

And now, almost five years later, she was there right in front of him, every man's dream – petite and demure and preternaturally attractive, but capable of administering the sexual arts with a savagery few could imagine, let alone possess. She was a worthy recipient of the refreshed title, and he would do his utmost to ensure that she was given every chance to restore it to its proper place and influence in the corridors of power.

She glanced around, her pale-blue eyes locking on his as if she was aware of his thoughts and approved of them. Her lips were parted, her pinky gloss still remarkably smear-free considering how fiercely she'd been sucking on the brown uncircumcised cock now wavering in front of her. She continued staring at him even as the man's hand went to her cheek, gently urging her to resume sucking him, and she palmed his hand away before reaching down to pull at her right buttock – the other two men were fully inside her, both passages filled with solid cock as she pushed back against them, deliberately scraping her steel-tipped heels against their thighs, scratching deeply as they strained to maintain their uncomfortable occupation. The photographer moved silently about the podium, his camera silently capturing the set piece, always careful not to capture her full-face. It was not his place to direct, to advise in any way, he was merely to record the event and leave behind all of the equipment he'd been issued with when he was finished. He'd already taken some video-clips. There was plenty. They could finish any time they wanted.

He couldn't help shifting once again as she gave him a broad brilliant smile before turning, reaching once again for the chubby man's penis, and soon she had him erect again, her fingers splayed across his thighs as she took him directly and deeply in a series of long slow strokes which made him quiver. The two men occupying her other holes re-established a fucking rhythm, and she complied, bucking herself higher with each of their strokes, forcing the crouching man to mount her completely, his trembling calves displaying the extent of his exertions as he struggled to keep himself in her behind.

When she turned again, the whiteness was swinging from her coated chin, a creamy band of it also clinging to her forehead, snaking a course over her nose and lips. And still she smiled, genuinely pleased with herself. Then she pouted, the gathering discharge forming a pooling thick globule on her lips which seemed to wobble defiantly for a split second before coursing down her chin to thicken the dangling ribbon.

He brought a hand to his crotch. A long time since he'd been so instantly impressed. The people in Prague had been right enough, and, if anything, the earlier evidence he'd seen of her prowess did not do her justice. She was, in the flesh, electrifying, and he knew he'd made the right choice.

Yes, her body was great. The breasts were high-placed and almost unnaturally pert – when she'd been riding on top of the men earlier, doing all the work herself, he'd been mesmerised by her tits, the solidity of them as she fucked up and down on the conjoined cocks. But she was entirely natural, something that was becoming increasingly rare among those who sought to impress the great and the good. And she was not, as seemed to be the fashion, thin. There was meat on her bones, but it was well toned without being unpleasantly muscular, retaining an evenly distributed layer of healthy fat which gave her entire body the impression of having been protected by a supersuit of perfect skin. And the skin was indeed perfect, utterly blemish-free aside from that one delicious birthmark, the dime-sized brown patch, almost perfectly circular, which virtually overlapped one of the dimples that appeared on both buttocks when she stood and tensed in a particular way. And, of course, there was the texture of her flesh. So unusual. He'd never ever seen such skin before, never even heard of it. Skin so irresistible that no one who ever touched it would forget the sensation.

Her face, too, was unforgettable – all the more reason to keep her well concealed. The eyes were startlingly blue, and of a paleness which was at once entrancing but slightly sinister – the effect was not nearly so shocking in artificial light, but he had once seen photos of her shot in bright Prague winter sunshine, images in which she huddled within a huge black fur, squinting at the camera. He'd never seen such brilliantly reflective, expressive eyes in his life – they appeared unnatural, as if made from cut-stained glass and slivers of diamond.

And the eyes were the highlight of a face which most men would be content to merely witness – her lips were full and naturally red, needing virtually no attention, just as her high cheekbones seemed to accentuate the genuine rosiness of her cheeks without recourse to cosmetics. The hair was straight and dark and, he'd been informed, prone to curling when damp, but that would not be a worry in any case – she had yet to receive her 'official' Kayla hairpiece, the lightly bobbed thirties-style handmade wig which would be her best guarantee of anonymity as well as the distinguishing article incontrovertibly declaring her to those in the know as the real thing, the one and only Kayla.

But vitally, and most tellingly, she had that most attractive asset common to all Kaylas when they were still experiencing the first flush of excitement – she was genuinely keen, and the relish she brought to the strenuous tasks assigned her was beyond mere duty.

The man straddling her, his dick impaled in her rectum, pulled himself free, standing to relieve the visible pressure on his thighs and calves as he emptied his load onto her back. She craned her neck as he spurted over her, shaking her head as if in a vain effort to capture his ejaculation while the man beneath her struggled to release himself as she bucked free and hard now. His length was suddenly freed, springing up to be enveloped by her strong buttocks as she pushed back hard, milking him with the clamping muscles, his vein pumping into prominence as he, too, discharged.

He renewed his grip on the chair arms and grimaced, desperate now to free his cock and rub it as Kayla raised a gloved hand to smooth the scattered droplets across the small of her back and over her pink behind. The photographer found yet another angle behind her, briefly interrupting the spectator's view. Perhaps just as well – he was terribly close to orgasm himself, and even the friction caused by moving fractionally in the seat threatened to trigger an irreversible come.

Just as swiftly as they had been summoned to perform on her, the men were gone, and Kayla was left to recover on the velveteen-draped dais. The photographer quietly deposited the small camera alongside the other equipment which had been made available for his use, then departed as instructed through the same gap in the drapes used by the trio of anonymous forty-something ex-civil servants. The dull flicking of switches was followed by a gradual but dramatic dulling of the light, and the man delved into his jacket pocket to locate his cigarettes and lighter. There was no rush. The girl would be waiting for his reassurance and praise no less than further instructions. And, of course, she would be expecting the blonde wig. Well, that could wait until a little later. He hadn't had to hint, at their first meeting, that she would be expected to make herself freely available to him at any time, and she'd demonstrated an eagerness to display her readiness even there, in broad daylight in the back of his car on a Parisian side street. But he'd declined, as he always did until the nature of their relationship had been firmly established and clearly understood. The time was now right, and he fancied she was still capable of a great deal more, had exerted but a fraction of her youthful energy with the three much older men.

It was too dangerous to take her back to his own apartment. It would have to be her hotel room. But the wig was in the car, safe in the box. The ceremony would be low-key compared to the traditional crowning of Kayla, but perhaps all the more moving and meaningful for that. Of course, his PA would be there – there had to be a witness to complete the formalities – but she was every bit as enthusiastic as him about the whole project, at times too keen, and the many stories he'd told her of Kayla's exploits had only served to intensify the mature woman's curiosity. She would, of course, be keen to savour Kayla's attention, but that was no reason for her to stay all night. He wanted her to himself at some point, and tonight might be the only real chance. Even then, she would have to invite him – he was nothing if not a gentleman, and some rules simply were not broken regardless of the circumstances – and he could not be sure that the young beauty was that keen to voluntarily claim the scalp of a sixty-year old.

She shifted in the dimness, her suspender belt twisted and awry, her stockings rumpled, one entirely detached from the clips. The corset too had been hauled out of shape and appeared to be damaged at the back. No matter. She had more outfits than she could possibly use, and the supply of whatever she wanted was assured. The investors had made sure of that.

He admired the gently shifting musculature of her shoulders and back as she raised herself, her fingers gently tracing the flesh which had been so desperately, brusquely pounded and kneaded by the men. She would be tender for a while, and he fully intended to soothe and pamper her. But the respite would not be a long one – her first assignment had already been confirmed, there was no going back now, and even though she didn't know it, Kayla was, quite possibly, only days away from her first confrontation with Charlotte.

He closed his eyes, tasted the sweetness of the memory, could even recall Charlotte's peculiar, utterly distinctive smell, the texture of her flesh and hair. The mere thought of seeing her again was intoxicating, but the prospect of seeing her being dominated and chastised by the gorgeous creature only a few feet away from him was unbearably arousing. Or would

Charlotte be capable of resisting, of re-establishing the dominance she'd once enjoyed over each and every person who crossed her path?

The possibilities thrown up by the impending clash were fascinating, but he calmed himself with the gambler's instinctive wariness – chance decreed that Charlotte would not come herself, but send deputies, others well capable of looking after themselves. There was Seona, of course, who'd excelled all those years ago during Charlotte's training and had been a strong contender for the title of Kayla. And Imogen, the blonde-haired beauty with whom Charlotte had fallen out so spectacularly. If their friendship had regained anything like the intensity he had himself witnessed then she would be a formidable ally. But as far as he knew she was in the States and had been for some years. She would have little to gain by launching yet another claim for the mantle, and yet – if their partnership had been repaired – who could foretell the possible permutations.

One thing was for certain – this young woman was about to give the chattering classes of Europe something to more than chatter about. By the time he was finished he'd have them shaking in their shoes, and that was before she'd even started in earnest. The foundations had been laid and tested and found strong – now, with the zealous intensity found only in those who have been deeply and grievously wronged, Dark Eyes saw the future as he had arranged for it to be, and there, smiling sweetly, the reborn Kayla assured him it would all be all right, it would all work out in the end and he could die happy.

Her sigh snapped the reverie, and he stood as if to attention, sparking the lighter to his cigarette, drawing the smoke in deeply, noisily. He coughed sharply, dropped the cigarette to the tiled floor and angrily flattened it.

'Come,' he said, 'we have to leave now.'

Kayla appeared startled, as if she had genuinely forgotten he was there, and, as she turned to face him, the dim blue-tinged electric light sparkling brilliantly in her eyes, he felt the fluttering in his belly and the dryness in his throat, and wondered if he would ever be cured of this mad addiction, the need to fall in love again and again.

The daydream resurfaced, little more than a flash card in his mind's eye, but there among the victims she'd claimed he saw those bastards who'd destroyed his friends, taken his dearest Librarian from him, conspired to remove him and his work from all memory, the last repository of known history, any form of truth. He would not be denied, would have his final say, but in the mountain of claimed and tormented flesh upon which Kayla had been scaling new heights over the past century, he knew that his own features, his own limbs and flesh and even, yes, his soul were inescapably bound. He'd already given himself to her, helped her rise to where she was meant to be, and the bastards would deny her, and his own sacrifice, no more.

'Yes,' Kayla replied softly, her apparent innocence causing his chest to tighten with sympathy, 'I know.'

Charlotte was struggling to keep up. Seona's feet pounded out the beat on the hardened mud, the path now dipping again, back towards the smallest of the ponds where the ducks and swans were still settling after the last interruption. The final stretch of the three circuits – less than a mile to go now.

The sun had long been shielded behind the stubborn banks of slate-grey cloud, but the air was loaded with static, the atmosphere muggy and close. Another storm was surely brewing.

A swift backwards glance from Seona, just checking that she was still there. Charlotte quelled the urge to demand a slowing of the pace – Seona, as the fitter, stronger woman, knew what her smaller friend was capable of, and wouldn't push her beyond reasonable limits, but that knowledge didn't make it hurt any less.

They simply had to get fit, and fast, purge themselves of the alcohol and be prepared for what would undoubtedly be a serious and possibly dangerous challenge. Imogen was due to arrive just as they'd set off on the six-mile run, but it had seemed wise to leave Sunita to show her up to her room and let her recover after her flight. Charlotte longed to see her again, but whether or not she would feel the same remained to be seen, especially when she received full details of the predicament they all now faced.

The tumultuous events of the weekend tumbled chaotically in Charlotte's mind. The police had been and gone yet again that morning, just to double-check the guest list and compare it with the list of witnesses they'd found at the scene two days before. The postmortem examination of Leo's debauched body was ongoing, but she'd been told by the chief investigating officer, via a series of grunts and arching eyebrows, that no foul play was seriously suspected.

The family of swans launched themselves into the pond again as Seona neared, the gangling grey cygnets splashing awkwardly in behind their parents as Charlotte passed them. The path wound away from the pond, and uphill yet again as they made the final ascent towards the hillock dominated by the ancient Scots pine.

Charlotte tried to ignore the pain across her diaphragm, the cramps now sparking in her calves.

She knew she had no one to blame but herself – the weekly round of golf had never felt like exercise, but the squash had been too much like hard work. Abandoning both in favour of riding had seemed a fair compromise, but her body now told her precisely the extent to which it had been neglected. She screwed her eyes shut to squeeze the sweat away, pumped her aching arms into the air between her and Seona and cursed her recent sloth. The neglect was over.

Seona slowed to allow Charlotte to join her as they broached the final uphill stretch and left the path, the soft relief of the grass underfoot a welcome blessing as they traversed the huge central lawn upon which poor old Leo had spent his final afternoon doing what he did best – entertaining his coterie of friends.

The first heavy drops of rain started to fall as if urging them to crank up the pace. Charlotte watched the gap increase as Seona gradually built up the sprint for the glass-doored lounge. Her lungs screaming for relief, every muscle demanding relief as Seona pulled away, Charlotte knew she was close to collapse, but the faint shouts coming from the figure silhouetted against the lounge light exhorted her to go on, to work that body.

The voice was familiar, although the physique was not – it was Imogen.

Sunita had already left out a tray bearing a large jug of ice and several bottles of fruit squash. Seona poured as Charlotte collapsed onto the sofa, unable to settle, her limbs twitching as though they had not yet received the message to stop. The pain was impossible to conceal, and, to Imogen's obvious delight, intensifying with every passing second.

'Poor dears,' she said. Thankfully, despite her three-plus years in Dallas she had not yet developed any trace of a twang. 'It must be this ghastly weather.

When you have to stay indoors half the year it's no wonder you overdo it when you finally get out.'

Charlotte was not yet capable of replying, but she registered Seona's expression of disgust as the glass of lime juice was passed to her. She sat up, crammed a cushion behind her back and unzipped the front of the tracksuit top. The sudden influx of cool air was as delicious outside as the icy drink was inside. She continued puffing between sips as Seona sat in front of the ornamental hearth, back poker-straight and her joined legs flat on the floor before her as she maintained gentle stretching – she was terribly prone to cramp and would have to keep moving for the next hour or so.

Imogen had probably had a few on the flight, and was certainly wasting no time topping up. The broad heavy-based tumbler was half-empty, but would surely have been full with gin and soda. She looked utterly different, but Charlotte resisted the urge to comment until Imogen had declared her hand. The name of Kayla had not yet been mentioned to her – too dodgy over the telephone or via any other electronic medium, and Charlotte could not be sure that Imogen would be too keen to resurrect that chapter of her past.

'Well, isn't this sweet?' Imogen said theatrically, the old familiar note of sarcasm creeping back in already. Christ, she was only back a few minutes and already the tension was building. 'I come halfway around the world and I don't even get a peck on the cheek?'

She held her arms open, still gripping the glass tightly, lips already pouting, and the exaggerated totter she affected displayed that she really was rather tiddly. Yes, the heels were sluttishly high and the shocking-pink pencil skirt was rather tight about the knee area, but she was hamming it up.

Charlotte drew her knees up, raising her face to receive the kiss, and couldn't help smiling as she imparted the warning, 'Best not get too close, dear, I suspect we're both probably rather gamey at the moment.'

'Gamey-schmamey,' Imogen growled, 'come here.'

The kiss was short but firm, no hand contact whatever, and Charlotte caught a glimpse of Seona's plain disgust before it was dispelled by a beaming smile upon Imogen's facing her to repeat the process. As Imogen bent, lowering herself to Seona's raised face, Charlotte noticed that her first lover had rather expanded in the buttock department and, although her waist appeared not to have undergone any significant expansion, the increased breast size was unavoidably dramatic.

'Have you –' Charlotte started to ask, but she had no need to complete the question as Imogen drew herself up, inhaled deeply and showed off her new assets.

'I thought you'd never ask,' she said as she raised her free hand to firmly cup her right breast. 'Finally took the plunge, darlings. Best thing I ever did.'

'You did not!' Charlotte gasped, genuinely alarmed. Of all three, Imogen had always been most adamant that she would never go under the knife, not for cosmetic purposes at any rate.

'I did too, and I'll do it again as and when.'

Imogen sipped again at her drink, and Charlotte caught just a glimpse of regret in her eyes, a momentary lapse in the overpowering ebullience which suggested she was not quite as happy as she wanted her old friends to think she was.

'Bobbo was ever so pleased. He'd been on at me for a while, but, well, I didn't –'

'Bobbo?' Seona asked incredulously.

'Oh Seona, dearest. Robert. Bobby. My little Bobbo. Surely you haven't forgotten him already?'

Seona made no reply, nor did she make any effort to hide her disbelief. Charlotte moved quickly – the whole point of the meeting might easily be lost if the reunion degenerated into a girlish squabble over respective menfolk.

'How is he, anyway?' Charlotte asked, her breathing still nowhere near normal, but small snippets of speech becoming more viable.

'He's very busy. Very happy, or so he tells me when I see him every other week or so. Very happy and very busy.'

Imogen turned away, scanning the unfamiliar room as if hoping to locate a well-stocked bar. Sunita had probably fixed the drink for her, and no doubt had given her a civilised, but unacceptably mean measure of spirit. She was on the hunt for more.

'So he won't miss you being around for a while. A fortnight perhaps?'

Imogen turned to face Charlotte again, and something in her expression was so yearning, so desperate, that Charlotte wanted to rise from the sofa and hug her. But not yet. It could be one of her ploys, just another attack of melodrama. But then the shield was back up again – that glistening, perfectly maintained smile was impenetrable, perhaps another affectation that dearest Bobbo had encouraged.

'I'll do what I want to do,' Imogen replied testily, although the smile didn't fade, 'and if he doesn't like it he can go and fuck himself.'

'Well,' Charlotte said, barely concealing the smile, 'I suppose that's clear enough. I'm sorry I was so mysterious on the phone, but, well, it's just that –'

Imogen's smile disappeared as Charlotte started to speak and she moved towards the floor-to-ceiling sliding windows which comprised the wall facing onto the front lawns. Tiny lamp-lit midges were starting to congregate beneath the wooden eaves, and the bolder of the moths were starting to venture close to the lounge as dusk claimed the landscape. She paused, scanning not the tree-dominated horizon, but the window-door framing.

'How do you shut these?' she asked, sounding suddenly sober and alert. Charlotte indicated the remote control behind Seona, and she quickly located the button that brought the huge glass doors silently together as Imogen watched their smooth union, the insects hovering and retreating in stutters, as if aware that danger lay beyond.

'I know it has to be serious,' Imogen said, and Charlotte could see that her old friend was actually talking to her own reflection. 'You wouldn't have invited me here otherwise.'

Charlotte was starting to wonder if perhaps, just perhaps, Imogen was on something other than booze when she saw the shifting of her arms and realised what she was doing, saw the reflection of the blouse-front being opened. Imogen raised her palms to her breasts and covered her nipples before turning around. Charlotte held her breath, afraid to utter a word, aware that her eyes were widening with every split second she took in the sight of the huge artificially enhanced tits. Seona's harsh intake of breath signalled her own shock. Imogen appeared to be looking beyond her old friends, beyond the room, perhaps into the past, but her words were clear enough, if perhaps tinged with a justifiable self-pity.

'Before you tell me anything, before we even discuss how we're all doing and how wonderful our husbands are, I want to go upstairs and make love, preferably with both of you. We used to do it. I still remember those times. Often.'

She looked down at her spherical boobs, her eyes already filling with tears.

'I don't recognise myself any more,' she said quietly, and Charlotte felt the sob rise in her own throat.

'You look fantastic,' said Seona, already getting to her feet. Imogen looked wary, fearful, but Seona advanced carefully, her eyes locked on Imogen's breasts.

'Come shower with me,' Seona said then, voicing Charlotte's own thoughts. Imogen looked down at Charlotte and extended her hand.

Charlotte rose and, despite herself, despite the sadness her friend was clearly experiencing, she knew from the knots in her own stomach that she couldn't wait to get hands, lips and tongue about those fantastic breasts.

Kayla would just have to wait until much later.

The utter blandness of the hotel bedroom was strangely comforting to Dark Eyes. Kayla's room was through the wall behind the bed. The rooms would, of course, be completely identical, but mirror images of one another.

It wasn't even really what he considered a hotel, more a resting-spot for travellers with conventional basic bed and bathroom facilities. The complex had not yet been completed, and the receptionist had been reassuringly moronic, seeming barely capable of ensuring that they were given the correct keys, let alone asking any potentially awkward questions. He'd completed the formal paperwork quickly using false names and paid cash with a little on top to help reinforce his request that they not be brought breakfast and be left undisturbed regardless of any calls or visitors.

Kayla had requested an hour. No matter. It gave him time to prepare. His PA seemed less able to relax, was obviously anxious to see more of the mysterious girl she'd heard so much about. She'd busied herself trying to tune in the television to anything viewable, despite his repeated insistence that the complex had not yet completed the satellite connections which would make any reception possible. She then inspected the bathroom, the light fittings and had partially dismantled the telephone as if convinced that she would, eventually, find some form of bugging device.

Poor soul. She was in her mid-forties and had come to him highly recommended from an old colleague whose security apparatus in an ex-Soviet bloc country had recently been dismantled, its staff scattered and disappeared. She was one of the fortunate ones whose skills marked her out as worthy of more than enforced retirement, but old habits died hard, and her paranoia still irked him after more than three years together. Still and all, there was always the chance that one of these days she would indeed find something, and caution was always an asset in their business.

In line with convention he had insisted that she answer to the title of 'Librarian'. He had been trying to forget her real name – it made things so much easier in the long run – but it was Karena, and she had a grown-up son who was doing well in South America; she spoke all the major European languages, understood most Slavic tongues and was still improving her Scandinavian prowess; although she couldn't possibly be aware of it, and he had no idea how such things had been determined, her files showed that she had an IQ of 152 and had a high pain-tolerance; she had no surviving family aside from her son and an elderly aunt whose whereabouts were unknown. Quite apart from anything else, she retained the exquisite looks which had first drawn her to the attention of the secret services and assured her success as a spy in her early years.

He removed the shirt and paced nearer the bathroom. The light inside was on and she had left the door ajar – she was folding a towel, but staring at herself in the mirror above the washbasin. She was still fully dressed, was merely preparing the bathroom for his use, but she'd already been in there a while. Perhaps she knew he was looking, perhaps not, but she continued stroking the folded edge of the towel, fingers bringing the sewn corners together, and when they did not match quite exactly she allowed the towel to drop open once again and repeated the process. She was angling her face, playing with the light as it concealed, then shone upon the lines about her eyes and forehead. She had never struck him as a vain woman, although he'd known many women – and men – who demonstrated much deeper self-love with much less reason. She was beautiful, and perhaps she could not appreciate how little her looks had faded over the past two decades. But then again, she did not have access to her files, and had been uprooted, changed identity so many times that surely she had little remaining personal evidence to show that yes, she was once young. He would show her one day. It was still too dangerous, but the time would come.

He advanced another step and cleared his throat. She instantly completed folding the towel and neatly draped it over the edge of the steep-sided bath.

'I'm sorry,' she said, 'you've been waiting.'

He raised his hand to gently lie upon her clasped hands. She had been his lover for long enough now to know that she was special, and yet, despite her past as a beautiful female spy and all that that entailed, despite her knowledge of Kayla and the nature of her business, he knew that she was nervous, anxious. They had both, in their own line of work, in their own ways, done many shocking things, things which would appal and disgust respective lovers. But this was different. This time, they would both be participating, and in a way, this aspect of their work would draw them together in a unique and unprecedented way. It was a big night for both of them, and he knew she knew it. He squeezed her conjoined fingers.

'It is going to be OK, but you have to trust me, and you have to trust this young woman, this Kayla.'

Karena – no, he reminded himself yet again, no, she was now the Librarian – looked down at his hand upon hers, and he felt the shudder of her stuttering breath vibrate through his fingertips.

'You will do exactly as she commands, tonight, and for ever after tonight. She is Kayla. That has been decided. Accept it and learn to love her, despite what she may do to you. Learn to succumb utterly and she will reward you, she will reward us both. I know you fear no one, but she is as worthy as any other of great respect. You are to be careful in your dealings with her and any associated with her. That is my order. Should anything happen to me, you become her guardian as there is no one else authorised. You understand?'

She looked up into his eyes, and he could tell that she wanted to be kissed, wanted him to make love to her there and then, but his final gentle squeeze of her fingers was, they both knew, a goodbye of sorts. The cosiness of the old straightforward business relationship was coming to an end. From now on, they would both have to answer to a higher authority in crucial aspects of their lives, and that authority just happened to be a 24-year-old woman.

'Do you understand what I have just told you?' he repeated, and she nodded, her lips tightened, the frown adding ten years to her.

'You are Kayla's Librarian, and I am her guardian, and may God help us all,' he said sternly, although he could not hold her gaze. 'And now, we must prepare for her arrival.'

'Yes sir,' she replied, and although she managed somehow to absorb the tears which had already been forming, he knew she would take whatever Kayla might throw at her.

An alarming clunking sound, near and loud and followed by a strange new silence, alerted them both, and the Librarian shifted a little closer to him as they both turned to stare at the tiled wall behind the shower unit. He held her close and gave her a final reassuring cuddle, but the slight shiver of apprehension was tinged with genuine relish.

'It's OK,' he said, still staring at the spot through the wall where he imagined the curvaceous petite body to be, 'it's just Kayla. She's finished showering.'

It was as if the preceding decade had simply not happened. Of course their bodies had changed, their circumstances and personalities and attitudes had been transformed, but if anything, it was better than ever before.

Charlotte and Seona sandwiched their old friend in the shower, strenuously responding to her urgent demands. Whatever Bobbo's attributes, Imogen's husband had clearly been unable to satisfy her sexually, and the release of her frustration and lust was volcanic, almost uncontrollable.

'Oh yeah, lick me,' she panted as the powerful

shower spray thundered against their flesh, Seona kneeling, her face buried between Imogen's thighs.

Charlotte raised the tube and squirted another thick worm of the coconut-scented skin-rub across Imogen's matted, dripping hair. The translucent green compound instantly frothed and bubbled, coursing down her back as Charlotte palmed it into the tanned flesh, leaving the water to bring the foam down her spine, swiftly channelling into the raised crevice of her backside. The cream was textured with flecks of something hard, the gently scouring effect surely adding to the sensations swamping their tiddly friend as Charlotte worked her open palm hard against the tight buttocks, Imogen's own hand moving back to pull and part her cheeks.

'Fingers,' Imogen gasped, 'please, fill me, fuck me.'

Charlotte declined to obey immediately, never prepared to demonstrate such submission – there had always been that competitive tension between them and, despite the intensity of the moment and her undeniable wish to do as she was being told, Charlotte instead slapped down hard on the slippery buttocks, both hands alternately cracking wetly against the taut foamy flesh.

'I hope you girls have some toys here,' Imogen said weakly, and the desperation in her voice was clear.

'Maybe,' Charlotte said teasingly, knowing full well what Imogen wanted – she was planning ahead, probably picturing that strap-on they'd used for the first time so many years ago. That tool had long been discarded, but there were others and Imogen surely knew it.

Seona got to her feet again, pushed back the wet hair from Imogen's face and started to kiss her deeply, strongly lapping at her lips as the water continued to pound onto them. Charlotte brought her hand up hard into the space between Imogen's legs and found that Seona's fingers were already fucking Imogen's pussy, three fingers bunched and working steadily in and out of the dripping juncture. Charlotte pooled the coursing foam, used it to help ream their friend's behind, not invading but merely slackening, softening the back passage. Imogen's thighs were trembling, her torso slipping, moving downwards as Seona gripped her head, applying the kiss as if trying to suck the life from her, and Charlotte helped keep her upright, moving both hands to encompass and raise the heavy breasts. The nipples were too slippery to get a proper grip, but the strength of her palms beneath the silicone-packed tits was enough to help steady Imogen as Seona's finger-fucking intensified.

'I need fucking,' Imogen whined, almost sobbing as Charlotte squeezed hard at the unusual firmness of the swollen tits, Seona's fingers now hammering into the woman at such a pace that her voice was quavering as she spoke. 'I need it now, please.'

They moved quickly, Seona helping her from the shower as Charlotte quickly towelled her down with the bath-sheet before seeing to herself. Imogen slumped onto the bed, eyes closed, muttering as though hallucinating, her own hands palming across her breasts and tenderly scanning her puffed and completely shaven sex as she waited for them.

Charlotte hauled open the drawer and had Seona select the strap-on she wanted. She opted for a short and ridiculously thick black rubber tool with broad leather strapping. They'd used it many times before, but it would be the first time Imogen had ever experienced its unnatural girth. Charlotte drew out her own favourite, the heavy flesh-coloured model which was, supposedly, a perfect replica of a well-known US porn star's cock. She wasn't familiar with the man, had seen none of his work, but the grotesquely veined foot-long instrument with the broad mushroom shaped helmet was indeed impressive, if slightly daunting.

Charlotte hauled the straps up hard between her legs and stretched the clip to connect at her right hip. Her flesh folded about the edges of the rubber, skin-clinging belts, the nipping pain annoying her sufficiently that her own determination to use the weapon hard and fast on the writhing Imogen was suddenly overwhelming. She licked her palm and circled the cock-bulb, running her saliva about the flanging glans. Seona was ready too, had already secured the thick black dildo in place and was mounting the bed, clearly intent on getting the thing into Imogen's mouth.

Seona was tracing Imogen's mouth with her finger, urging the woman to open, slipping her thumb in between the gleaming teeth. Imogen opened her eyes to see the thick black dick-head hovering over her face, and she reached up to grasp it before Charlotte reached forwards and landed a stinging smack across her thigh.

'No hands, dear,' Charlotte snapped, 'you know the drill. Open wide for Seona.'

Imogen did as she was told, and Seona used her hands to force the tool down as she straddled Imogen's head, her still-wet thighs forming a triangle at the base of which Imogen's gaping face now waited for the artificial cock to be pushed into her mouth. Charlotte steadied her own tool, briefly stroking it hard against her. It was solid, and any contact with the shaft was instantly transmitted to her trapped clitoris. The harder she fucked Imogen, the better her own climax would be.

Seona was already circling Imogen's lips with the black rubber thickness when Charlotte motioned her to stop while Imogen's body was shifted just a little further down the bed – with her backside now so near the edge, Charlotte would be able to remain standing as she fucked her, and the position would allow her the extra degree of force she needed to enhance her own come.

'You must be nearly ready, dear,' Charlotte said, smiling as she witnessed Imogen's mounting frustration.

'Oh yeah, you know I am,' Imogen rasped, her lips tight, expression angry, 'and what goes around comes around, Charlotte, you'll be next.'

'That's for me to decide,' said Charlotte as Seona shifted forwards again and unceremoniously stuffed the broad rubber tool into Imogen's mouth. She released a muffled cry of anguished shock, but there was little time for her to protest before Charlotte was tapping the heavy end of the fleshy cock down hard against the bare clitoris, eliciting simultaneous grunts from Imogen as her mouth was stuffed, her throat already starting to bulge as she was forced to take the dildo deeper.

'Knowing you,' Charlotte said as she slid two fingers into Imogen's pussy, 'it won't have been that long since you were double-fucked, or does Bobbo have you on a tight leash these days?'

Imogen's eyes opened briefly, her angry stare confronting Charlotte for just a second or so, but she had no chance of answering as Seona leaned forwards and pushed down harder, her fingers guiding the breadth of the rubber into Imogen's mouth although she was clearly unable to take any more.

'And you used to like it so much,' Charlotte continued teasing, 'if memory serves you even liked taking two at a time in here, didn't you?'

Imogen's growl was bestial, loaded with lust as well as anger, and Charlotte brought the head of the cock to Imogen's lips, her fingers now tapping, gently slapping the hard clitoris. It was true, and Charlotte knew that Imogen would recall the occasions just as clearly as she did – that time, in Madrid? Or was it Barcelona? It didn't matter now, but she still recalled with perfect clarity the sight and smell of two cocks working in and out of Imogen's pussy as Charlotte watched close up, her own sex similarly packed. She couldn't remember the men's faces, the details of how they'd ended up there or what the point of the exercise was, but it had been an official Kayla job, just one of many they'd crammed into that insane ten-year period. It had never ceased to amaze Charlotte that she could recall the various sexual encounters in such detail, while the context, the circumstances, were so easily dulled and dimmed with age.

Imogen's hand moved towards her sex as Charlotte started to shove the long tool into her, but she stretched her fingers open, hovering over her mound, perhaps mindful of Charlotte's warning as the thickness was relentlessly driven inside her. Charlotte opened her hand and pressed down hard on Imogen's belly, feeling the vague sensation of her friend being slowly but surely filled with artificial cock. She used the heel of her hand to compress and shift the beleaguered clitoris as Imogen's hand shook with the restraint she was having to exert. Charlotte drew her thumbs down to further part the already well-open pussy lips, inching forwards again to bring the tool as fully home as possible as the bulging rubber testicles were brought against Imogen's arse.

'You said you wanted to be fucked?' Charlotte asked, and Imogen groaned, Seona's hand still firmly holding the black rubber in her mouth.

'OK dear, let's see how much fucking you can really take,' Charlotte said, and she had barely finished the sentence before Seona leaned forwards fully, supporting herself on outstretched arms as she started to face-fuck Imogen. Charlotte withdrew her dildo almost fully, steadied the juice-coated shaft, wiggled it hard, the head still inside Imogen, then released it, plunging it back into her friend with such momentum that the artificial scrotum made an audible smack against the woman's dampness upon meeting her flesh.

The rhythm was instantly established – brutal and relentless, it was only a matter of seconds before Imogen started to jerk, her stomach muscles spasming into prominence as the dildos were slammed into either end of her, her hands now pawing at Seona's tits and arse as she drew the rubber into her throat. Charlotte gripped Imogen's hips, hauling her torso nearer against the brute force of the fucking which was shifting her back further up the bed, and Seona helped too, pushing Imogen's body down, urging her to buck against the gleaming length of hard pinkness as it glided in and out of her.

'Maybe you need more down there,' Charlotte said as Seona drew the cock out of Imogen's mouth, already shifting again – she knew what was going to happen next.

Imogen needed little encouragement to stand up, but she had little chance to voice any objection or observations as Charlotte immediately forced her to bend, her stretched mouth now forced to accept her own pussy-juices as Charlotte drew her head onto the bobbing pink shaft.

'Seona's going to sit there nice and steady, dear,' Charlotte said quietly, slowly, as if instructing an idiot, 'and you're going to sit your bum down on that thing. OK?'

Imogen's eyes moved, her mouth still stuffed as she moved a hand behind her to where Seona was now seated on the edge of the bed, the broad short black pole thrusting upwards from her sex. Her fingers located the end of the thing, and she had barely registered the thickness of the central section of the shaft when she pulled away from Charlotte's dildo and angrily shook her head.

'No chance. It's way too thick. It's been absolutely ages and I don't –'

She was gagged again as Charlotte roughly stuffed the wet cock-end back between her lips, forcing her to screw her eyes shut and concentrate on taking the pliable rubber in the new position. Her hand moved back down to the black cock behind her, fingers once again assessing the girth of the tool as if perhaps willing it to thin and wilt. Seona was sitting back, her shoulders hunched as she regained her breath and smiled at the sight before her – the old friend who'd so often claimed to be the best of them, who'd even staked her own futile claim to be Kayla – now she was being humiliated at her own request, about to be buggered despite the weak protestations which were undoubtedly more than theatrical defiance.

'Sit on it, and don't speak again,' Charlotte ordered.

Imogen shuffled back and started to lower herself, her mouth still clamped about Charlotte's dildo as Seona steadied the heavy tool, one hand raised to help part the tight buttocks and expose the damp but firmly shut anus.

Seona helped raise Imogen's thigh aloft as she gingerly lowered herself closer to the dildo – as soon as the slender head was positioned correctly, Seona nodded up to Charlotte.

Imogen must have anticipated Charlotte's next move, but she made no effort to stop it – Charlotte brought her hands to Imogen's shoulders and pushed down hard. Imogen squealed as her backside was broached and she found herself impaled on the dildo, her sphincter snapping about the rubber in an effort to restrict its entry.

'No way,' Imogen cried as she yanked Charlotte's dildo from her mouth with such force that a long swinging ribbon of spittle slapped across Charlotte's belly. 'I can't, it's just too –'

Charlotte wound one hand into Imogen's hair, and with the other she located her left nipple, now hard and dry and pronounced at the peak of the breast. Charlotte squeezed hard, drawing a high cry from Imogen as she yanked her head away, but only so far as Charlotte's tight grip allowed.

'I said, sit on it,' Charlotte commanded through gritted teeth, and Imogen opened her eyes, her defiance receding as she yielded to the inevitable. With eyes shut again, Seona's fingers sunken into her thigh-flesh by way of assistance, Imogen allowed her weight to drop onto the vertical shaft, and Charlotte watched, transfixed, as her old friend gaped, sound-less, breath suspended and chest magnificently thrust, nipple still painfully clamped between thumb and forefinger as her reluctant backside was judderingly filled with solid rubber.

Charlotte cupped Imogen's cheeks in her hands and allowed the thick wet dildo to bob against her friend's chest as her frown deepened and she pursed her lips, puffing lightly as she fought the urge to stand and free herself of the implement.

'How that does feel now?' asked Charlotte, and Imogen did not answer, but when her eyes opened again they were milky, glazed with resignation and relief.

'Now you can lie back and relax a little. This thing wants to get back inside,' Charlotte said, and Imogen obeyed instantly, lying back to be embraced by Seona's hands covering and moulding her breasts as Charlotte steadied the pink tool briefly at Imogen's sex before once again sliding it in fully. The thick rubber filling her backside was clearly felt, even via the tool, and Charlotte savoured the completeness of the entry as she started to concentrate on her own satisfaction.

Charlotte closed her eyes, gripped Imogen's hips, and started pumping into her. Seona responded likewise, jerking the thickness in and out of Imogen's backside as far as space would allow.

Their moans and cries melded, became a single voice as they worked their way towards their peaks, and Charlotte felt years of nostalgia and sheer joy build in her eyes – it was just like old times.

Four

Kayla assessed the scenario carefully, but swiftly – her training had not covered every eventuality and she did not have a manual to which she could refer.

The Librarian had donned the outfit Dark Eyes had described, but Kayla hadn't quite expected it to transform the rather dowdy woman so completely. She stood in the corner of Dark Eyes' room by the thin netting curtain which had been drawn across the door opening out onto the tiny balcony overlooking the motorway. Pulsing headlights briefly illuminated the corner, bolstering the dim light from the small bedside lamp that struggled to impart its weak crimson glow from beneath the satin handkerchief which had been draped over it.

Kayla's own outfit was plain enough – the court heels added length and tone to her legs, and emphasised her behind, which was rather uncomfortably bound within the skin-tight rubber dress. No underwear at all this evening. She'd slaked her hair hard against her scalp with gel once again, aware that the hairpiece would be added later, and the most time-consuming part of the preparation, as usual, had been the make-up. The dim lighting in the room helped to underscore the pallid foundation she'd worn to emphasis the dark eye shadow.

But the Librarian was altogether more demurely attired – the glimmering sheer texture of the black silk stockings contrasted beautifully with the thigh-high suede lace-up boots. Her corset was also black, an intricate front-lacing design of lace and what appeared to be rubber-coated boning which dramatically drew her waist in, elevating her breasts to such a degree that they appeared almost like succulent dishes which were being presented in shallow platters, and the dim outlines of nipple-flesh were only just visible. Her elbow-high gloves appeared to be made of plain black cotton, but Kayla was intrigued to see that she'd replaced her rings and bracelet over the tight black material. She, too, had spent time on her make-up, her naturally olive complexion concealed beneath a dense layer of what surely had to be stage foundation, lips fantastically bright and glossy-red, eyes concealed beneath the broad leatherette blindfold which wound about her tightly ponytailed dark hair.

She shifted her weight as Kayla neared, bringing her heels together as she stood up straight, face raised slightly as if trying to confirm the scent of her new mistress. They had kept her waiting for more than an hour, blindfolded and standing. She was surely getting pissed off as well as tired.

'You are the Librarian,' stated Kayla, and the woman nodded once, angling her head again, the better to hear over the dull throb of the pulsing traffic below them.

'And I am Kayla,' she continued as Dark Eyes silently perched himself on the edge of the bed.

'We both know that these are not our real names, but for our purposes, and for the duration of our business together, they are the only names we can have. You agree to this?'

The older woman nodded again, her lips lightly parting to reveal strong, well-maintained teeth.

'You agree to help protect me and my identity regardless of the circumstances?'

Another nod.

'You devote yourself to me utterly?'

She nodded again, but Kayla raised her forefinger to the woman's chin, lifting her face just a tad higher.

'You may answer me.'

'I am devoted to you already,' the woman said, her voice low, steady, self-assured.

'And your devotion will be intact despite what I am about to do to you?'

The woman appeared to hesitate, her lips pursing, but she was merely swallowing, clearing her throat.

'I am prepared for whatever you may wish.'

'Good. Now you may see me.'

Dark Eyes moved on cue behind the taller of the two women, carefully unstrapping the blindfold before lowering it to the Librarian's raised and protruding breasts where he allowed it to lie, the slender straps draping down to dangle over the lacy corset cups.

Kayla stepped back from the Librarian, hands on her rubber-sheathed hips, and she blatantly measured the older woman up from top to bottom, allowing her eyes to linger at those points of interest which were already arousing her.

'What experience have you of punishment?' asked Kayla, staring at the woman's thick, silk-coated thighs, the corset straps elongating the hem so that it glimmered in the dim red light. The woman's flesh seemed to tighten at the attention, as if her body was so receptive, so sensitive that even the eyesight of another could be detected.

'I have given and received it many times,' came the reply, but there was no boastful tone about her; it was a plain statement of fact. Kayla knew from what Dark Eyes had already told her that the Librarian's early years had been very difficult and she had indeed been subject to real pain. For her, this play-acting was nothing.

'And do you have a preference?' Kayla asked, aware that a note of sympathy had entered her tone – she would have to be careful, eliminate it at once. The woman blinked several times, stared at the pink-lit carpet below as if seeing snippets of past experience in the darkly swirling pattern.

'I know not to express preference,' the woman replied matter-of-factly. Her fingers, clasped together in front of her belly, tensed slightly. If she was afraid then she was doing a good job of concealing it, but she was far from nonchalant.

'You are not curious? I could take offence,' Kayla said as she turned her torso, elevating her tits within the suit, bringing her upper arm in against her chest to emphasise her cleavage. The woman's eyes scanned the space between them, rose up Kayla's calves, assessed the firmness of her thighs within the tight rubber, lingered at the ridge of her slight belly, the smoothed contours of her breasts. Then, finally, the woman's eyes shifted up again, to Kayla's face, and when the dark eyes met hers Kayla felt a surge of excitement, raw and undeniable – the older woman was truly beautiful, must have been stunning when younger, and her rather solemn expression was transformed by the brightness of her eyes.

'You are most beautiful,' said the Librarian, and Kayla smiled.

'And you are kind,' Kayla replied softly, 'now give him that blindfold.'

Kayla turned fully, her back now to the woman. Dark Eyes' face was superficially expressionless, but

Kayla could see the bewilderment rage in his eyes –
he'd suggested the course she might like to pursue
with the Librarian, but she'd insisted that she reserved the right to proceed as she saw fit considering
all circumstances. To punish the Librarian, however
lightly, was too predictable – the mere fact of her
being so much younger did not mean she necessarily
had to impose her will so violently so soon. The
Librarian's eyes told Kayla what she needed to know
– that the woman had already seen and done things
which were beyond Kayla's considerable experience,
and there was no reason why the younger woman
should not take the opportunity to learn as much as
she could. Punishment was not her forte, but she
could tell that this woman most certainly had exacted
revenge on her tormentors, and in more ways than
one. Now was the perfect time to find out just what
this servant was capable of, and in so doing she
would set a precedent, stamp her own identity on
proceedings right at the outset.

He clearly wasn't too happy about it – the sporadic
twitching of his jaw declared as much. But he would
not dissent. Not now. He would find no other, and he
knew she knew it. He'd spent years looking for her,
stumbling aimlessly from city to city, country to
country, continent to continent, always hoping,
searching, but quietly resigned to death and failure,
his lifelong dedication scorned and unmarked. And
all those years he'd been searching, travelling, she'd
been waitressing and pot-washing right there in
Prague, a mere forty kilometres from his home town.

He liked to speak of a Cosmic Joker, especially
when he'd had too much brandy. Then he'd cuddle
her close and whisper that God had given him to her,
but only after testing him in ways that she would
never ever understand. To her it was a simple matter

of being in the right place at the right time, and she was quite content for him to ponder the more esoteric features of their first encounter. But so long as he kept his promise to free her, allow her to find the independence she craved, he could be every bit as esoteric as he damn well liked.

No – he would not dissent, not now that she knew enough about him to destroy him and what remained of his beloved legend. If she decided that Kayla was no more, there wasn't a thing he could do about it.

'Tie it,' she commanded, and the woman passed the blindfold to Dark Eyes before stepping back again, hands clasped before her as she awaited further instructions. He rose slowly, examining the dark, soft band closely.

'You will punish me to the fullest extent you are capable of,' Kayla said carefully, 'and you will not spare me pain. You may not draw my blood, you may not scar me. I leave the manner of my punishment for your judgment, but be aware that I am strong and I do not cry easily. I have hurt many men and women, and I know what they are capable of receiving, as you surely do. Do not allow your status to affect your application to the task I am setting you. Do you understand?'

Dark Eyes grunted assent, and the woman breathed in deeply, as if fully absorbing the instruction before committing herself to a response.

'I understand,' the Librarian said quietly.

Kayla raised her face as the blindfold was secured tightly, felt her hardened hair yield to the pressure, crackling slightly as the solidified gel was broken, her scalp-flesh registering the narrow band as it was pulled tighter and strongly tied.

Dark Eyes' hand took her upper arm, led her to the corner where the Librarian had been standing when they entered. She was aware of the quickening of her own breath, but experienced it as if from beyond herself, objectively, calmly. She was getting excited, fearful, and soon she would be punished. The fear was delicious, had long since become addictive, it spurred and emboldened her. And it seemed the more she acknowledged the fear, the more she drew from it. She had not run away from the men who had challenged and threatened her. She had taken on each and every one of them, called their bluff and quickly located the source of their own fear, the root cause of the macho bluster she so detested.

He drew the sliding door fully open with a metallic swish that made her start. Cool air swept through the opening along with the horribly increased volume of traffic noise – so late now, surely not far from midnight, and still the traffic pounded along the bypass. She felt the netting brush against her side as the breeze brought it billowing towards her, and still Dark Eyes led her, urged her forwards. Her heels on the wooden balcony and the sudden swirling of cool air within the tight rubber dress told her that she was outside, and bringing her hands up before her, she found the rail at waist height, cold tubular steel firm in her grasp as the footsteps of Dark Eyes and then the Librarian followed hers onto the small third-floor balcony. There would be no one below to witness her punishment. Passing motorists might perhaps catch a glimpse of the silhouettes, but such witnesses would be few and far between. They could do what they liked to her.

She drew in the air as the Librarian started to work the rubber dress up over her knees, and a light tap on her thigh indicated that she should get her legs together while the tricky upheaval of the tight rubber was completed. The Librarian had clearly handled such material before, and Kayla had to strengthen her grip on the rail lest she be pulled away from it as the older woman hauled at the thick dark rubber, pulling it clear of Kayla's body before allowing it to fold back on itself, thus creating a powerful, tight band of thicker material. The action was repeated four, five times, Dark Eyes concentrating on the front of the dress as, between them, they brought the dress up about Kayla's waist and diaphragm so tightly that she strained to inhale even shallow breaths.

The air about her backside and sex was welcome, soothing after the constriction, but she was allowed little time to enjoy it. As Dark Eyes lowered the top of her dress, fully unzipping the back as far as it would go before gently folding the material to overlap the already thick band engulfing her midriff, she resisted the urge to raise her palms to the painfully stiffening breast-flesh, her nipples reacting powerfully to the air, swelling swiftly, skin goose-pimpling as she shuddered. Dark Eyes' broad long palm rested on her hip, his fingers curving around to lightly press on the juncture of thigh and crotch. Through his fingers she could feel herself tremble, the tightening of his grip perhaps meant to reassure her. The notion that he had perhaps misinterpreted her reaction to the cold as that of raw fear suddenly enraged her, but she bit her inner lip and tried harder to inhale fully despite the increasingly uncomfortable constriction caused by the rucked rubber.

Dark Eyes' hand moved to her bare shoulder, gently led her, made her turn to her right and grip the shorter rail at the side of the balcony. She turned carefully, positioning her heels together as she secured her grip. The breeze now moved against her face directly, the coolness washing across her torso, chilling her flesh further.

Despite the tight blindfold she could see what she imagined the landscape to be – the twinkling lights of the city in the distance sparkling beneath the dull orange sky above, the great pulsing vein of the motorway snaking away over the gently rising hills to the south. Even now, bared and voluntarily submissive, her tender flesh glowing under the dim red light from the room, she saw herself as if on a stage, declaring her presence to an indifferent world. But no one cared, and not a single reason could she think of why they should.

The bodies shifted behind her again, but she had issued her instructions, declared her readiness to remain submissive. There was nothing else for her to say, but when the first blow landed across the back of her thighs she couldn't help gasping aloud. Perhaps it was his trouser-belt, maybe the Librarian was using one of her own, but the strap was broad and stiff. She gripped the rail harder and lowered her face, clenching her teeth together as Dark Eyes' fingers moved over her chest and neck, smoothing softly.

The Librarian's boot heels shifted again – she would be perfecting her stance, checking her balance before the real punishment began. Cool fingers – the older woman's – pulled at her thigh, forcing her to bend further, raise her behind. The hard slap on her inner thigh, precisely on the most tender spot close to the crease of her buttocks, made her part her legs. She complied, but another sharp blow to the other thigh was demanding more separation. The posture became more difficult as her ankles strained within the shoes, now twisting, arching painfully as she endeavoured to keep her arse raised. The light slap on her now taut buttock indicated that the required position had been achieved, and she tried to gulp some air before the inevitable thrashing commenced.

The crack of the strap across her backside was like distant gunfire. Pain swamped her, and although her eyes were screwed shut behind the blindfold, a brilliant array of shifting spangling colours seemed to explode in her view, as real and awesome as any firework display. Her stomach muscles strained, solidified as she instinctively braced herself, every inch of her now charged and hardened to protect against the assault. But the Librarian knew what she was doing, and the blows were timed so that the first blast of pain was only just starting to fade when the next blow was applied, the pace only marginally quickening as the discomfort became more bearable. Dark Eyes' hands were stronger now, squeezing at her dangling breasts, taunting and teasing her nipples as the punishment intensified, the cracking slaps of the broad leather length now coming in a steady rhythm, the strength constant as the Librarian worked higher, overlapping the previous stroke slightly with every blow.

The pain levelled out, and the severe constriction of her breathing combined with the adrenalin to inspire an hallucinogenic vista before her eyes – the face of the previous Kayla appeared as it had in the images she had seen and committed to memory, and the bobbed blonde wig, far from being effective as a disguise, seemed to frame and highlight the irresistible features of the English woman called Charlotte, the one who had clearly made such a lasting and profound impression on Dark Eyes. She was petite indeed, similar in build to herself, and her demeanour, her style, had inspired Dark Eyes' long and lonely wanderings around the world. The image expanded, the face still clear as the greater context of the image sharpened into brilliant technicolour, and there she was, commanding the action as her friends lay on the platform, limbs entangled, heads furiously working at one another's sex as the men entered them, moving according to the English girl's choreography.

The vision dimmed only slightly as Dark Eyes moved her again, this time shifting her to the opposite rail so that the punishment could resume. The breeze seemed stronger now as it pulsed against her raised, strapped behind, and once again the Librarian slapped at her thighs, moulded her buttocks, made sure the position was just right before she heard the strap slice through the air yet again. Dark Eyes was at her legs, smoothing the fullness of her thighs between his broad palms, eagerly fondling her strained calves and ankles as the Librarian picked up the pace and settled into the rhythm once again.

Breathing was becoming laboured, truly uncomfortable, and she yearned to free herself of the rubber dress, suck in the evening air. She twisted her fingers hard against the steel rail, felt her arm and shoulder muscles twitch, resisted the building compulsion to throw her hands back in defence, announce that the punishment was over. She'd never gone quite so far, allowed so much pain, but solace seemed to come again from recalling those moments which had been captured and shown to her in such secrecy – the English girl's friends being penetrated, writhing as their mistress oversaw their debasement, gently bending the crop in her gloved hands, her expression displaying little more than mild amusement at the scene before her. If Dark Eyes had indeed laid the foundations properly then the woman, surely now in her mid-thirties, would respond, and soon. She would not, could not allow her name to be so crassly revealed. She would come. Yes, she would come to reclaim her anonymity, demand that the role of Kayla be laid to rest.

The giddiness became suddenly overwhelming, and she was aware of her knees buckling, her shoulders slumping, backside slackening as her bladder opened and the piss sprayed from her, splashing onto the wooden balcony, droplets registering on her ankles and calves as the warm liquid came away from her. Resistance receded; strong hands, male and female, moved quickly to support her as the pain reached a crescendo, thighs and buttocks now burning, screaming for relief.

But even as she fainted, even as she was aware of control leaving her and her weight being relieved by the Librarian and Dark Eyes, Kayla saw the face of Charlotte, close and clear and smiling sweetly, and the lips, so beautifully painted, so luscious, were mouthing the same words over and over again. Kayla heard herself ask what she was saying, what did she want, but the face of the English girl splintered and shattered in a blaze of blinding light, the parting glimmers disappearing beyond her field of vision, leaving a deep and silent darkness where pain was instantly softened and blissful sleep was hers to take.

Charlotte passed Imogen the glass of water, but her old friend was engrossed in the paper, frowning as she reread the translation. Dawn was casting a tangerine undertone to the eastern clouds, and the house was quiet. Seona had gone home to pack a bag and would meet them at the airport.

'According to this,' Imogen said, the disbelief clear in her voice, 'Kayla is just the code-name for a notorious English spy who has been infiltrating foreign intelligence services for decades. The latest Kayla recently tried to sell her story to a news agency via a journalist based in Prague, but persons unknown moved quickly to remove her from possible scrutiny and her whereabouts are unknown. The journalist was detained and questioned by police on suspicion of aiding a kidnap attempt, but was released without charges being brought. He, too, has disappeared and his employer says he has filed no reports since his release, although his story would obviously guarantee the newspaper a huge boost. Understandably, they want to find him as soon as possible.'

Imogen laid the sheet carefully on the coffee table, avoiding the little circle of water caused by the glass Charlotte had just deposited.

'So,' Charlotte summed up as she sipped at the strong coffee, 'you can see why it was important for you to know all of this. I'm not expecting anything, but you had a right to know.'

Imogen had drawn her bare legs up to her chest, settled back in the high-backed sofa and was cuddling her knees, the frown deepening. Although her hair was lank and her face devoid of make-up, she was still quite radiantly beautiful – they'd made love for hours, gently after the initial lust had been expended, quieter still when Seona had finally fallen asleep. The years had, if anything, intensified the mutual passion.

'Is it blackmail?' Imogen asked. Charlotte weighed her answer carefully and stared down into her coffee before sitting in the armchair opposite Imogen.

'A blackmail attempt would involve demands. There haven't been any. And blackmail also implies shame, concealment. We've nothing to be ashamed of, and concealment was integral to what we did.'

'For Queen and Country.' Imogen added sarcastically, but Charlotte didn't smile.

'For whoever. It was never our place to ask, and we never did. That was the deal, it was always understood. Dark Eyes and the Librarian fled because they'd manipulated the machinery. They got caught. Too bad. They used you every bit as much as they used me and Seona. But they never did it for anything so venal as cash. If anything, it was about power.'

'And our leaving effectively removed the machinery,' Imogen continued, picking up Charlotte's thread, 'made them redundant. They were operators, senior of course, but with no machinery to operate they were useless, their function was gone.'

Charlotte put down the coffee cup and stood, arms folded. Her nipples ached terribly and she gently massaged them as she paced across to the window.

'But now, if there's a real prospect of Kayla being discussed openly, just another scandal, another sleazy story for the vultures to get their teeth into –'

As if on cue, a half-dozen dark crows swooped silently from the old Scots pine and glided off down towards the ponds in search of some breakfast. Imogen, the poor dear, was still tired and very probably more than a little hung over. This had to be terribly hard for her to get her head around, but there was no other way.

'We really are in considerable danger,' Charlotte said tersely, and the shifting of Imogen in the sofa confirmed her complete attention.

'Our silence was always taken for granted, and rightly so. But think back Imogen, think back. Over the years we fucked some pretty important people. OK, they might not be in the public eye, half the time we didn't even know who they were, it was fun, little more. But we know they stay in the shadows by choice, that they have the power to remain anonymous. If there's any real possibility of Kayla being revealed, even if she is a fake, then some of those people will move quickly to remove the real sources, the real players. That's you and me, and of course, Seona. We can't ignore this. He's warned us. That's what this is all about. Using poor old Leo as a messenger was just a typical piece of flamboyance on his part.'

Imogen looked up, quizzical, confused.

'Dark Eyes is smart,' Charlotte continued, 'he had to show us that he's still on top of things, that he knows who's who, that he has people in place everywhere who can update him any time he likes. The simple fact that we haven't seen or heard of him in years doesn't mean he hasn't been keeping very close tabs on us.'

'You mean he's had people spying on us all this time?' Imogen retorted, genuinely appalled.

'It's not impossible,' Charlotte replied, 'and Leo croaking it like that really is a bit much to take.'

'Oh really, darling,' Imogen smiled, the first real smile Charlotte had seen since her arrival, 'Leo, a spy? I can't imagine anyone less suitable. He's, I'm so sorry, he was utterly harmless.'

'Quite so, and all the more useful for it. He was used. Pure and simple. Used as a very effective mailbox to get to us. Any other avenue would have left traces, and Dark Eyes knows we're more than capable of chasing them up. Leo received enough, just enough to bring it to my attention, but the police will scour his computer, find the links to anonymous senders in Central Europe. They'll dismiss it all as the sordid web-surfing of a rather sad character and the case will be closed. No foul play, nothing amiss. An overweight alcoholic had one too many on a hot day, his heart caved in. Nice and clean and tidy, no messy loose ends.'

'Come on, you don't really believe Leo was murdered.'

'I'm just saying it might not be as straightforward as it looks,' Charlotte said as she returned to face Imogen, took her seat and cradled the cooling coffee cup in her palms.

'Look,' Charlotte said quietly as Imogen's eyes glinted, wide awake now. 'Dark Eyes loved us. He really truly loved us, and Seona too. He simply could not accept that we had our own lives, that he didn't own us. He overstepped his own remit, ignored the rules he was responsible for enforcing. We killed Kayla. It was our decision and he could not accept it. Shifting the operation to France was, for him, ostensibly a stopgap, a desperate attempt to convince himself that it wasn't over. But it was over the day we seduced the Librarian at the House. You know as well as I do that, to a man like Dark Eyes, what we did was unforgivable. He cannot possibly allow that to go unchallenged. But he doesn't want simple revenge. If he did then we would not be here now. He wants us back again, Imogen. He is the only person capable of resurrecting Kayla, and that's precisely what's happening. And he also knows that we're the only people capable of stopping him.'

'It's simply too fantastic,' Imogen said, shaking her head as she reached for the water.

'Maybe so, but I'm going to find Dark Eyes and get this sorted out once and for all. Seona's coming too. Will you join us?'

Imogen frowned into the water, as if it had suddenly become bitter.

'If we don't find out for sure we'll never know. It could all blow up again, and next time it might not be in such an obscure newspaper,' Charlotte mused. Imogen sighed.

'I suppose my dearest Bobbo will just have to struggle by without me for a few more days, then,' she said, feigning self-pity. Charlotte smiled broadly, squinting into the dawn as the first strong rays of the new day penetrated the skyline.

The Librarian was jaded, desperate for sleep, but she knew it would not come. Not yet. She was still too angry.

The sun was on the rise. The dull shifting next door told her that Dark Eyes or Kayla was up and about, but what they were doing she could not guess.

Her punishment of Kayla had been rigorous and, under most other circumstances, would have been hugely enjoyable, but she'd wielded the strap with misgivings – the girl was young and strong and full of ambition, and the Librarian knew full well that the punishment would, in due course, be applied to her, and its severity might well be more extreme.

Kayla had slept for almost an hour as she looked on, and Dark Eyes had never left her side, waiting for her awakening. When she had eventually recovered, her thighs and backside balmed with cooling moisturiser, he had presented her with the blonde wig which meant that she had, officially, assumed the role of Kayla and all it entailed. He had dismissed the Librarian then, telling her only to wait until he summoned her again. Her function as witness had been fulfilled.

Hours had passed. She'd removed her boots and unlaced the corset, tried to sleep to no avail. The jealousy raged through her, clashing with her undeniable attraction to the young beauty. And yet, he had made her no promises, had warned her not to allow her feelings to overlap with the business in hand. Typical bastard man, always looking to have his cake and eat it. Do not overlap business with pleasure, never confuse the two. So easy for him to say, perhaps even easy for someone like him to believe. But it was a different matter when he was horny, when he expected her to stroke and suck him. And was it purely business when he forced her to don the clothing which aroused him so? Merely business when he mounted her like some rabid animal, pumping at her as if she was no more than a fleshy vessel into which he emptied himself as and when required?

And now, with a woman half her age at his disposal, he had no use for her, could dismiss her without so much as a glance. She cast the thin sheet aside and felt her thighs, still tightened by the silk stockings. Her breasts ached to be free of the constricting corset, but her nipples had not yet relaxed, kept throbbing to remind her of the unsated lust.

She drew her fingers across her sex again – the dampness had dried, but her clitoris remained exposed, protuberant. She'd been so close, so damn close as they carried Kayla to the bed and removed the rubber dress. The young woman hadn't even stirred throughout the difficult procedure, emitting only sporadic groans which seemed to be inspired more by dreams than any discomfort. They'd had to use liberal quantities of talcum powder to get the material free of her skin, and eventually the young stunner lay, sound asleep, completely naked, coated in the fine white powder. It had been so difficult not to explore her then, to probe and use her. If he hadn't been there she surely would have done, and she knew why.

Her clit pulsed weakly and she savoured the brief tingle in her sex, the glimmer of possible arousal. Something in the scenario she'd just envisaged – she rewound the thought, settled on the body of Kayla, powdered and prone and utterly relaxed. The pale complexion, the perfectly sculpted face, the large eyes, closed, the gentle movement of the hidden eyeballs tracking the dream she was viewing. Running her hands freely across that young body, savouring the high firm breasts and fantastically velvet softness of her thighs and arms, the curve of her neck and hip bones. Yes, yes, it was all there, so familiar, so comforting. It could have been her. She had looked like that, so long ago. She had seen so many men's faces change the same way Dark Eyes' had earlier when faced with her beauty.

Her palms returned to her stocking-hems, felt the relative coolness of the material on her upper thighs. If she kept her eyes shut, if she forgot what age she was, it was possible, yes, it was possible to imagine that she was that young beauty next door, that she was being feted and crowned and adored. What difference was there? Some lines and a little extra fat here and there, a bit less shine in one's hair, less sparkle in one's eyes? And yet, what a difference it made to one's treatment.

Anger surged to swamp the self-pity yet again and she clasped her sex firmly, forcing her middle finger down hard against her tender clitoris. The pain was brief as she instinctively allowed the digit to slip to the side, but she forced her fingers hard together and resumed pressing with tips now trapping the tiny button of flesh, forcing herself to push against the pressure, intensify the sensation. If only she could come – those few seconds allowed her to travel back through the decades, to regain the beauty of that first moment, the instant when she'd become a full woman.

It had been recalled hundreds, probably thousands of times, but picturing herself as Kayla threw in the necessary spice to make the vision vivid, sustainable.

She drew her legs up, dropped a hand to cup her buttock just as he had in the minutes before it happened.

Her first male lover. Did he ever think of her? Had she been just another conquest in the back of his restaurant? He'd been toying with her, urging her to touch him despite her persistent refusal to do so. It was dirty, it wasn't right. But he'd gently run his length up and down her hair, grazing her enough to spark the feelings she'd never felt before. Put it in for me, he'd said, but she'd bitten her lip and shaken her head and refused again as the hot thickness nudged her thighs, his scent blending with hers as she held her legs further apart to ease the increasingly frustrating itch so deep within her. Then he'd entered her with a finger.

The Librarian parted her own thighs as far as they would go, raised her legs higher. Yes, it had been just like this. Her legs had been bare. She rolled the stockings away from her thigh-flesh, using toes to fully run the silky material away from her limbs as she savoured the smoothness of her skin; recalled how his hands had continually stroked them, his mouth even rising to lick at her toes as he'd continued tapping his cock against her, stroking her thighs with it, begging her to touch it, rub it, imploring her again and again to put it in for him.

Her middle finger slipped inside her easily now, not as strong or as thick as his had been, but the other finger was eased in to simulate the sensation. She kept her digits static, bucking against them lightly as his voice resurfaced, and in his eye she saw Kayla, young and fresh and resistant, hanging on to her virginity by sheer will and nothing else as the thick cock swayed above her, waiting for her to take it. He would not force, would never do that, and had told her so. It had to be her decision to give herself to him, and he would not allow her to be passive, to absolve herself of responsibility.

Something about her own scent now, perhaps more in her sweat than her sex, brought his odour back to her, the most difficult memory to conjure. And recollection of his aroma was forever tied to the sight of his cock pointing up at her, her own shaking hand reaching up to grasp it firmly. Self-disgust and arse-slackening excitement gripped her in that split second, as she'd tightened her grip and stroked hard for the first time, watching the strange contortions of the thing as it shifted, the great purple peak of it paling, thinning under her grip. His groan was deep and long and he shifted higher with every stroke, and then she was opening her mouth, sticking her tongue out, eager to taste the clear fluid pooling in the eye of the thing, curiosity now rampant and shattering any further restraint.

His fingers found her clitoris as she engulfed him with her mouth, cramming in as much as she could. She gagged and he pulled back, staying inside as she sucked inexpertly, the sounds coming from him now erratic, punctuated with muted gasps.

Whatever he'd done then, with his fingers, she'd pulled him from her mouth and forced him down, angling the solid shaft towards her, bucking upwards the sooner to get it inside. He'd entered her with one long steady stroke, filling her and remaining still as she hammered her sex against his, the unfamiliarity of orgasm frightening her beyond belief, and even as she struggled to control the surging reaction, fought the shuddering which seemed to be afflicting her every muscle, he was fucking her, his arms holding her hard against him, his chest-hair grazing her face as he drove into her again and again.

The Librarian suddenly remembered who was next door – Dark Eyes and Kayla may or may not have heard her. She didn't know if she'd cried aloud as the orgasm engulfed her, but she didn't care any more.

Her clitoris complained, pulsing uncomfortably as she drew her damp fingers to her chest and curled her legs, became small and quiet, her breathing slowing.

She drew the thin cool sheet across her as the memories of scent and sound faded completely, the here and now returned. She was still 43, still alone and unloved with not even the name she'd been born with to call her own, and she knew that when she next awoke the anger would be back, deeper and stronger than ever before.

Five

The approach could not have come soon enough.

Charlotte was beginning to tire of acting as pig-in-the-middle with Imogen and Seona, and the second full day in Prague had been fractious, nerve-grating for all three.

The hotel was splendid, the weather was rather humid but mercifully rain-free, and they'd enjoyed touring the city amid the throngs of tourists taking in the sights. With hindsight it would probably have been better had they opted for single rooms rather than the self-catering flat, but it had seemed safer at the time.

Requests to meet with the journalist who'd been approached by Kayla had been steadfastly rebutted despite the strenuous efforts of a splendid translator. The newspaper had not heard from him since the incident at the office, the alleged kidnap attempt and subsequent coverage. Their best guess was that he'd gone to ground, probably working on a piece about the incident, but they could not and would not release a contact number or address under any circumstances. The well-fingered photocopy Leo had given her the day he died contained no substantive clues as to the man's whereabouts, and there had even been denials that the man had ever worked for the paper at all. It turned out he was freelance, had briefly been employed there some years ago and occasionally contacted the editorial staff. The translator did, eventually get a lead of sorts – an anonymous call to his mobile, taken when they were all at lunch the previous day, had recommended that he cease working for Charlotte and her glamorous friends or there would be grisly consequences for him and his family. He'd switched off his mobile, smilingly related the content of the call, then requested full and immediate payment in cash for services faithfully rendered before promptly disappearing into the crowds.

And yet, Dark Eyes was there, somewhere. Charlotte knew it, and the others concurred, miserable though the waiting was, that their presence would not have gone unnoted. He would get to them, in his own time, and the waiting was part of his game plan. So, wait they would.

They were sitting outside the restaurant, nursing cocktails, watching dusk creep across the stonework as evening fell on Wenceslas Square. When darkness fell completely the ladies of the night would appear, nonchalantly strolling, pausing to chat to one another as their pimps kept a careful eye on them from the narrow cobbled alleys and darkened closes of the old town's centre. It would then be time to return to the villa, drink some wine, and take turns to sleep.

Charlotte had resumed smoking, and was lighting her third of the day when the man approached.

They'd already been made many offers over the two days – cheaper accommodation, guided tours of the beautiful countryside, gaudy souvenirs and free invitations to late-night clubs, all of which had been politely declined. But this guy was different, and both Imogen and Seona joined Charlotte, turning in their seats to scan him, instinctively reacting to her wariness as he neared confidently, pacing rapidly across the square directly towards them.

He was in his early thirties, and wore a plain white shirt and black slacks which were fashionably cut to mid-calf, his bare feet sandalled. Reassuringly, he was not wearing sunglasses, although many of the men they'd encountered seemed to wear them day and night.

Charlotte extinguished the cigarette as he mounted the three broad steps to the restaurant's piazza. He paused, only three or four yards from them, his eyes already fixed on Charlotte, a meagre smile developing on his lips as he took another step, more tentative now.

'Miss Charlotte?'

The voice was ludicrously deep and resonant, as though he was trying to imitate someone else. Charlotte tried to ignore the face Imogen pulled out of the man's view, feigning alarm. Charlotte nodded towards a vacant seat at the next table, but he gently waved a hand to decline the offer.

'Thank you, but I am only here with a brief message,' he said, the basso profundo tone almost comical.

'How do you know my name?' Charlotte asked, not really expecting an answer. The man smiled broadly, exposing teeth which were clean and bright but horribly overlapping and awry, as though a once-normal set had been removed one by one and replaced in the wrong holes.

'Please, miss, I am so sorry that I cannot tell you anything at all apart from the message I have been given.'

Charlotte returned the smile, which seemed to bolster his. Seona and Imogen also started up at him, both waiting. He smiled some more, nodding as he surveyed the women.

'Will this take much longer?' Charlotte asked, eyebrows raised.

'Oh no. I am sorry,' he repeated, still nodding and smiling as he clasped his thick brown hands in front of him and closed his eyes, perhaps picturing the exact sequence of words he'd been sent to impart.

'Please return your books. They are some years overdue and fines are payable. If you cannot pay the fines we will understand. Thank you.'

He bowed slowly, still smiling, apparently content that the errand had been successfully completed. Charlotte flipped open the cigarette carton and raised it to him. He opened the broad hand again, his body already shifting into retreat-mode.

'No, thank you. It is a filthy habit.'

'How do we pay the fines?' Imogen asked. The man seemed alarmed by her voice, as if he regarded her tone as implausible as she did his.

'I am sorry,' he said, turning away, palms open and facing the ground, 'but now you have the message and that is, what is it you say? That's it, folks. Thank you.'

The anger brought Charlotte to her feet. The occupants of the tables nearer the restaurant's facade stopped chatting and the waiter who'd been serving them appeared quickly, moving towards the stocky man.

'Who sent you?' Charlotte snapped, but the man's eyes were fearful, aware of the disturbance her reaction was causing, and he moved quickly down the steps, glancing back only briefly before breaking into a trot as the waiter occupied the top step, staring defiantly after the troublemaker.

The fifty-something waiter apologised as he replaced Charlotte's ashtray, and the three friends watched as the man's white shirt grew smaller, shifting shape every now and then as he turned, perhaps to make sure no one had given chase.

'The Librarian,' Seona stated flatly. Imogen snorted.

'She must be, good God, it doesn't bear thinking about. She must be kicking on for seventy by now.'

Imogen's disgust was momentarily infuriating, but a quick mental check confirmed that she probably wasn't far off the mark. Dark Eyes' most loyal assistant had to be beyond conventional retirement age by now.

Charlotte drew out another cigarette, toyed with it.

'So what do we do now?' Seona asked, the exasperation clear in her voice. Charlotte sparked the lighter, lit the cigarette.

'We do what we're already doing,' she said, puffing the smoke above her to billow into the warm evening air. 'We wait.'

The Librarian put down the binoculars and snapped her fingers. The men rose instantly from the small table where they'd been seated for hours, drinking tea and playing cards.

'It's time,' she said, and the taller of the fair-haired men buttoned his shirt, his shorter colleague already slipping on his jacket.

She went to the front door and opened it slightly. The old elevator was already descending, but she could hear the echoing footsteps pounding up the flights. He'd almost made a mess of it, had allowed himself to be quizzed, however briefly, and she'd have to be sure to impress upon him that she'd seen his every move.

The men were good, no doubt about it, and she'd personally confirmed to her own satisfaction that they were physically up for the job, but she wasn't entirely confident that they knew exactly what they were letting themselves in for. No matter – if she had any serious problems with any of them then Dark Eyes would be informed, and she'd witnessed first-hand how his presence terrified them. Even after so long, there were aspects of Dark Eyes' life that she clearly knew little about, but she did know better than to ask.

She briefly checked her hair at the small wooden-framed mirror atop the dressing table. Dressed purely for comfort, she felt good. The sports bra lent her the support she suspected she might need, but she'd shunned any other underwear given the annoying humidity. The two-piece linen trouser suit was baggy, the shoes low heeled and soft.

There had been no word from Dark Eyes for more than 24 hours, and she did not expect any – when she had Charlotte, then and only then was she to contact him. He'd taken Kayla north, but declined to tell her exactly where, leaving just a mobile number which was only to be called when Charlotte was available and willing to speak to him directly. But without Charlotte safely in her custody, the Librarian knew perfectly well there was no guarantee that she would ever see Dark Eyes again. She had to get her, and the sooner the better. Tonight.

The men waited at the front door, alert as Pavel entered, breathless and smiling.

'You told them?' she asked. He nodded, leaning on his own knees, a series of sweat-drops dripping from his forehead, forming a line of exclamation marks on the oak-stained floorboard.

'She wanted to know who sent me, but it's OK, I told her only what you told me, no more,' he gushed in one breath before panting heavily.

'They are still staying in the same place?'

'Yes. They have already paid until the end of this week. I guess they will return there within the hour, and when they go inside they stay inside. That is what has happened before, both nights.'

'And you managed to get access?'

Pavel raised his loose shirt-front and delved deep into the front pocket of the thin trousers, his thick tanned fingers drawing out the slender brand-new key.

'There is no one above them, the flat below is unoccupied for now. There is no security camera covering the entrance. It is easy, I think,' he said, 'there is nothing to worry about.'

She returned to the window, pulled back the netting and looped it, as before, about the back of the chair. Raising the eyeglasses, it seemed that, even in the space of a few minutes, the Square had become dark, the streetlights suddenly brighter, positive identification made more difficult. But there they were right enough, elbows leaning on the thin steel circular table, deep in conversation as the waiter deposited another round of brilliantly coloured cocktails. It was impossible to make out Charlotte's features, but the Librarian had seen enough over the past two days, knew the woman's body language. And she could tell that Charlotte, cigarette in hand, shoulders tense and strained, was not a happy woman.

'OK,' she said, laying the glasses down carefully on the loosely scattered playing cards as she beckoned the three men to follow her, 'let's see what you three little boys are really made of.'

Dark Eyes examined the whisky in the glass, allowed it to swirl as it reflected the light. The acerbic aroma drifted up to him, always surprisingly unpleasant. Kayla shifted in her chair, but he didn't look up.

Almost midnight. Still no call.

She sighed, but not extravagantly. She was good company for him, seemed to enjoy silence every bit as much as he did. Or else she realised how much he liked it and forced herself to shut up. Either way, her presence was more than bearable and she did not object to him looking at her as he might enjoy a favoured painting or sculpture. Of course, he'd asked permission.

He allowed his eyes to wander to her feet, bare and petite and lightly tanned, soft creamy stripes where summer sandals had concealed her flesh from sunlight. The toenails were free of paint, naturally shiny. She curled them into the carpet as if aware of his attention, but he glanced up to see that she was still engrossed in the book she'd selected from the library next door. An illustrated history of England.

If she had one identifiable weak point, it was an irrational, almost obsessive love of London. She was convinced that it was the centre of the world and that she would one day live there and have *a lot of babies*. He'd tried, over the weeks, to establish the source of her fixation, but with no success. There were no easily identifiable links to the country in her past and she knew no one there. But he'd already promised that he would make sure he personally accompanied her on her first tour of the great city, would show her the sights. It was the only time he'd seen her weaken, eyes filling with tears as she realised he was not joking, that he really would do that for her, and soon.

And he surely would. It had been a long time. The humiliating manner of his departure from England still rankled, embarrassed him, and although there were few who had known him there – even fewer who would have noticed his absence – the prospect of enjoying a final English summer was appealing. To do it in the company of this beauty would be something special indeed, but he quelled the thought – there might not be another summer for him, and his hand moved slowly to his chest before settling on his thigh again.

He felt her eyes follow him as he passed the hearth. The summer lodge was not his, but the financier friend who'd gladly given him the use of it had warned that a gang of in-laws and accompanying coterie would be heading up to the private estate by the week's end. Matters would have to be resolved before then. The prospect of moving on did not appeal at all, but he was damned if he was going back to Prague yet again. Too cramped, too humid. At least here, in the country's northernmost mountains, so close to the borders of both Poland and Germany, they could breathe fresh clean air while waiting for events to unfold.

He brought his face as close to the window as possible and squinted into the night. Total darkness. No moon, no clouds, no stars. The tree line beyond the lake was indistinguishable from the sky – a uniform sheet of utter blackness. They'd walked late the previous evening, and Kayla had spoken little as he told her some of the things he had done in his life. But there would be no walking tonight.

The low drilling tone of the mobile was alarmingly loud in the silence, and he turned quickly, snatching it up before it rang again.

'Yes?'

'She's here. You wish to speak to her?' It was the Librarian's voice, slightly out of breath but he could hear the smile in her tone.

'At once.'

The static seemed to last forever, the shifting of the receiver as frustrating as it was perplexing.

And then she spoke.

'Hello?'

He turned so that Kayla would not see the elation which he knew was illuminating his features, but his voice could not conceal the sheer joy of the long-awaited moment.

'Charlotte?'

'How do I know it's you?' came her voice, soft and calm, although she was clearly a little more than irked. He bit on his forefinger to suppress the chuckle of glee bubbling in his chest.

'You don't recognise my voice now?' he said, and she paused, sighed.

'Who is this woman?' she asked then, and he could imagine her defiantly staring at the Librarian, daring her to utter a word.

'I can tell you everything, but not like this. We must meet. She is there to receive you, escort you.'

'By breaking into our apartment and scaring us half to death? Your manners, your methods were never so crude.'

He turned to see that Kayla was staring up at him, teeth gently nibbling her lower lip. She was dying to know what was being said, dying to hear Charlotte's voice and he knew he was struggling to maintain anything resembling the cool facade Kayla had come to know. He cleared his throat and deepened his voice, deliberately slowed his delivery and avoided Kayla's fascinated, unblinking stare.

'Come now, Charlotte, let's be adult about this. You didn't come to Prague for a vacation, and I'm quite sure dearest Imogen didn't fly halfway around the globe to embark on a wild goose chase. You know why you're here and so do I. But, as always, there are rules. There always were. You, more than anyone, know that. The post of Librarian became

111

vacant. More than that I cannot tell you right now, but the successful candidate is entitled to the same respect as all previous administrators. If you want to meet then I hope, I trust, you will give her her proper place?'

Charlotte paused again. Dark Eyes drew the receiver away from his mouth – his breathing was laboured, almost panicky, and she might well detect it. The moment expanded, filled with awful possibilities – she could so easily just decide that she did not want to play the game, that she would return to England tomorrow and let him do his worst. She had no way of knowing that he could and would do nothing if she did. Not unless he slipped up now.

'Charlotte?'

'Yes. I'm still here. We can meet, certainly, but I have one condition.'

'Name it.'

'I must see this woman, this so-called Kayla.'

He looked down at her, sitting with her hands still clasping the closed book, her knees drawn up on the sofa, soft thigh showing as she waited, breath suspended.

'Is she – is she *with* you there?' Charlotte demanded.

Dark Eyes did not reply, but passed the mobile to Kayla. The girl was cautious, but the excited smile accompanied her acceptance of the little grey unit, and she brushed the lightly curled dark hair behind her ear before raising it and gently saying hello.

He turned, hyperventilating. The moment had been long anticipated but he'd never guessed he might react so viscerally to the disembodied voice. The years had somehow been stripped back in those few syllables uttered by her lips, time had been thwarted, and the surge of fear and love was almost overwhelm-

112

ing. He leaned on the mantle and tried to control his breathing as Kayla spoke.

'. . . so I believe . . . it is not my place to say . . . to the best of my knowledge . . . I look forward to that.'

Dark Eyes watched as Kayla's expression changed, the colour infusing her cheeks before suddenly draining to leave her frowning and livid as she returned the phone to him, her eyes fixed on the coffee-brown dust jacket of the old book.

He raised the phone – it was dead.

'What did she say?' he asked firmly. Kayla replaced the locks of hair pinned behind her ear and smoothed an open palm across the book.

'She said that whatever the Librarian does to them, she's going to do to me.'

He swallowed hard, trying to imagine Charlotte's face, and his cock hardened swiftly as the Librarian's many talents flashed across his mind's eye.

He extended a hand, and Kayla took it. It was time for them both to rest.

The Librarian took the mobile back from Charlotte, checked that it was disabled, then passed it to Pavel.

The two fair-haired assistants remained near the door of the apartment's main lounge while Seona and Imogen affected nonchalance, strolling about the huge room as if defying the intruders to challenge their every move. Imogen had even taken one of Charlotte's cigarettes and was doing a very good impression of a seasoned smoker, while Seona cast dirty looks at each of the men in turn, saving full-blown scowls for the Librarian.

'That takes care of the formalities,' the Librarian said quietly, raising her face to meet Charlotte's icy, static stare. 'I dare say you would rather not be here, but let's make this as pleasant as possible.'

113

The English girl had aged very well indeed. Her figure was fuller, certainly, but her face was virtually unchanged. The eyes, just as the Librarian had been warned, were electrifyingly attractive, not only for their darkness, but the energy which seemed to swirl within them. It was easy now, seeing her in the flesh, to appreciate why she had held the title of Kayla for so long and had been the only woman ever to voluntarily relinquish it.

'Your idea of what is pleasant might not chime with mine,' said Charlotte, and the Librarian did a rapid mental vocabulary check. Chime. Concur. Agree.

'Indeed. But that remains to be seen,' she said, summoning Pavel's attention with a raised finger. 'Arrange drinks, my dear,' she said, and he moved away to explore the layout of the apartment.

'It's through here,' offered Seona helpfully, and the young man stopped dead in his tracks.

The Librarian turned slowly, smiling.

'You must be, let me see now, you are Seona.'

Seona nodded, glancing at Charlotte. She appeared to be physically more powerful than Charlotte, but there was no mistaking her submissive role in the relationship. Charlotte shifted, just out of the Librarian's view but significantly enough for her to have to turn back.

'You will not dare to hurt my friends,' Charlotte said, the voice strong and deep and calm. The Librarian wet her lips.

'Hurt is such a subjective term. You must show me what you think it means.'

The Librarian waited. Rage burned in the English-woman's eyes, but even now she managed a smile.

'I will, gladly,' Charlotte said softly, and the Librarian had no cause to doubt she meant it.

'I will bear in mind your promise to Kayla,' she said as she unbuttoned her suit jacket, the thick bone buttons tight, requiring both hands to release them, 'and I will do to you what I imagine you may wish to do to her.'

She parted the jacket to reveal her breasts, high and tight within the white bra, and watched as Charlotte's eyes moved to assess her.

'Won't you ask your friends to relax?' she asked then, aware that Seona and Imogen were both watching. Glasses clinked in the kitchen. A car with rumbling exhaust made a slow, bumpy passage along the narrow street below.

Charlotte turned and nodded to the others as the Librarian unhitched the clip of the trousers. She'd purposely left herself alone since the anger-inspired self-administered climax two evenings previously and the tension had been steadily building. Yes, she'd made her formal 'assessment' of the men sent to her, but that had been little more than mild entertainment – Pavel had come closest to arousing her with his tongue, and the two blond men were adept at following instructions, had managed to fuck her for some time without loss of control. But even the eventual occupation of all her orifices was not enough to make her come against her will. And her will had been strong enough to save her energy, intensify it in preparation for this encounter.

She slipped her feet free of the soft beige leather shoes, stepped away from the crumpled trousers, stooping to retrieve the garment, still watching Charlotte closely, breathing in deeply to catch the faint scent of her perspiration.

'Pavel!' shouted the Librarian, and he appeared almost at once bearing a broad steel-rimmed tray on which he'd carefully arranged some glasses and a pitcher of iced water. He deposited the drinks, ice clinking softly as the Librarian indicated the switch panel at the door. The shorter of the blond men turned and fiddled with the three knobs until the little spotlights and concealed lighting behind the bookshelves were all but completely dimmed. She stepped nearer Charlotte, her eyes still sharply reflecting the available soft orange streetlight.

'This has to come off. Now,' she ordered, and Charlotte complied, raising her hands to ease the slender cotton straps away from her shoulders, the floral-pattered knee-length skirt falling swiftly away to course down her body, only briefly gathering at her hips. She fingered the material away from her pelvis and it silently settled, forming a light tangerine-coloured puddle about her feet.

'I will show you what Pavel has, you can decide what is to be done with it,' she said then, and the shortest of the men, smiling broadly yet again, moved eagerly but with surprising light-footedness across the room, fingers already hauling at his trouser belt.

'Nice and steady, that's right,' she said as he bared his thick dark thighs, and the Librarian watched Charlotte's eyes as they scanned the juncture of his limbs, looking for his manhood. It sprang into prominence as he stood up, flinging the trousers over onto the empty two-seater. Charlotte's eyes appeared to take in the uniformly daunting girth of the thing before her eyes returned to defy the Librarian's. Still maintaining the eye contact, the Librarian extended her right hand and gently stroked the cock as Pavel removed his shirt. She traced her forefinger from the slowly rising peak of the member, continued through his thick pubes and up, following a straight line which contoured the ripples of his belly, the protuberant stomach muscles, only opening her palm fully and

116

stopping to bury her parted fingers in the thickness of his chest-hair.

'He is insatiable,' she said. 'I suppose it's because he's still quite young, aren't you, Pavel?'

She brought her hand back to his dick, gripping the end tightly and squeezing hard. He groaned. 'Shhh, Pavel, haven't I told you before? You're too noisy when you start. Nice and quiet for Miss Charlotte and her friends, let them see how good you can be.'

She released her grip, still holding him aloft as he filled strongly, the expansion of his glans already visible, the rounded edges of his helmet gleaming into prominence as she gently stroked him.

'No one is insatiable,' said Charlotte, and the Librarian chuckled.

'Well, I suppose you will want to prove that, and I'm happy for you to use Pavel as a guinea pig in that regard,' the Librarian said as she strengthened her stroking, the man's cock now hard and vertical in her grip.

'Seona,' Charlotte said quietly, 'get over here and make this boy come.'

The Librarian stepped away from the youth and moved behind Charlotte to get as close to her as possible without making any contact at all. The Englishwoman was surprisingly short, but no less attractive for it. Her hair had taken on the faint scent of the city, but the underlying aroma was clean, reminiscent of the simplest of soaps. Her shoulders and neck, barely illuminated by the weak streetlight, were slender but not skinny, and her posture was superb, undoubtedly the result of her upbringing and regular riding activities. She was every inch the little dynamo described by Dark Eyes.

Seona kept her clothes on as she stood in front of Pavel and examined him, fingering his face, angling it into the light as he retained that wide and seemingly irremovable smile.

The Librarian brought her hands up between Charlotte's forearms, higher again before cupping the tender breasts, so velvety and yielding, the tighter harder skin about her nipples hardening already as Seona's hand gripped the big cock and started to stroke it almost languidly.

'Come on Seona, let's see how insatiable this chap is,' Charlotte said, and Seona's grip hardened about the man's cock-base, his helmet swelling alarmingly, veins standing up in the light, testament to the force she was now exerting on him. He raised his face into the meagre light, and the Librarian could see now that his smile was gone, replaced by a tight-lipped grimace, eyes firmly shut as Seona lowered her face and blew lightly onto the cock-flesh only inches from her mouth.

The Librarian cupped Charlotte's breasts softly, parted her own legs slightly as she felt the English-woman's hand slowly move behind to graze over her thickly haired sex. This was proving to be easy, but who could tell what surprises the former Kayla had in store?

Moving her sex against the tentative fingers, the Librarian brought her lips to Charlotte's neck, parted them as widely as possible, and gently bit into the smooth flesh, her low moan reverberating against Charlotte's responsive skin.

The faint popping sound brought her attention back to what was happening before them, and it was clearer now as they all got accustomed to the dimmer light – Seona was still standing, but she had bent impressively to take Pavel's cock orally, one hand having located and cupped his testes, pulling them down and away from his cock as the other hand steadied the thick shaft. She was pulling the cock up

118

and down, working her hands rather than using her head, forcing him to buck lightly as she hauled his swollen flesh into her face.

The voice of Imogen broke the relative silence, but the Librarian didn't want to interfere now. The manoeuvring of the bodies was unfolding according to the unwritten rules which governed such scenarios, and she knew it was wiser not to intervene, not to impose her temporary authority too strictly. They were not trying to escape – Charlotte's submission had guaranteed as much – but if they were anywhere near as effective as Dark Eyes claimed they had been, then they too would try to impose their own strength, fully exploit their own skills.

'What are you two looking at?' came Imogen's voice, strong and mocking, and slightly tiddly. The men shifted uncomfortably, looking towards the Librarian for direction. She had Charlotte's beautiful breasts in her hands, and the Englishwoman's fingers were already finding their way through her pubic hair, teasing her clitoris. She wasn't going to leave to direct them.

Charlotte's head moved back, nuzzling into the Librarian's as she continued her gentle biting of the slender neck, teeth teasing and testing the tendons, sporadically closing just that little bit harder to test the smaller woman's reactions. Seona had steadied into a rhythm, her hands pulling Pavel's cock into her mouth with relentless vigour, and although his hands were at her, one on her head, another on her back, he was seeking to keep his balance more than urge her on to greater efforts. He was already beginning to totter, and his contorted expression suggested that the most athletic-looking of the Englishwomen had indeed succeeded in swiftly bringing him to the point of release.

And Imogen wasn't wasting much time either. She'd folded down the tight bright pink top to bare her surgically enhanced tits, smoothing her palms across them as if posing for a photo-shoot, the thin white miniskirt already hauled up to expose the broad lean buttocks beautifully framed by the high-slung white G-string. She was taunting the blond men, daring them to make their move.

'Come on, chaps, one of these each, and as much of this as you can handle,' she snapped, voice loaded with anger and impatience as she gripped the G-string and brusquely hauled it up, roughly manipulating her sex as the men watched, 'or is it too much for you to handle? Eh?'

Pavel gasped, deep and hard, his torso doubling, almost concealing Seóna's head as she forced him deeper into her face. He yanked his hips backwards, and the audible pop again suggested that she'd had him deep in her throat. He backed off, thighs buckling, and he stumbled before reaching the two-seater, his eyes still closed as he raised his hands to haul himself up. He barely had his arse on the edge of the leather seating when Seona was on her knees, hands grasping at his solid dick, her mouth agape as she wanked him with painful-looking strokes, compressing his balls with every downward thrust. He managed to slip back fully onto the sofa, his back supported, thighs fully parted as her fingers gripped his scrotum again, briefly fingering at his flesh to locate both balls before teasing them away from beneath his arse and running her tongue the full length of his central cock-vein, only pausing to flick rabidly at the visibly gaping eye before once again engulfing him.

'I'd give him another twenty seconds,' Charlotte said, and the Librarian didn't have to turn Charlotte's face to know that she was surely smiling.

'Let's see, shall we?' the Librarian replied, moving a hand down to press gingerly at Charlotte's pussy, smoothing the tender flesh below her bellybutton before allowing her middle finger to start its descent to the shaven sex, all the while breathing into Charlotte's ear, her lips grazing the petite lobe as they both watched Seona start to deep-throat in earnest, her distended lips widening about the meaty orange-lit shaft, the head of it now surely being compressed by her as she squeezed hard on the big testicles. His own jerking must have signalled the imminence of his climax as Seona drew her head away, hands replacing her throat to encompass the slender shaft-head as she pumped the semen from him, the initial burst arching high, missing her mouth but catching her fringe and forehead, the supplementary ejaculations closer to home as she directed him, hand firmly milking the spitting cock in synchronicity with his lunging hips.

The Librarian pressed against Charlotte's fingers, urging her to delve deeper, breach her lips as Seona slowed her strokes of the tamed cock, her hand wiping the dripping discharge from her head as Pavel stared down, mouth agape.

'What did I tell you?' Charlotte asked, but the Librarian resisted the temptation to gloat as Seona glanced up towards Charlotte with an expression of concern and disbelief.

Pavel's cock was thickening. Even as Seona's tight fingers drew the final vestiges of creamy semen from him, the shaft broadened and stiffened again.

'And what did I tell you?' asked the Librarian as Charlotte's fingers finally parted her lips and started to ream her.

Seona got back to work on Pavel as the Librarian's focus shifted to Imogen. She was standing as bold as could be, hands on her broad hips, buttocks clenched high and taut within the G-string as she pushed her chest out. It was as if she thought herself in a movie, and her display was certainly forcing the men into action. The shorter of the two was down to his boxers, his cock prominent and straining while the other had simply opened his flies and was firmly wanking himself, his eyes glued to Imogen's pneumatic breasts.

'Do I have to stand here all fucking night or is one of you sad specimens going to do something?'

The Librarian knew that neither man's command of English was good enough for them to respond to her taunt verbally, but they clearly understood the tone of her outburst and it was the older, taller man who moved first, swiftly pulling off his jacket and hauling the shirt over his head rather than waste time unbuttoning it. He slackened the trouser-belt, pulled down his trunks and allowed his cock to spring free while his shorter colleague got his boxers off and advanced upon Imogen, mouth lowering instantly to her left breast. The other man reached out to fondle her other tit as she maintained her Amazonesque stance. She felt for the older man's face, her fingers scouring his scalp for a grip in his hair, but it was too short and she cupped her hand behind the strong neck, pulling him to suck on her tit as the other was being eagerly licked and fondled high. The men's hands appeared at her buttocks, pulling at the string-thin band of white material, yanking it higher between her legs, and her sporadic grunts were interspersed with muttered threats and further taunts before she lowered her own hands to her backside and snapped the flimsy underwear apart, leaving it to cling to her cleft as they pawed at her sex.

'I think your friend could use some help,' said the Librarian, and she felt Charlotte's attention turn to

Seona, whose brilliant white T-shirt was now drawn up to expose her chest. Pavel's dark stubby fingers worked deeply, kneading her tits as she continued to suck at his thickness.

The Librarian moved away from Charlotte, leaving Charlotte to do as she wished – Imogen was virtually wrestling with the two blonde men, her high sharp laughter seeming to further embolden them as they now had her off her feet, hands drawing her thighs higher, her breasts still in their mouths as they jostled to get their cocks nearer her widened pussy, the torn G-string still held in place by the groping hands.

The sudden crack of flesh being slapped made the Librarian turn as she advanced towards the standing trio, and there was Charlotte in action – Pavel had been forced to straddle Seona, his cock still in her mouth as he leaned over her, his backside raised, arms supporting him as Charlotte smacked his buttocks furiously, one hand gripping his testes hard and high.

The Librarian dropped her hand again to find that her sex was open and wet – Charlotte's gentle exploration had opened her, but now she needed to be filled and fucked. The business side of the mission had been accomplished, and now she could see to her own needs. Imogen was aloft, her legs winding wildly about the men as they held her high, hands parting her broad plump buttocks.

So, this was the woman who had tried to claim the crown of Kayla for herself, who had precipitated the eventual destruction of the role? Clear to see now how intense her passion was, what courage she showed in the face of what she considered to be a challenge. The Librarian raised her hands to join the men's, eagerly massaged the heavy globes, ran her fingers down the warm crack of her sex.

Her fingers slipped in easily, and Imogen bucked back hard, impaling herself on the Librarian's digits with a grateful long groan, turning her face briefly to check who was invading her. Her expression was wanton, completely devoid of restraint or self-consciousness.

Reaching down to grip the first cock which came to hand, the Librarian buried her face in Imogen's backside, mouth widened and tongue lapping at the woman's softening orifices. The men continued to suck and lick at the heavy breasts while holding her aloft. She slapped the hard dick to one side, felt it return strongly to the vertical, slapped it again, hardening it further with every strike, and then she gripped it again, fingers encircling the scrotum while she secured the firm hold.

'Put her on it,' she ordered, and the men shifted, the older moving to occupy a more central role as his colleague helped position Imogen for the descent.

The deep grunts of Pavel quickened from the other side of the room as the painful slapping continued, Charlotte now urging him to get his cock into Seona doggy-style – she had turned to bend over the sofa, torso resting, her behind raised and waiting as Charlotte guided the thick cock towards her.

Then, as she knew it would, it all came together within a few seconds – the men appeared to lose grip of Imogen for just a splitsecond and she shifted down with alarming speed, the Librarian's hand forced away from the cock she was holding. Imogen cried painfully, gripping the taller of the men and hauling his head into her chest, muffling his own grunting. The Librarian thrust her hand back down to find that he had indeed dropped the woman directly onto his shaft and he was buried fully within her pussy. The shorter man was still obsessed with Imogen's tits, his face a picture of frustration as he tried to secure a grip on them despite the awkwardness of the access, but she would give him something else to concentrate on.

The Librarian grabbed his erection and pulled on it, drawing him away from the breasts which so fascinated him, further away and behind her as she bent over, legs straight and widened, arse raised. She used the same slapping technique to bring his cock to full hardness and gripped her left buttock, pulling hard and high to bring her open sex into his view as she lowered her face to Imogen's cock-filled posterior, stabbing her tongue at the woman's behind, nibbling her plump buttocks.

The cries from the sofa confirmed that Seona had been filled by Pavel and was surely appreciating the attention, and the Librarian raised both hands now to part and grip Imogen's velvety cheeks, lashing her tongue at the woman's arse as the cock hammered higher, each thrust seeming to bring all flesh closer, the impending climax nearer. The short man gripped the Librarian's hips and slid into her fully, not stroking but merely filling, pressing further with every thrust but not withdrawing at all, pushing her face further into the raised, cock-packed pussy.

The come sparked deep in her belly as he withdrew and started to pound into her, breathing now impossible as her face was entirely smothered with Imogen's flesh, the man's scrotum slapping against her chin with the severity of his thrusts. The mild panic of breathlessness helped to quicken her orgasm, bolstering her oral attack on Imogen as she was overwhelmed, kept upright only by the strength of the youth fucking her from behind.

Imogen's own hand came to her behind, slipping in between the Librarian's lips to assist her tongue's probing, widening herself further. The Librarian's billowing orgasm seemed to further invigorate the youth behind her, and his balls slapped noisily against her cheeks as he sped towards his own release.

The accumulated tension of the previous days burst apart with the climax, and she screamed her release into Imogen's flesh as her own cries were joined by others, some undoubtedly real but others imaginary, fragments of briefly surfacing memories. As the peak was passed, the blinding vista of colours shifted into dark giddiness as she pulled her face from Imogen's sex and panted for air.

The hard part had been done – Charlotte was on board and Dark Eyes would be happy. She would see him again. And before then, she still had the two other women to explore.

Suddenly, life didn't seem so bad after all.

Six

Charlotte sat bolt upright, sweat soaking her scalp, the cold film coating her bare torso.

Angling her watch into the available second-hand streetlight filtering through the blinds, the hands showed it was almost three in the morning.

The Librarian and her three goons had left almost two hours previously, but the clearest indication of what might happen next was a vague assurance that she would be kept informed and things would take their course. There was no hurry.

Seona was sound asleep right beside her, looking peaceful in her slumber. Charlotte swung her legs over the side of the bed, making every effort to make as little noise as possible. She leaned over and tapped Seona's shoulder but her friend did not stir.

Only a dozen paces to the door separating the rooms, but she took each and every one with great care, aware that the old floorboards were liable to creak easily under any weight. And she squeezed the door handle down carefully too, allowing the door to inch open until the bundle that was Imogen became visible, and the slight shifting of the shape indicated that she was awake.

'Imogen,' Charlotte whispered, and her friend's face appeared, frowning and wary.

'For God's sake, darling,' she said, 'haven't you had enough for one evening?' but Charlotte beckoned her to get up and raised an erect forefinger to her pursed lips.

Imogen's knee-length slip seemed to glow in the dimness as she got up and tiptoed across the bare floor. Charlotte gripped her hand, squeezing it hard as she whispered to her.

'There's someone here. Someone's watching us.'

Imogen raised a hand to her open mouth, releasing a tiny squeal of alarm.

'Where?'

Charlotte didn't answer, but led her friend back through her own bedroom and towards the door leading to the huge lounge.

'They've come back?' Imogen whispered, but Charlotte was busy listening, the hairs on her neck and arms poker-straight, every fibre of her instinct telling her that someone was next door.

Then she realised that it hadn't been a sound which awoke her, nor was it some obscure instinct. It was a smell. The scent of a man, but not the Librarian's companions. It was there, as definite as an airborne fingerprint – a man was next door in the lounge, and he was close to the door. Charlotte urged Imogen to take a step back, and she positioned herself carefully, toes well clear of the door's trajectory as she prepared to pull it open. She looked briefly to Imogen, and her friend nodded to signal that she was ready.

Charlotte plunged down the old brass handle and yanked the door open. The dark figure was only feet away, a shifting silhouette which moved awkwardly away, the panicky breath audible, scent now powerful. Charlotte flicked the bedroom light switch and Seona's cry of alarm was joined by Imogen's scream as Charlotte flung herself after the man. She leaped on top of him, throwing him off balance, the pair of them tumbling over the two-seater as Imogen moved swiftly to help add her weight. Seona was with them in seconds, her hands at the lightly bearded man's throat as he struggled beneath the women, her fingers digging deeply into his windpipe, and within a further few seconds he was limp and quiet.

Charlotte got off the body and wiped the sweat from her face as Imogen helped Seona shift him into the recovery position. Even the smell of alcohol was not strong enough to mask his body odour, pungent and unpleasant, but Seona was fastidious in her attention, loosening the shirt and hauling the collar free of his neck to assist his breathing.

'Who the hell is he?' Imogen pondered, her voice close to breaking. Charlotte bent to examine the face closely. Perhaps early thirties, lank dark shoulder-length hair, embryonic patchy beard and moustache, thick dark eyebrows. She'd never seen him before.

She eased the filthy coat from beneath his body and rifled the pockets – cigarettes, a lighter, a set of keys. Seona helped raise the body to assist emptying the inside pockets, and there Charlotte found what she wanted.

In a small leather-bound credit-card wallet, a tiny photograph of the man in happier times. It was an International Press Card.

'I think we've just found the journalist Kayla spoke to,' she said, and the wretched, semiconscious man, as if responding directly to the mention of Kayla's name, started to cough raucously, doubling up, hands wrapping about his belly as he spat blood-streaked saliva onto the carpet.

Kayla had always thought the notion of pinching oneself to double-check that an experience was really truly happening was mere hyperbole, but she found herself doing it for the umpteenth time as the helicopter touched down.

Conversation with Dark Eyes had been all but impossible since takeoff, there had been little to see given the heavy cloud cover and only a faint violet pulse on the horizon to indicate the approach of sunrise. They'd been in the air for almost an hour, and he had given no indication where the Pagoda was based, but she did know that the mountain retreat was so close to the borders that they could quite easily be in any one of five different countries.

Following Dark Eyes, hunched and with ears firmly covered against the painful noise of the air-craft, Kayla was vaguely aware of a deep and unvoiced fear. He could be kidnapping her and noone would ever know. She had placed such total trust in him that he could do as he wished with her and they both knew she would not object.

The Pagoda came into view, starkly silhouetted against the gradually lightening cobalt sky as they mounted the gentle slope, movement-sensitive ground-fixed lamps blossoming as they progressed, dimming back into darkness as they passed. Behind them, the helicopter briefly increased its throbbing assault on the ears before swooping back into the night.

'So,' he said, waiting for her to catch up with him, extending a hand which she gratefully accepted, 'this is it.'

He paused, panting from his exertions as she followed his gaze – the gracefully curled edges of the building's roofs appeared like the pages of a book being blown in the wind, each level slightly smaller than that below. He had spoken of the place so many times, shown her the plans, described how he dreamed of it long before it ever appeared on any draughtsman's drawing board, how it had turned out precisely the way he'd always imagined it would be. As they got nearer she kept looking up to the sculpted eaves, remembering his description of five great pages of the mysterious and wonderful book being turned by the gentle night-time wind.

The assistants were well prepared, opening the broad timber doors just as they mounted the steps, the warm light beckoning them inside. She noticed that the Oriental women did not look at her at all, and he spoke softly to them in what she imagined to be Japanese as they were led down the narrow dim corridor.

The tiny windowless room to which they were brought had no chairs, just huge, flat silk-covered cushions upon which they sat as the tea and food was served. He ate little, seemed content with the green tea, but Kayla enjoyed the little sweetmeats, the sugared biscuits and batter-coated lumps of meat and fish, also spiced nuts of a shape she'd never seen before.

'You will need a lot of rest before they arrive. It's unlikely that you will be disturbed until they do. Or, I should say, if they do.'

'You still think they might not?' she asked, genuinely surprised that he appeared pessimistic. He'd appeared so thrilled that Charlotte had accepted his invitation, albeit under some measure of coercion.

'They will come,' he said, lighting a cigarette as the silent assistant seated at the doorway rose to fetch him an ashtray, 'but whether or not you will get to see them is another matter.'

She didn't like to expose ignorance on any subject, but was not afraid to confront it when it did arise.

'I don't understand,' she said, 'I thought you wanted me to meet this woman so much, that I was to learn from her.'

'You surely will,' he replied, now smiling, 'but she must earn the right to that meeting. It was Charlotte who destroyed years of work. I understand her reasons, and I also accept my responsibility in that regard. I was negligent, had allowed things to turn beyond my control. But I reckoned without her stubbornness. And that stubbornness is what brought her in search of us.'

Kayla shook her head. The fatigue was beginning to draw her eyelids down, his words were confusing. He massaged his thighs lightly before getting to his feet.

'I will show you. Then you will understand.'

The assistants stayed well behind them as he led Kayla further along the same corridor, then around a series of corners which, she was quite sure, should have returned them to their original position. But the plain, unadorned walls brought them to a small dark room with one wall made of what appeared to be solid glass. As soon as she entered behind him and saw the bodies so close to the pane she instinctively drew back, cautious, but he raised his hand to take hers and gently lead her inside.

'Don't worry. They can hear nothing.'

The portly middle-aged man only feet from them on the other side of the paned wall was lying on a waist-high table, thick towels spread beneath him. The two little men shaving him were elderly and stern faced, going about their business as the tall black woman supervised them, chatting to the prone man.

'Gisele is the mistress of the first level. She supervises the preparation of the guests.'

He reached forwards and flicked a switch on the small console built into the pane-frame. The voices came loud and clear and frighteningly near, shattering the illusion that they'd merely been watching a gigantic silent movie.

'. . . practice makes perfect, I suppose,' laughed the grey-haired man as he was urged to turn over by the silent little men, one slaking the thick creamy foam in great broad stripes across his shoulders and back as the other fetched up a small container and repeated the same process on his calves and thighs.

'There's no shame in it,' the tall black woman said, shifting her weight from one booted foot to the other, gently swaying in the elevating heels as she examined her fingernails, 'most men can't get past three. Women tend to be better.'

The man chuckled deeply, as if receiving this information as something of a rebuke.

'Well, my dear, I can assure you, I'll be trying my level best to redress the balance.'

'I'm sure you will,' said Gisele, stepping forwards to playfully slap the man's chunky buttock before pacing off, checking her watch as she crossed to the foot of the steep wooden staircase situated in the far corner of the huge room.

'Five minutes,' she said cheerfully before exiting through a sliding door in the shade of the stair-flight.

Dark Eyes flicked the switch again. The grey-haired man, still smiling, closed his eyes and said something but the lips moved silently again, the two small Oriental men working steadily with the lightly curved open blades as they shaved him.

'This man has been here before, perhaps three or four times. He comes all the way from Australia. He has never progressed to level two. Quite honestly, I doubt that he ever will. From what Gisele has told me he is very content to stay here.'

'What is this, this level one?' Kayla asked, transfixed by the speed with which the man's flesh was being denuded.

Dark Eyes rubbed at his chin, he appeared to be

enjoying the simple question as he exited the tiny room, the assistants pressing themselves close to the wall to allow him and Kayla to pass as he delivered his careful, slow answer.

'Level one is, for some guests, the best of all. If they are capable of satisfying our people here then that is enough for them. As you will see, those who have been deemed suitable are not so easy to satisfy, and so it can quite rightly be regarded as something of an achievement.'

Dark Eyes paused. There seemed to be only plain low-ceilinged walls, and Kayla felt momentary discomfort, a nagging claustrophobia as the assistants neared her from behind, but then the taller of the two ladies passed by her and Dark Eyes and shifted a section of the wall, the light spilling from within to illuminate the corridor. Kayla wondered how many other doors were concealed along the lengthy passageway, but had little time to ponder as Dark Eyes entered a room identical in every respect to the previous viewing booth.

The vista was more colourful than the first, great garish drapes of pink and orange providing a startlingly bright backdrop against which the contorted flesh and limbs writhed in a bewildering heap only feet from the floor-to-ceiling pane. Dark Eyes smiled, but Kayla declined to ask the source of his amusement.

The woman lying on her back on the broad low platform was also middle-aged, perhaps in her early forties – her voluminous blonde hair appeared to be a wig, but she was otherwise bare. Her breasts were enormous and lay quite flat across her chest, sagging heavily onto her upper arms, her knees drawn up, something dark and long and barely visible sticking from the juncture of her thick thighs where either

134

pussy or arse was holding it in place. Clearly, she was the centre of attention for the three men who surrounded her, all on their knees, all naked apart from thick leather belts around their waists. One was a Caucasian, one an Oriental and the other a black man. All were completely bald, even to the point of having no eyebrows, and all were gleaming, completely covered with some kind of glistening oil.

Kayla neared the pane. The black man lowered his hand to the woman's sex and pulled at the dildo which had been inserted into her. She grabbed his wrist and forced him to replace it before resuming her frantic stroking of the cock she'd released. The Oriental and the Caucasian were positioned at either side of her, their dicks within easy reach, and Kayla could see that the black man had recently come, a slender string of whiteness swinging from his slowly wilting cock as she brought both feet up to squeeze the drooping member.

Once again, Dark Eyes flicked the volume filter and the angry exhortations of the woman filled the anteroom.

'Come on, you fucker, let me see it, come on, I want it all over me, I want it in my mouth and over my tits, come on!' she bellowed, and the Caucasian screwed his eyes shut, his reddened shaft thrust forwards as far as he could manage without toppling as her wanking grew more furious. He released a long low grunt which coincided with the blast of spunk and the woman raised herself, panting her satisfaction at her own handiwork as the strong white burst of liquid snaked down onto her face.

'You too!' she yelled, turning her face towards the Oriental man as he lowered a hand to his testicles, squeezing hard as she used both hands on his slender length, rotating his glans in the cup of her palm as her other hand pummelled into his groin. His pre-orgasmic cries were clearly too much for Dark Eyes, and he switched off the volume, leaving Kayla to watch in silence as the woman hauled at the man's shaft, forcing him to lean forwards, arms supporting him as she brought him off into her mouth, no evidence of his release visible as she took him deeply.

'So, you see Mademoiselle is happy. She will have a little rest, perhaps some wine, and later, who knows, she may ask the boys to come and see her again or she may request to see a couple of the girls. It will be as she wishes. She has only once ever gone upstairs to level two, but she prefers it here.'

'Please,' Kayla asked, 'can you tell me about these levels? I'm still not so sure what it is all about.'

Dark Eyes made a basket of his fingers and raised it to his mouth. Again, the self-satisfied smile returned, and she could not help but suspect that he was in some way testing her.

'It is quite straightforward. Level one, our people are difficult to please, but their pleasures are simple and come from use of the hands. That's it. The men masturbate the girls, the women do likewise with the boys, other permutations as and when required. There is no penetrative sex on level one.'

Kayla nodded. She could see it coming. It was just a question of demarcation, what had been decided, in what order.

'Let me guess,' she said, 'level two is normal sex, intercourse?'

Dark Eyes shook his head. He was enjoying it right enough.

'Then it must be oral,' she said, and he nodded.

'Then level three must be when conventional penetration first occurs,' she stated, allowing a smile to confirm her enjoyment at solving the riddle.

136

'And four?' he posited. She raised her eyebrows and affected the expression of one who has more choices than can be comfortably tackled.

'There are no straightforward couplings at this level. Of course, it hardly needs saying that all activities are cumulative throughout the levels and should be expected as one progresses upwards. Level four is really rather gruelling. That's why no guest has ever passed it. The guest faces a group whose individual tastes are secret. The guest must discover for him or herself exactly how to satisfy each and every one, but there are certain limitations of time and so on. Obviously, the size of the group confronting a guest will vary with circumstances and personal preferences, but the demands are tough indeed, particularly when one has just graduated from a lower level. I know of only three people who have ever passed through level four, and I am one of them. The Librarian is the second. The other will be your personal assistant whenever you stay here. Perhaps you will meet your assistant shortly.'

'Perhaps?'

'The formalities of filling that post have not yet been finalised. I was hoping you could perhaps meet this evening, but we shall have to wait and see.'

'Am I required to pass through these stages?' she asked, more than a little concerned at the prospect.

He moved away from the pane, indicating that she should now leave first and he would follow. The assistants now walked quicker, and Kayla almost had to trot to keep up as he set her mind to rest on the business in hand.

'Kayla, my dear, you are level five. It has taken me as many years to find you. It will not be necessary or desirable for you to undergo the process. No, I have seen you prove yourself many times, and the decision is made at my discretion. It is also for the benefit of the guests, and I do not want you to meet our other people here. Not yet. It will happen over time, but one must be very careful. There is contempt in familiarity, and it is crucial that Kayla commands the deepest possible respect among all of our people. That is why you will rarely meet any of them, and when you do you will be fully costumed, your face obscured. I know the idea may be unpleasant to you, and it does require that you spend extended periods of time with only your assistant and perhaps myself and the Librarian and a few others for company. It will be difficult for you, knowing that so many interesting diversions are happening elsewhere below you, but you cannot participate. I can only trust that you accept such periods of boredom and loneliness as part of the role you have accepted.'

'I do, of course,' she replied immediately.

'Good. The girls will show you the other levels and your own spaces, both private and functional. I hope you will find the tour interesting and instructive and your quarters to your satisfaction.'

Kayla glanced at the two women, but their eyes were instantly averted before she could make any form of contact. He checked his watch.

'I will come to see you later this morning. We can chat a little. Perhaps you will have some questions about tomorrow.'

'Tomorrow?'

'Yes. I expect we will have the young woman, Seona, tomorrow. She will be, how can I say this, a trial run. Charlotte has many skills to be sure, but her friend has also been her lover and closest assistant for many years. Whatever Charlotte is capable of, Seona will almost surely be able to emulate. In any event, bringing Seona here will ensure that Charlotte follows, and that, my dear, is the object of the exercise.'

'I understand,' Kayla said, invigorated and fully awake once again, her own sex now glowing, ready to be touched, to be further inflamed by the strange sights and sounds unfolding overhead.

He made as if to leave her then, but turned, almost apologetically delivering his afterthought.

'The girls are yours. After your little tour it is quite possible that you will require some relief. If so, and you are so minded, use them in any way you wish. They will comply.'

Kayla turned sharply to assess the females' reactions to the casual manner of his remark, but their eyes had already found the floor in front of her feet.

Dark Eyes' soft footsteps on the wooden corridor floor were soon gone. The girls remained standing, hands clasped in front of them. Kayla wondered if she should introduce herself, but dismissed the notion – she really would have to get used to the idea that such basic politeness did not apply in this world where anonymity was prized and pseudonyms were the norm. These women were there for her, had been assigned to her. She looked them up and down as they waited silently. Even in the dim corridor light she could see that they were identically groomed, right down to the colour of their nail polish and the shade of mascara. Their clothing was strangely old-fashioned, reminding her of the uniform she'd had to wear in the restaurant – plain white high-buttoning blouse with little elasticated green bow tie, plain knee-length black skirt and skin-coloured hose with low-heeled pumps. Their hairdresser was undoubtedly the same person, and the shoulder-length straight locks had been firmly pulled back into neat ponytails. Perhaps they too were Japanese, but she didn't know if she should even bother checking – perhaps that, too, would be deemed inappropriate.

'You speak English?' Kayla asked flatly. The girls nodded.

'Please look at me when you answer,' she added, voice low but menacing, mentally reminding herself that the *please* word was also unnecessary for one in her position. Eerily, both women looked up at her at precisely the same moment.

'We both speak English, mistress,' said the slightly bustier of the women. Her voice was little more than a whisper.

'Good. Please show me level two,' Kayla said, and the girls both nodded and lowered their eyes once more as they turned and headed off down the corridor, advancing only ten yards or so before yet again drawing back a sliding panel in the left-hand wall to reveal a plain broad-stepped wooden staircase.

Kayla smoothed her skirt as she followed the women, was aware of light perspiration on her forehead, the uncomfortable dampness at her armpits. She wanted to shower and rest, but the intriguing scenarios Dark Eyes had shown her had aroused more than simple curiosity and she doubted whether she would be able to hold out until her mystery assistant was revealed. If she had learned nothing else from Dark Eyes it was that he never rushed, made no commitments whatever which tied him to anyone else's timetable, and it might well be hours before she saw him or anyone else again.

The prospect of using her own fingers to bring relief was tempting, but it wasn't beyond the realms of possibility that the women assigned to look after her would make a more interesting nightcap. She scanned their calves and well-shaped behinds as they mounted the steps before her and the notion became more alluring.

But the tour took her mind off her escorts, albeit temporarily. The suffocating sense of *déjà vu* she experienced when following the girls along the corridor was unnerving and not at all pleasant – if Dark Eyes had indeed been responsible for every detail of the building's planning then he had gone to extraordinary lengths to ensure that any intruder would find it all but impossible to access the viewing rooms. She could only surmise that the women used some system of counting the ceiling beams or floorboards to pinpoint the exact location of the sliding doors, and whatever method they used to open the handleless doors was too subtle for her to catch, perhaps involving the application of pressure to very specific points on the identically painted wooden panels.

In any event, she stopped worrying about such trivia within seconds of entering the first of the second level viewing rooms. The figures on view were further away than before, but there was more than enough light in the room to illuminate as much detail as she needed to see.

The woman was heavily made-up and wearing an extremely tight rubber balaclava-style headpiece – with luridly red hairpiece attached – which encased her own hair, so it was difficult to determine her age, but she had a strong, well-toned body and extraordinarily long but muscular legs which were being held together and aloft by the man whose cock was stuck in her pussy. Her breasts were concealed by the dark-red corset, but her legs were entirely bare.

She appeared to be enjoying watching the man as he pumped at her, her dark-gloved hands behind her head. He seemed to be in some distress, his face red and bloated as he faced the ceiling and cried out, but

Kayla didn't want to hear him. Clearly he was at or near the point of coming, but the woman was not. It was not difficult to guess who was the guest, and his chances of advancing to level three.

'Show me another,' Kayla commanded, and the two twinlike women moved again exactly as before, one sliding the door open and waiting until the others had left before silently shutting it to become just another section of the corridor's wall.

The second room was altogether more interesting, and the two women attending to the one man appeared to be fighting over him. The body language was playful, the punishment he was receiving seemed mild, but Kayla found the interaction intriguing, particularly as the man was wearing an elaborate harness about his own sex which, in effect, meant he had two erections for them to contest. She had never seen such a device, but she could easily imagine how useful it might be, particularly upstairs. The thought of taking two cocks simultaneously, although not at all new to Kayla, was suddenly unbearably arousing, and she wanted to tell the women what to do, direct them onto the double-headed, semi-real phallus. But they were having too much fun spanking him, teasing him as he stroked himself, measuring his own member against the amazingly lifelike stalk which was firmly strapped above his own. The women, both short-haired blondes, perhaps in their forties and completely naked, eventually toppled him to the floor and tormented him with mild tickling before settling down to suck on him, their faces joined at the cheek as they contested their throating abilities with the double-dick, the man exhausted as his palms pressed their heads further onto him.

Kayla chided herself again as she overcame the instinctive reluctance to masturbate in front of strangers, and she dropped her hand to her sex, pressing hard through the skirt to ease the burgeoning throbbing.

'I want to see upstairs now,' she said, 'level four.'

'I'm so sorry, mistress,' said the escort, 'but we have no guests on level four this evening.'

Kayla looked down to follow the focus of the woman's eyes, and the slight darkness of her nipples against the thin white cotton was brought into focus by the extent of her breasts' arousal, both nipples now prominent and pressing hard against the material.

'I suppose it'll just have to be level three then,' Kayla said chirpily, now desperate to see some real fucking.

As soon as they'd mounted the staircase leading to the third level, Kayla knew she would have to be fucked and soon. The moisture on her inner thighs was pleasantly cool but the heat seemed to intensify with each floor ascended, and she knew that the air conditioning was very probably state-of-the-art.

Within seconds of the viewing-room's door being opened she knew she could wait no longer.

A man and a woman, both black, were fucking a petite blonde. The black woman was dressed entirely in latex and was wearing the most viciously thick strap-on dildo Kayla had ever seen, fully a foot long, poker-straight with impossibly gnarled vein-work. The man was in possession of a real cock which wasn't too much smaller. The long-haired blonde was on the floor, legs tight together, sitting back on her haunches as she tried to cram both cocks into her mouth, the couple kissing one another deeply as they gently stroked one another's members.

Although she knew full well that they could not see her, Kayla could easily have believed that the scenario was being enacted solely for her benefit. One of her favourite imaginings involved dominant black women, and this beauty before her now was as close to her fantasy ideal as she had seen. Her knees weakened, and Dark Eyes' warning about the frustration of not being able to participate suddenly crashed home with an aching, nipple-straining relevance.

'I need to be fucked,' she said, pulling the hem of her skirt up, squeezing her legs together to glide the gathering material over her thighs as she feasted on the sight before her. The black woman was saying something. Frantically, Kayla reached for the console. The first switch she flicked brought a faint blue strip light flickering into life, and she angrily flicked it off before throwing the other. It suddenly felt as if the glass had disappeared.

'Two big black cocks for you, little lady, that's right,' said the woman, her accent American, 'and if you suck real good you're going to get both of them in you. Would you like that?'

The blonde moaned her agreement, but the woman pulled her heavy artificial penis away from the slender white woman's face, waving it gently as she wound her fingers into the platinum-blonde hair and roughly pushed her harder onto the real cock still stuffed in her mouth.

'I said, would you like that?' repeated the black woman as she pulled the man's cock away, holding it vertical and pointing away from the blonde, who now raised both hands to grip the solid bases of the shafts denied her.

'Yes, I want them in me, please, now,' said the woman, but she was not American, her English was faltering, unsure.

Kayla turned to the escorts, both standing impassively.

'I need fucking right now,' she said, and the slightly plumper girl nodded, then turned to her colleague before facing Kayla again.

'By us?' she asked politely, as if requesting how many sugars Kayla took in her tea.

'Yes,' Kayla gasped, reaching behind her to find the wall which would support her as she started to finger herself, her soaked panties already hauled aside.

'Get me something, I don't care, but fingers aren't enough. Get me something.'

The quiet escort left, and Kayla heard her feet make rapid progress down the corridor as the other woman cleared her throat, her awkwardness evident as Kayla slipped a finger into herself and started to frig in earnest.

'Please, mistress, if you require anything, you have to tell me,' said the woman, her voice slightly more confident. Kayla looked around. The woman looked so utterly calm, unmoved by what was happening on the other side of the screen, the imploring cries of the blonde as she begged to be fucked. Kayla raised her face, settled her head against the wall and forced her sex forwards, the skirt now tucked into itself.

'Lick me,' she ordered, and the woman immediately got to her knees, both hands placed firmly on Kayla's thighs as she plunged her tongue straight to the apex of her excitement, her salty sweetness rising under the woman's fingers as her lips were parted and smoothed to allow fuller access.

She'd clearly done it before, and Kayla found it difficult to focus again on the scene beyond the glass as her clitoris was gently sucked and simultaneously nibbled while her labia were flicked and further parted – the blonde had risen and managed to get the man's cock back in her mouth while the black woman, with the heavy dildo resting on the blonde's shoulder, reached down to part the broad pale buttocks, smoothing her latex-gloved hand down the moistened channel.

Kayla cupped her breasts through the cool cotton, squeezing, looking back down to see the glistening dark hair of the woman working hard against her, palms now cupping her buttocks and pulling her onto her lashing, rasping tongue.

The quiet one came back in, the small black case that she carried placed on the floor in seconds and clips released to reveal the selection of toys. Kayla could scarcely believe how quickly it was happening – the expression of the woman licking at her pussy was as passionate and genuinely preoccupied as the other's was virtually indifferent, and yet, when Kayla indicated the toy of her choice, the quiet woman withdrew it swiftly before shutting and shifting aside the case.

'Put it on,' Kayla ordered, 'and hurry. Hurry, please, I'm going to, oh no, not yet, not yet –'

Kayla pushed the woman's face away, her tongue still protruding and waving from side to side, her eyes shut, nose and chin thickly coated with Kayla's wetness.

The quiet one stepped carefully out of her skirt and into the strap-on, carefully working it up her legs, securing the straps tightly, pressing the short dark length against her sex as her colleague, still on her knees, shifted across to secure the buckle at the back. Kayla moved forwards, raised her palms to the great thick glass pane, and parted her legs.

'Hurry up and get it in me,' she gasped, voice already breaking, cracking with the strain, 'in my pussy from behind. And I want to be fucked as hard as you can manage. Understand?'

'Yes, mistress,' said the quiet one, the first time she had spoken, and she'd barely uttered the words before the tool was slipping into Kayla's pussy, eager hands parting her buttocks to make sure the correct orifice was being filled.

'Get back to licking,' Kayla said then, and the slightly chubbier woman complied instantly, working her way between Kayla and the glass wall to resume lapping madly at her pussy as her colleague secured a good solid grip on Kayla's hips and started to fuck her as if her job depended on it.

Kayla closed her eyes, savouring the dual attention as the blonde's cries were suddenly muffled again, and when she next opened them it was to see that the black woman was sitting on the hard-backed chair, the gigantic dildo firm in her grasp as the man gently fucked the blonde woman's face. Kayla could see now that the black woman's fingers were deep in the woman's pussy, and she kept them there as she widened the opening to make space for the brutally thick dildo-end.

'That's it, baby,' said the black woman, her latex stockings and corset gleaming darkly, brilliantly highlighting the creamy paleness of the thirty-something blonde as her thighs tensed and she sat down on the black shaft, groaning her relish as her cheeks were sucked in, one sinking to accentuate the high fineness of her cheekbones as the other bloated with genuine cock.

'Oh yes,' Kayla groaned, her own breathing now starting to match that of the blonde as she began pumping herself up and down on the dildo, the black woman's fingers working at her arse.

'You like your tight little ass finger-fucked baby?' asked the black woman as the blonde's grunts quickened, and Kayla responded, bringing her own

147

hand behind her to probe at her anus as the strap-on was relentlessly pumped into her pussy.

'Oh yeah,' Kayla moaned, 'fuck me harder, go on, do it harder –'

The orgasm crashed over her in tandem with the blonde's, but how long it lasted Kayla could not tell. It subsided several times, each signalling a false climax, the next resurgence stronger than the one before, and by the time she was able to think about getting her breath back the figures beyond the pane had shifted yet again, the black woman now on the floor with the blonde on top of her, the giant dildo buried deep in her pussy as the man completed masturbating over the woman's ecstatic face.

'I have to sleep,' Kayla said, slumping to the floor as the panting, perspiring escorts wiped her with cooling wipes.

It had been a long night for all involved, but Charlotte was keen now to get to Dark Eyes to demand some explanations. The Librarian had promised that they would know when to leave, would be given proper directions in good time, but there had been no contact as yet.

The journalist was still in the bathroom, had been there for some time. He'd insisted that he wanted no medical treatment, that the blood was no more than the result of a kick to his face – his nose was swollen and the bruising on his body was consistent with the beating he'd described.

He seemed plausible, and yet she felt unable to trust anyone fully any more. He claimed that he'd been lying low since the Kayla interview, that he knew there were powerful people involved and feared for his own safety following the farcical staged kidnap in the newspaper office. The tip-off regarding

Charlotte's whereabouts had been given to him by someone in the old place, probably at the editor's behest, but he couldn't say who it was for sure. For the past two days he'd been casing the place, waiting for an opportunity to speak to her, but he'd reckoned without the Librarian's security. The two blond men had given chase and beaten him unconscious when they spotted him upon leaving the girls' apartment. When he came to, he was in the darkened room which turned out to be their lounge. Why they'd decided to deliver him to her was unimaginable, but Charlotte knew that the Librarian would have good reason, and, of course, she still had the copied key which allowed her and the goons access at any time. They must have carried him in and dumped him quietly while the girls were all asleep.

She checked her watch – the girls had gone to do some basic shopping and should be back soon. Then they just had to wait for the Librarian's directions. But she still had some questions for him and wanted to ask them before Seona and Imogen returned. She poured a drink for him and was setting it on the coffee table as he entered.

He looked almost boyish after a shower and shave, reminding her of someone she'd known long ago but could not place. He accepted the large Scotch with a mild nod of gratitude and sniffed it deeply, taking a little sip before balancing it on the gently curving sofa-arm and then drawing the collar of the towelling robe close against his neck. It wasn't even vaguely cold in the room.

'They'll be back soon,' Charlotte said as she sat down in the identical two-seater opposite him, 'and I don't know if we'll get a chance to speak privately again. I believe what you told us last night. I'm sorry if you felt we were a little rough with you, but we had to be sure you weren't just here to throw us off-track.

149

But I need to know anything else you might know, even if it seems trivial. Please.'

He sipped at the whisky, grimaced. Charlotte leaned forward and poured some of her iced mineral water into the tumbler to dilute the neat spirit.

'I went to Kristina's old place,' he said quietly, holding Charlotte's gaze steadily.

'Kristina?' Charlotte asked, and he frowned, as if genuinely surprised at her apparent stupidity.

'That's her real name. I'm forgetting, you think she's called Kayla.'

Charlotte couldn't help smiling at the mistake. So easy to make. She'd lived that double life for almost a decade, and had taken years more to finally rid herself of the schizophrenic symptoms.

'Kristina Maria Prystnykz. Twenty-three next month. She told me herself. It took a bit of digging but I found where she worked until she disappeared three months ago. It's a small place, a family restaurant about two miles uptown. She was there for three years. It's a woman who runs the place, a most unpleasant character, but perhaps she was merely being protective. She wasn't happy about me talking to customers, wouldn't allow me to speak to any of the staff, but from what I could find out it seems Kristina was a quiet and popular girl. The men remembered her very well, and all of them mentioned her eyes. Her eyes and her skin.'

He picked up the whisky as if suddenly angry with himself and downed half of the contents, coughing fitfully afterwards as Charlotte lit a cigarette and offered it to him. He declined.

'And this man who called you?' she asked, before drawing lightly at the smoke.

'I knew I was being used right from the start, but the alternative was to leave the bait for someone else

150

to take. He didn't speak to me directly. He called the office where I used to work, told the editor that he had an explosive story that would dominate the front pages for weeks if it broke. My old editor was interested. He called me first, offered the job. I asked him for a direct contact but he refused, said that was impossible. The best he could do was arrange a meeting with a young woman who knew the full story. I would be permitted to take some images, but those would be subject to the approval of her boss before being made available. I agreed an advance with the editor and packed a bag. That was it.'

'Did you fuck her?' Charlotte said, and the shock on his face was immediate.

'No. I did not. And if you don't mind my saying I find your language offensive.'

'I don't mind you saying anything except the truth. Did she come on to you at all?'

'It's difficult to say. I don't know.'

'You don't know if she tried to seduce you?' she asked, making her incredulity plain, and he raised the glass again, finished what remained.

'Women who look like that, who naturally look like that? Who can ever tell what they are doing, how one is supposed to respond? If she was a girl in a club and she was looking at me like that, I would say yes, she wanted to make love. But in a dirty office on a rainy day with a complete stranger? And besides, she is no ordinary girl, by no means. There is something very unusual about her. Strange.'

He pulled the towelling collar closer yet again, as if the mere memory of Kayla chilled him, and Charlotte pondered his reply, his whole demeanour. He was certainly attractive, albeit with rather unconventional looks. Something about his eyes and demeanour aged him well beyond his years, as though he was weighed down with knowledge which had been given to him too soon in life and the burden was a source of constant discomfort.

'You have to know that you've been set up,' Charlotte said softly, aware that he was already hurt and humiliated and probably fearful. He stared into the empty glass and nodded.

'They won't allow you to write about this,' she continued, 'Never. And even if you do, noone will ever publish.'

He looked up sharply, a spark of defiance accompanying the slight smile.

'I'm serious,' she said, 'you won't work again.'

'Not unless I can get a source. Someone who really knows everything that happened. Someone who won't spin it into something it isn't purely for personal gain.'

'And you have someone in mind? You imagine you can find a 'Deep Throat' to satisfy your curiosity?'

He avoided her gaze and nodded to himself, clearly confirming the thought before voicing it. When he looked up again Charlotte knew what he was thinking.

'Yes,' he said, 'I think perhaps I can.'

She checked her watch as she stood. The girls would surely be back soon and they could get going. Dangerous as it might be, it was difficult to avoid the only sensible conclusion – he would have to come with them. Far safer that she keep him close where she could keep an eye on him, and the incentive for him was clear.

'I'll tell you the full story,' she said. He looked up, making no effort to disguise his suspicion.

'There's only one condition.'

He frowned, angling his head as if afraid that his hearing might suddenly fail.

'You can get all the sordid details you want. Names, dates, the lot. But I'll only part with them when I'm back home safe and sound in England, and until then you don't leave my sight.'

The footsteps nearing the door brought a welcome end to the tense exchange, and Charlotte opened it to reveal Imogen, loaded down with bags, pale and panting heavily.

'Where's Seona?' asked Charlotte, already alerted by Imogen's expression that something was wrong.

'She's been taken,' Imogen blurted as she staggered through the doorway. 'It was the Librarian's boys. They've got her.'

Seven

Dark Eyes had enjoyed watching the dawn, eaten well and showered before completing his diary entry and dozing lightly in the easy chair.

The painful erection had woken him. He went to the bathroom and soaked a hand towel in cold water, folding it once before wrapping it about his swollen cock. Three days since he had ejaculated at Kayla's hand, but he was determined that he would not do so again while there was a chance that he would see Charlotte again.

He removed the little towel and allowed it to soak up more cold water before replacing it – even the memory of her, the sound of her voice still fresh in his mind was sufficient to bolster the blood flow to his dick, and he squeezed hard, flicking some of the water to tighten his scrotum.

He had never ceased wondering – was it a miracle or a curse? The eternal erection, constantly returning, demanding attention. Each ejaculation was merely a staging post, a temporary respite from the awful need, the irrepressible desire. He'd tried so hard, for so long, to quell and control it. But nothing had worked.

He returned to his study. Kayla's room was right through the wall, but he had no direct access. Just as

154

well. She would still be sleeping, and the longer the better. They would be arriving within the hour, and not too much later Kayla would be facing her first challenge on her own turf. He moved to the window and opened the paper-coated wooden shutter – the sun was already high and strong, the air warmed. No matter. The shutters were always drawn in the guest rooms at all levels. Once Seona had arrived and been prepared, she would see no more daylight until Charlotte had followed and their business had been concluded.

He sat back in the seat, felt his cock cool against his thigh, the flesh already warming and stirring once again. He closed his eyes and folded his hands atop his chest, the fingers knotted together to prevent them straying to his member. It was so maddeningly tempting, the possibility, the simple freedom of having the choice. It grew and pulsed, the bulb shifting along his tender thigh-flesh, sharp stinging pain as it tugged at the fine dark hairs. No. Not yet.

Charlotte's face appeared again, as clear as the last time he had seen her. But her hair would surely have changed, her weight, her height – the years moulded them all, left their marks in many different ways, but he knew that her eyes would be exactly the same.

His dick jerked upwards. He took a deep breath and exhaled as slowly as possible. Imagining Kayla instead of Charlotte did not help. They were so different in so many ways, and yet, in that one unquantifiable respect, they were the same – their eyes gave the clue to the quality they possessed. He'd never been able to pin it down, analyse its make-up empirically, but whatever it was, they had it. She'd had it too. His wife. His only wife.

It seemed a lifetime ago now, and for some people it was – 33 years since she'd died and still he could not forget her smile, her smell, her laugh. Noone had ever come close to affecting him in the way she had, but he knew that the years spent in perpetuating the legend of Kayla had been nothing if not a tribute to her as well as a futile – always futile – attempt to bring his love back from the grave.

His cock had wilted, and he drew another breath inside him, releasing it more naturally as the curse was temporarily relieved. Minutes, hours before it rose again? It didn't matter. Nothing really mattered any more. He would soon join her, or he would decay into dust. Either way, the erections would continue until he expired, and he was determined to enjoy each and every one of them as fully as possible. If Kayla could be resurrected at the same time? So much the better. He could pass on knowing that he had left something in the world which would help, in a civilised and peaceful manner, to satisfy those urges, those desperate needs which masqueraded as pleasures.

Charlotte's face appeared in his mind again, but before his cock could react the door was lightly rapped and he rose to answer.

It would be the head of security, and he knew why. He had stressed that he was to be disturbed for one reason only.

Seona had arrived.

The Librarian had been growing ever more anxious during the drive out of Prague, and if anything she'd become positively hyperactive since their arrival at the Pagoda.

Seona continued to fix her eyes on her own reflection as the girls scoured her flesh. She raised her arms when commanded, ignoring the growing pain in her shoulders as the small Oriental women shaved her armpits. By focusing on her own eyes in the full-length mirror, the guilt seemed to be assuaged – the longer she stared at her reflection the easier it was to convince herself that the naked body reflected in front of her was somehow that of another, that of someone who could do what she had done. And the guilt was not hers alone to bear – those who had used her over the years would have to accept their share, feel some of that pain.

The smartly dressed women allowed her to lower her arms and paced back, facing her as they whispered, staring at her torso. They were speaking in tongues. She closed her eyes, swaying lightly. Sleep during the drive and short helicopter flight had been all but impossible, but the exhaustion had been building, grinding at her senses since the previous morning. Now, with the mission all but accomplished, she realised that she would have to push herself beyond any limits she had ever endured as Charlotte's trusty companion. Her every fibre ached for sleep, and she'd been assured that a chance would come. But now, with the petite women deciding that she needed to be shaved still more, she knew that the chances of rest were diminishing.

They allowed her to lie back on the hospital-style trolley as they slaked the warm foam across her sex, kneading the citrus-scented cream hard into her flesh. She felt herself relax, her jaw open, her arms and thighs soften, the memories of the past few days melding with those from years ago as she slipped in and out of wakefulness. She was briefly aware of the Librarian's return, her strong voice sternly dictating whatever orders she had to impart to the two women before the hard clicking of heels on wooden flooring indicated her departure.

The Librarian. Seona still recalled the Librarian she had known and been so afraid and fond of – the blonde older woman whose expertise with her tongue was unmatched. Perhaps this new Librarian was just as good. Maybe. There might well be a chance to find out in the days ahead.

Her thighs further parted and raised, something firm slipped beneath her behind to raise her, fingers still smoothing the thick cream over her, the ingredients starting to heat her, slightly stinging as the shaving started. Her calves felt high and widened, but no strain – some form of support was there, but she didn't have to see it, there was no need.

Even the fear of Charlotte's reaction had now dissipated. Anger wasn't the right word. There would be grief and rage and, most certainly, a deep sense of betrayal. Perhaps she wouldn't believe it at all, refuse to accept that her dearest friend, good old reliable predictable Seona could even consider setting her up in this way. But better that the truth emerge. Along with all the other emotions, there would, finally, be great relief.

The sudden sharp pain at her breast startled her awake. One of the women had plucked a tiny hair from her chest and was peering closely at the spot, already rubbing something into it. The fleeting discomfort stirred her, she was fully awake once again as the Librarian's heels signalled her imminent return and appearance at the open shutter.

'Dress her. Now.'

The woman working at her sex stroked harder with the blade, the final movements short and precise, ticklishly close to her backside. The lotion started to cool upon her breasts and belly as she was gently urged to sit up. The Librarian remained, and Seona could see now that the woman had donned a plain black jump suit which covered her body entirely, the outfit completed with a broad neck-hugging collar, blue-black gleaming elbow-high rubber gloves and kitten-heeled boots. Her broad hips and large breasts were emphasised by the tightly fitting suit, but she didn't look pleased at all – if anything, her anxiety seemed to have given way to barely concealed anger, and she scowled at the women and Seona in turn before repeating her order and smartly turning, tugging at her gloves with rather sinister purposefulness.

Clearly affected by the Librarian's tone, the women now worked quickly, all but bundling Seona into the shower unit and swiftly rinsing her from top to toe beneath the powerful stone-cold jet spray. She gasped, covering her nipples as the powerful jet swept over them, her flesh tightening under the dramatic temperature change. Almost as alarming was the roughness of the women as they dried her with warm but hard-fibred towels, the strong small hands gripping her limbs firmly as the coarse material was vigorously rubbed over every part of her. Her flesh felt raw and hypersensitive by the time they had finished, mild nausea swamping her as her senses struggled to make sense of the assault, but the final cleansing was instantly ameliorating, tiny moistened wipes being used to once again treat every inch of her, the herby oil calming her flesh at once.

They directed her to use the toilet. She didn't want to, didn't need to, but they insisted. She tried, but managed little more than a weak trickle. This seemed to please the women, and they wiped her again before bringing her through to the anteroom where her outfit had already been prepared.

She sat as directed on the tall four-legged chair which could quite easily have been a bar stool, and one woman checked her foot size while the other attended to her hair, working quickly. The lace-up high heels were smart, very close in style to the shoes Charlotte had once favoured in her Kayla days, and she flexed her ankles, pushed her toes as the woman waited, watching her face for approval before slipping the shoes back off again.

Her hair dried and thoroughly brushed, the woman pulled it into a tight hard tail, securing it with what felt like a metal band, and her scalp protested as the locks were firmly bound, the tail then wound and pinned high. The woman then took a pair of scissors to the piled hair, snipping loose ends.

The confusion of studded leather straps then brought by the smaller of the two women was like some strange puzzle, snaking curled lengths of inch-broad blackness madly entangled, and the woman raised the jumbled pile between her and Seona, staring hard, studying it. She teased two lengths apart, pulled gently and Seona watched as the connected harnesses peeled apart like some living thing, the oiled leather squeaking as it formed the shape into which she was expected to fit. The bands were slipped over her feet and drawn up her legs. She stood, the woman behind her still working at her hair, snipping stray hair from her nape as her colleague worked the warmed leather ensemble up Seona's body, pausing to gather and tweak her flesh, slipping the steel-studded lengths over her hips, gently manipulating the flesh, sculpting it within the zones being delineated, framed by the outfit.

The woman behind her connected the straps, pulling tightly before buckling the belts, and Seona was forced to breathe in deeply as the slightly broader belt about her waist was firmly secured.

The make-up was also swiftly applied, only her eyes and lips receiving attention. The fine latex stockings were shockingly bright blue and wonderfully tight, toning her already reinvigorated legs before her feet were once again encased in the brand-new shoes. She was eager and excited now, ready for anything. But the women had one final lotion to apply.

She was asked to part her legs slightly as the woman dipped her fingers into a small ceramic pot, gently stirring the liquid, drawing it up to pool and drip from her fingers. It appeared to be some form of jelly, and the faint scent which wafted towards her was vanilla-laced, sweet with an alcoholic undertone. The woman stirred again, drew the liquid up and seemed satisfied that it was the correct consistency – she lowered her hand to Seona's sex, and with one firm stroke from anus to clitoris she coated her with the gel, standing back to admire her handiwork as Seona held the position, feeling the gel cool against her shaven flesh.

Fast moving heels clicked hard along the corridor outside the closed shutter – the Librarian was returning and Seona saw the mild panic register in the woman's eyes, but as she stepped back, rubbing the residual gel between her fingers, there was a suggestion of a smile on her face and she spoke for the first time.

'Good luck,' whispered the little woman as the shutter was whisked open and the impatient Librarian entered.

'It's time,' she said.

Seona drew in a deep breath and walked towards the older woman. She felt good in the outfit, tight and pampered, flesh tingling and still smarting from the vigorous attention. It was too late to go back now, no excuses would wash with Charlotte.

Dark Eyes flicked the sound-monitor off and folded his arms. He hadn't expected to be quite so excited at

the prospect of seeing Seona. He'd always been fond
of her, was a keen admirer of her skills, but he knew
there was a side of him which feared witnessing the
passage of the five years, how her own ageing might
simply confirm the worst – the idea that he might find
Charlotte repulsive was, of course, absurd, but there
was no telling how he might react. He would just
have to wait, but Seona's condition would afford a
valuable clue and he was genuinely concerned that
she might not be quite as delectable as he recalled.

As she entered the room behind the Librarian, his
fears were shattered. She was stunning. The outfit was
simple but accentuated her fuller figure, her still
youthful, high-placed breasts and crimson nipples.
But more impressive than her figure was her bearing,
her attitude as she scanned the room and listened to
the Librarian's orders. She was smoothing her hands
across her own nipples and licking the palms as if
preparing for a particularly irksome challenge, but
the slight smile on her darkly painted lips was
unmistakably excited.

The two naked men tethered to the far wall had
already been waiting for more than an hour and had
been told only that a special guest was coming to pay
what might well be a very quick visit. They were both
reliable chaps in their early twenties, still very keen
and capable. Their wrists had been tied and attached
to the short chain which had been pulleyed up to the
ceiling and they were back-to back, unable to create
a space between them. Of course, being tethered to
the same chain, there was nothing to stop them
turning to face one another, but presumably they
preferred to enjoy what shreds of privacy remained.
The strain was already beginning to show on the
shorter of the men, his stomach muscles tensing,
sweat evenly spread across his chest and shoulders as

he watched Seona nodding, accepting the Librarian's instructions. The taller man appeared calmer, not under quite as much strain as his colleague, and Dark Eyes could see that the man's cock was shrunken and withdrawn. Perhaps he was simply afraid, aware that this 'special' guest was important, aware too that his reaction to her might not be satisfactory.

He didn't have long to wait to find out. The Librarian stepped back towards the door, folding her arms and watching stern-faced as Seona advanced on the men. She was smiling broadly now, her strong long legs shuddering beautifully as she strode towards them, her glistening thighs thicker than he remembered but every bit as powerful, the flesh flawless and delightfully pale.

She paused in front of the men, looking them up and down. She spoke, but still he resisted the urge to receive the sounds. The shorter man now looked wary, smiling nervously as she straightened herself to full height, flexing her arms and placing a hand on each hip as she gently swayed her torso, her nipples already standing as if acting as antenna registering the proximity of her target.

The taller man stared down at his cock as it started to pulse, thickening quickly. He closed his eyes and raised his face to the ceiling as if wishing the erection away but it continued to grow as Seona watched, commenting on it, the smaller man puffing as his own dick started to swell. Whatever she was saying, it was working, and the men shifted, arms tensing and straining as their backs rubbed together, arching feet to help part their own thighs to allow the respective erections to grow unhindered.

Dark Eyes ignored the swelling in his own trousers. His resolve was harder, although he was aware of the coolness of pre-come on his briefs. Nothing was

163

going to sway him – only Charlotte would be allowed to relieve him, if she was minded to grant him that honour. In the meantime, he would not touch himself at all.

The twinge of pity for the tethered men was short-lived – both of them appeared to be genuinely distressed as Seona continued talking, her arms now folded, one leg thrust forwards, her toes describing an arc in the air as she swivelled her ankle on the sharp shoe-heel. The smaller of the men started bucking his hips forwards, his stubby dick now virtually parallel with his belly, the bare red balls rising into view as he fucked the air. His larger colleague was also fully erect, the long member at a right angle to his lean midriff as he too jerked, trying to twist himself around to face Seona. She stepped back a little as if fearing they might be able to swing towards her, but still she kept her arms folded, pacing around behind them, her expression scornful as she examined their bodies closely.

The memories flooded back for Dark Eyes, crystal-clear recollections overlapping with the reality through the glass. He'd witnessed her learn the basics, seen her losing her anal virginity, watched enthralled as she managed to accommodate four men simultaneously, draining them as one, dismissing them before returning to the arms of her beloved Charlotte. Seona had never had much use of men, found them shallow and easy to manipulate. He knew as much, had always admired her ability to dissociate the mechanics of lust from that which really mattered – now that she had agreed to jeopardise her relationship with Charlotte, her cynical attitude to men and their primitive desires might well take on a more vengeful edge. He hoped so, and her current attitude suggested strongly that she was already wielding an

164

altogether more effective weaponry than he'd ever known her to possess.

As if to confirm his suspicions, she brought her hand hard across the buttocks of the taller man, screaming at him. She looked genuinely angry, but he saw the grin flicker across her lips as the man raised himself on tiptoe and turned himself completely, his long cock slapping hard against the smaller man's hip as he swung around. She yelled again, this time right into the face of the smaller man, and he screwed his eyes shut, teeth bared in a pained grimace as he, too, struggled to turn himself around. She stepped forwards, grabbed his hips and drew him higher on tiptoe until he could go no further, arm-veins now prominent as he attempted to grip the chain above his wrists for relief. His short fat cock was pointing at Seona as she pulled again, and for a second or two Dark Eyes thought she might take him in her mouth. Instead, she shuffled forwards in the heels, secured her grip and spun him, his feet coming off the ground as he twisted and slammed against the taller man. They instinctively jerked away from one another as if magnetically similar, destined never to meet by nature, but Seona seemed happy now, smiling broadly as she retreated again, arms once again folded. Whatever she was saying now, the men appeared to be concentrating only on getting their bodies as far away from one another as possible. But that wasn't far.

Dark Eyes smiled. She was smart. She had a wicked sense of humour. And she undoubtedly knew that she had a long day ahead of her. No point getting her hands dirty and expending valuable energy when there was a clear and simpler option.

It was the shorter man who first succumbed to the need, rubbing himself against the taller man's hips, the cocks clashing, bending one another as they continued to writhe. The taller fellow resisted as long as possible, unable to avoid the bucking of the other, but he soon accepted what Seona had clearly told him to do, and they were soon rubbing madly against one another, legs firmly planted, arms straining on the shared chain as their cocks settled into a hard, grinding rhythm, the shafts barely visible as they pounded one another's groins together, the cocks occasionally slipping away under the intense pressure to point briefly away from the conjoined hips before the mutual handless masturbation reached a peak.

The dripping of their come from between the joined legs acted as a signal for the Librarian to step from the dimness by the door and beckon Seona. She appeared to do so reluctantly, enjoying the sight of the glistening men as they slowed and slumped against one another, the bright whiteness of their shared discharge dropping to the floor in a steady thin stream.

He flicked on the sound, and it was immediately dominated by the frantic panting of both men, their groans muffled and desperate as they recovered from the orally inspired wanking. They would recover soon, but no doubt it had been the first such experience for both of them and they would not forget Seona in a hurry.

'Very impressive,' said the Librarian, but the note of sarcasm in her voice was blatant.

'I'm not here to impress you,' Seona replied, clearly in no mood to take the impertinence unchallenged.

'You wish to proceed to level two immediately?'

'Unless you need a rest, dear, I can't think of any reason why not,' Seona replied, the enjoyment clear in her tone.

Dark Eyes' cock pulsed again. Her voice hadn't changed a bit. She was here, she was real. And Charlotte would soon follow.

He adjusted his swollen dick as he stood. She had reduced the men to trembling, dripping wrecks in a matter of minutes and barely laid a finger on them. Tempting as it was to go upstairs and see what Seona decided to do with the black man and his energetic mate, he had calls to make. Besides, the longer he spent watching Seona's prowess the more likely he was to succumb to the building need for release.

He had made the promise to himself, but it was really for them, for Charlotte and his long-dead love. It would be a sort of sanctification. He would have to dampen the lust again, wrap the cool wet towel around himself. But it would be worth it in the end.

All being well, just hours to go now. Mere hours, stretching ever longer as the almost paralysing lust increased, but the final hours of many thousands, the last grains of sand slipping through the slender glassy vial to join the countless others he had already lost.

The Librarian was already cursing the damn bodysuit before they even got to the second-level room where the black couple had been waiting for Seona's arrival.

Dark Eyes had been adamant – she was not to take part, had to remain covered up until Charlotte arrived, his reasoning being that she should, like him, show proper respect for the meeting of the old and new Kaylas by showing total restraint until permitted to release their tension as a form of tribute.

She slid the shutter open and waited as Seona strode in. The Englishwoman looked fantastic, so different from the rather quiet, almost shy female Dark Eyes had told her about. Perhaps it was the outfit, the flattering web of belts, or maybe the make-up, but whatever it was, her entire manner had been transformed and the Librarian could only wonder how self-assured and mesmerising Charlotte must have been if this beauty hadn't been successful in her application for the role. But of course, now, Seona was bidding to get involved again, reckoned she could give the girl upstairs a run for her money. The poor soul didn't know, couldn't know that Dark Eyes had already made his mind up, that the formalities had been completed and Kayla was in place. The best she could hope for was to be offered the chance to once again become Kayla's personal assistant. The Librarian struggled to remember the English phrase – something about always being a bridesmaid.

She drew the shutter across after checking that the two escorts were stationed outside. This encounter would certainly take a little longer than downstairs, but when the Librarian turned she found that Seona had not waited to be introduced, appearing every bit as keen to do whatever was required to advance as swiftly as possible.

The man stood. He was wearing one of the light-blue linen Japanese-style robes which were issued to all guests, but it was evident from the bulging curve in the material that he was already in a state of some arousal. The woman remained seated, her expression unsmiling and vaguely disgusted as she scanned Seona from head to toe. It would be an interesting confrontation – the woman had long been popular among regular guests as a favoured dominatrix, and it was plain that she cared nothing for the reputation of this newcomer, and would be more than keen to demonstrate who was the more powerful and persuasive of the two.

The black woman's boots were flat-heeled knee-high tight-fitting beige suede, her chunky thighs bared and their length enhanced by the hip-hugging lacy white basque whose suspender belts hung freely. Despite the height of Seona's heels, the black woman was clearly the taller of the two, and her broad shoulders, well muscled, would make her the favourite in any straightforward physical confrontation. Her fantastically full breasts were almost absurdly elevated by the strong cupping, but the Librarian knew from experience that they didn't require such uplift, they would barely droop when released from the lacy white trappings. Her hair had been tightly gathered and tied, the waist-length ponytail painstakingly braided to form an intricately detailed but heavy, whiplike snaking black column whose end she fingered calmly as she stared out Seona.

'I like your little outfit, dear,' said the woman as she stepped nearer Seona, raising a hand to smooth her finger along the strap which formed part of the rough triangle cupping Seona's left breast. Seona smacked the fingers away. The dark-skinned beauty released a long high sarcastic whoop of mock fear before turning to her seated partner. He appeared amused, but the Librarian could tell he was wary.

'Looks like we've got a little minx here and no mistake,' said the woman. 'I think she wants to play.'

Seona raised her hand to smooth it over her tight hair, tongue wiping her front teeth before she smiled broadly, hands on hips, legs steady and parted, toes pointed directly at the pair. The stance was uncompromising, a clear declaration of intent rather than availability.

'I'm not here to play,' Seona said quietly, the amusement in her tone belying the menace of what she was saying. 'I'm here to fuck you both, and I don't have time for any of your insolence.'

The dark woman laughed loud and hard, genuinely shocked, speechless, mouth gaping as she struggled to accept what had just been said. The Librarian moved a little closer, but maintained a safe distance. Physical violence was always tricky, had to be watched very carefully lest it spiral out of control. If Seona wasn't very careful she would find herself on the wrong end of a swift left jab or perhaps a painful kick to the chest – the woman was adept at a range of martial arts and also had a very short fuse, so it wasn't entirely impossible that she might react badly to Seona's antagonistic tone.

The dark woman's smile disappeared, and she adopted a similar stance to Seona, only two yards from her, breathing in deeply to further enhance her high heavy breasts as she frowned and adopted a much more measured, careful tone.

'I don't know who you are and I don't care. Special guest or no special guest, anyone who comes in here and threatens me can expect to be dealt with very harshly. So get it straight, lady, this is my domain and I decide who does the fucking and who gets fucked. See there?'

The woman indicated the wall behind Seona, who turned without moving her feet to see the range of dildos and strap-on cocks carefully arranged on the red-spotlit shelves by the gigantic glass pane.

'Now,' continued the dark dominatrix, 'seeing as how you're a newcomer and don't know the rules, I'm going to make an exception and allow you to select what you'd like me to fuck you with.'

The Librarian watched carefully, holding her breath steady as Seona turned again to view the implements on show – the range was bewildering, from tiny slender pocket vibrators and chunky little ribbed toys to bestially huge dildos whose function was primarily symbolic, so thick that few people would ever entertain the idea of trying to accommodate them. It was the telling moment, and the Librarian found herself at a loss, unable to decide

170

which way it would go. The woman had never ever been challenged in that manner, and clearly hadn't been expecting it from the special newcomer. The gauntlet had certainly been accepted.

Seona turned back to face the waiting woman whose arms were now tightly folded beneath her gently glistening ebony breasts.

'You're very considerate,' Seona said, affecting a coyness which the Librarian could instantly tell was utterly feigned, 'but I've a better idea. Why don't you pick one for me?'

The woman smiled, nodding, and briefly glanced at the silent man before striding over to the wall. She moved slowly, checking the available tools, then stopped and looked back at Seona before reaching up to take down one of the larger strap-ons. And smiling at it, slapping it against her palm as she returned, unclipping the restraint and smoothing out the large leather pussy-panel, she gently kissed the broad flanging helmet.

'What do you think of this?' she said, holding it out for Seona to assess. Seona took the heavy foot long solid rubber veined truncheon from her and weighed it. The fake balls were low slung at the base of the obscene dull stick and Seona squeezed them, fingering their breadth and roundness before gently stroking the shaft as she might a real cock.

'Splendid,' Seona said, 'nice and heavy. It'll do just fine thank you.'

'Good,' said the black woman, reaching out to accept return of the implement, 'I like a woman who's up for a challenge. Not many can take it.'

Seona smiled, firming her grip on the tool as the black woman's frown deepened, and she looked over to the man, the panic suddenly transforming her expression into one of sheer fury.

'Thanks so much,' said Seona, 'it'll be my pleasure I'm sure. Now get over there and maybe, if you're good, I'll let him fuck you to slacken you up a bit.'

'You are joking, yeah?' said the woman, the telltale tremble now appearing as she stammered, disbelieving. Seona raised a foot to slip into the harness, shaking her head and still smiling.

The Librarian tightened and clamped her thighs together, desperate now to lower the zipper and find her sex, frig it madly for instant relief. But the game was barely beginning and she knew she daren't take her eyes off what was happening. This Seona really was very good.

'I'm afraid not, dear,' Seona replied chirpily, 'but if you don't get over there and start getting some cock inside you I can guarantee that you'll find out first-hand just how serious I am.'

The Librarian felt her face freeze as the black woman looked to her imploringly, her eyes searching for some sign that there had been a terrible mistake, that the interloper was out of order and could somehow be stopped. The man was also looking to her, waiting, and the pregnant pause was interrupted only by the sound of Seona's hands working to secure the fearsome looking tool to her pelvis, the broad pussy-pad and straps forming a further layer of dark patches against her leather-bound flesh as she tightened it in place. The Librarian gently shook her head and raised an eyebrow – there was no mistake. It wasn't a joke.

The man drew his robe apart, shifted forwards in the sofa and parted his legs slightly.

'Honey, looks like you finally met someone who won't take no for an answer,' he said with a tone of mock regret as his partner stared down at him with blatant contempt. She retreated to the sofa, scowling at the advancing Seona as she reached down to grip her partner's dick.

'Just remember one thing,' the woman snarled as she started stroking him, curling her legs up protectively on the sofa in a futile effort to protect her sex, 'what goes around comes around, lady, and I'll get my chance.'

Seona smiled condescendingly as she tapped the end of the secured dildo, testing its solidity as it bobbed slowly before her, pointing at the woman's behind. 'Yes, dear,' she said, 'whatever you say. Now get busy and don't speak again.'

The woman kept her eyes on Seona as she raised the cock-end to her mouth and took the dark bulb inside completely, not sucking but allowing him to start gently pressing into her, her fingers digging deep into his thickening column.

Gripping the steel frame of the whipping post helped the Librarian keep her hands away from herself, but she was getting moist and the maddening tingling in her sex was redoubled as Seona started slapping the black woman's broad buttocks, the smart blows administered every couple of seconds until she had assumed the required position, kneeling on the sofa, her head now working up and down the man's erect cock.

No considered foreplay now, no more talk. Seona reached down beneath the parted black buttocks, her forearm muscles jerking as she located and worked hard at the pussy with one hand, the other firmly steadying the dildo-head as she started to enter the pussy in a series of short sharp stabs, each eliciting a muffled grunt from the woman. With the tool embedded, Seona leaned back, surveyed her handiwork, then rained a rapid sequence of loud slaps on the taut arse-cheeks, each making the flesh shudder about the

173

black rubber rod. The black woman started to work herself back, only the slightest suggestion of movement in her hips, the small of her back descending as she started to accept the thing. Seona moved quickly then to fill her, gripping the woman's basque with one hand, the other around the juncture of thigh and hip as she raised her own torso and pushed down hard to sink the remaining half of the dildo home. The woman pulled the cock from her mouth and yelled, high and plaintive, mouth gaping, eyes screwed shut as she wildly rubbed the real cock against her flailing tits, bucking madly against the wrist-thick tool embedded in her.

The man's hand moved to his cock, finger pressing hard into the base, suppressing the central vein as he quelled the imminent come. The woman's hand was still pulling him furiously, as if hanging on to him for support as the huge dildo was pummelled into her pussy, and she continued to stroke as Seona withdrew, ordering her to get up and face him.

The black woman straddled him as he held his cock firm. Her lips, clearly parted and easily visible from behind, slid over the thick end easily, and she lowered herself onto the smaller real dick with obvious relief as Seona stood, feeding the wet black rubber into the woman's mouth, gripping the long braided hair tightly to force the woman's face around. The man was clearly trying to stave off the inevitable, but the breadth of his cock and upward progress of the prominent balls indicated that he was on the brink. Seona pulled the heavy dildo away again, gripping the shaft firmly as she brought it down to press against the cock-filled hole. The woman's noisy gasping quickened as she realised what Seona was going to do, and the prospect was perhaps too much for the man – he started to come, thrusting up into

174

his partner's sex as Seona positioned herself between his widely parted legs and started to cram the rubber phallus into her, compressing his cock as she claimed joint occupancy with the slippery rubber bulb.

Whiteness started to rim the darkly crimson fringes of her sex as Seona breached the inner lips and sank the tool inside, not fucking now but merely holding it firm and allowing his orgasm to dictate the depth the woman would have to take, and she howled as his strong hands forced her further onto him, the thicker black rod now conjoined with his as the black woman started to scream.

'Anything to say now?' Seona snapped, her voice anger-laden but still with that suggestion of a smile. 'I can't hear you now.'

'Yeah,' cried the woman, 'oh yeah, it's almost, yeah, oh my God, you dirty English bitch, you can't —'

Her words became another high shriek as the man's spunk was squeezed out of her by the invading thickness, but his wilting cock remained in place as Seona drove in further, both of her thumbs now pushing into the woman's backside.

'Time for you to come now,' said Seona, and the woman slumped over the man, his teeth nibbling, pulling at an engorged nipple.

Seona sank her thumbs as deeply as they would go, her other fingers forming twin arcs of deep dimples in the silky dark buttocks as she gripped ever harder and pumped the tool fully inside.

'I said come! Now!' Seona cried, and the woman yielded, started fucking back against the rubber rod, her own hand coming down to encourage Seona's fingers as she bucked towards her orgasm.

As soon as the woman started to climax, Seona pulled away. She retreated two steps, unbuckled the strap-on's harness and let it fall with a thud to the floor.

The black woman was still jerking on top of the limp cock, still groaning and struggling to keep her head up as Seona turned from them.

'That was most refreshing. Thanks ever so much,' she said, making her way back towards the door.

'Level three I presume?' she said as she passed the Librarian, and the older woman couldn't help but smile.

Eight

The call from Dark Eyes could not have been more to the point, or more infuriating.

Charlotte clamped the ear-protectors closer to her head and groaned. Noone would hear her anyway inside the copter cabin.

He'd blatantly ignored her demand to know Seona's whereabouts, said only that if they managed to get to the private landing pad before six, they would find the aircraft waiting. If they did not, fair enough. He would understand. She'd cursed him then, sworn to kill him if any harm came to her friend, but the signal died.

If the journalist had not known the precise whereabouts of the heavily wooded hill in which the helipad was concealed, they would never have got there in time, and she was worried again, the old paranoia resurfacing – why else would they have dumped the writer in their apartment? They had to have a guide, and with the Librarian and her henchmen busy kidnapping Seona, someone had to bring them to her captors. And yet, she couldn't help believing him – the bruises on his ribs and the badly swollen nose and jaw were proof enough that if he was a co-conspirator, he was an extremely unpopular one. But something else about him rang true – he was desperate for the truth. She could see it in his eyes, hear it in his voice. He was quite prepared to face those people again if it meant he might still have a chance of capturing the elusive story of Kayla.

Dusk had not yet fallen completely when they touched down, this time having to descend steeply through the gigantic sky-scraping pines. It had taken less than an hour, and with every passing minute her anger had increased.

She was first out, throwing her headgear back inside the cabin as Imogen disembarked from her seat beside the pilot. When Charlotte turned to see the two blond men descending the slope towards them, she pointed to them and mouthed a warning to the journalist. He saw them, glanced back at Charlotte, then unclipped his harness and, with Imogen's help, got out.

The men advanced as Charlotte and her two copassengers made as hasty an exit as they could manage from beneath the frightening blades, and Charlotte moved ahead as the blond males neared, raising her palms, screaming at them to back off. They mimicked her gesture, palms open and raised as if butter wouldn't melt, but she carried on, making sure that Imogen and the journalist were right behind her as the hellishly noisy craft rose above them, the swooping departure mercifully swift.

'Back off, bastards,' Charlotte yelled, and she could feel her eyes widen, the tightening of her lips. They had no means of defence between them, and Dark Eyes had to have known that. He was asking too much, just as he always had.

'Miss Charlotte, we are only here to escort you, nothing more,' said the shorter man, although he kept firing rather nervous glances at Imogen. The taller of the two appeared more likely to be a danger

– something about his eyes was unsettling, too cool. Charlotte gestured to him to raise his arms and he did so without complaint as she frisked him. She repeated the process with his shorter colleague, then indicated the journalist.

'Don't you have anything to say to my friend here?' she asked, and again it was the shorter man who spoke, and his tone was genuine enough.

'I am, I mean, we are sorry, we both are sorry. It was the orders we had. I hope maybe you will understand.'

Charlotte couldn't help releasing a nervous laugh. 'Orders. I was just following orders. What a fucking typical excuse.'

The man looked embarrassed, sincerely contrite, for all the consolation that might be to the battered writer standing beside her. She folded her arms and stepped nearer.

'We've come here for my friend. Seona? You may remember her. You kidnapped her this morning.'

The shorter man looked to his larger colleague as if seeking confirmation of the translation he had just done in his own head, but his friend stared blankly back.

'Kidnapped?' said the smaller of the two.

Charlotte advanced two steps and brought her open palm across his face with such a crack that the man staggered back in shock, colliding with his colleague before tumbling eavily onto the short grass.

'You take me for a fool?' Charlotte snapped.

The man was ashen, the slender red lines left by Charlotte's fingers already appearing on his cheek as he rose, aided by his friend.

'There has been a mistake somewhere,' he said, rubbing his cheek. 'I don't understand. Kidnap? Noone kidnapped anyone. We are not kidnappers.'

179

Charlotte knew she was close to losing it entirely – she very rarely lost her temper, but when she did, the results were fearful. If he repeated the lie once more . . .

But his expression and his tone told her that he was not lying.

Her stomach flipped. It could have been the flight, but she knew it wasn't that which was causing the sudden nausea. It was the realisation that he wasn't lying and they hadn't kidnapped Seona.

She'd gone willingly.

Gripping her belly, bending to ease the overwhelming disgust, Charlotte turned from the men and retched into the carefully manicured lawn.

Dark Eyes slid the paper screen over – he'd seen as much as he had to. Charlotte was there. Making her way up the long path from the woods. He wasn't too happy about the man accompanying them, but he appeared to be moving slowly, carefully, and shouldn't present any problems. The real problem right now was directly behind him, sobbing miserably.

'Please,' she begged for the umpteenth time in the space of five minutes, 'I can't stand it any more.'

He turned to view the Librarian once again. She was distraught, jaw clenching, cheeks smeared with tears borne of sheer frustration.

'Will Seona make it?' he asked, and the Librarian bit her lip, as if she was close to telling him that she didn't know and didn't care.

'I've never seen anyone so effective. I don't suppose she'll be that long, no,' she said, and he moved to her slowly, hands clasped behind his back. It was at moments like these that he yearned for his old Librarian, but his own feelings could not be denied and he would not punish her nor banish her. Not yet.

He raised a hand to lay gently on her trembling shoulder.

'You are honest with me. That's what is most important. You could have touched yourself, I would never have known.'

She shook her head miserably, eyes shut, new tears trickling down her reddened cheeks. 'You would have known,' she sobbed, 'you would eventually have known because I would surely have told you. I can't break a promise to you. I never can.'

'I know,' he said, drawing her to him, cuddling her close, 'but I was serious, and you knew I was. That's why you will have to wear the restraints. I'm sorry. But the job has to be completed, and we both pledged ourselves to this. Did we not?'

She looked up to him as he wiped her eyes.

'Witnessing the lust of others is never easy. It arouses so much that we would prefer to suppress. Being older makes it no easier. Believe me, I know.'

He stepped back from her, replaced his hands behind his back and knotted his fingers tightly. These moments were so unpredictable and potentially so costly. He had not spent a lifetime creating a myth just to have it collapse into a free-for-all orgy because one small but important cog became detached at the vital instant. Yes, she was insanely aroused by what she had just witnessed and needed relief – as did he – but if she did not agree to wear the tight leather protective belt then she would have to be incarcerated, at least until Charlotte had been given the chance to confront him and Kayla.

'You will wear it?' he asked quietly, facing her again. She stared at his bare feet, her gaze travelling up his shins and knees to the hem of his gown. He parted the gown to reveal his nakedness. His cock hung limply, testes low-slung, the scrotum fully relaxed. She breathed noisily through her nose, flecks of snot fringing her lips as she stared unblinkingly. He looked down at his sex, held the gown behind his back as it started to fill and thicken.

'Control of these feelings is what conveys power my dear. You know this already, you've seen it proved time and again. But everyone has their limit, their breaking point. You've reached yours tonight, but this is the time when you have to be stronger than ever before. If you do not break now, it will take even more to ever break you again, and with that resistance comes the power I promised you would one day understand.'

'I know,' she said flatly, still fixated on the cock, now gradually pulsing into the air, bobbing towards fullness, his veins visibly pumping him harder. 'I listen and I understand. Understanding it is one thing, but doing it is another.'

'I need to know you will be strong tonight,' he said as his dick swelled to its fullest, the bloated head pointing directly towards her.

She closed her eyes, lowered her face and took in a deep breath.

'I will. For you,' she said.

'Thank you. Now return to your duties.'

As she neared the shutter he summoned a cough and she turned. He glanced down at his sex and she followed the cue – he was entirely limp once again. She blinked, checked again.

'Tonight,' he said as he closed the gown across his body and loosely tied the belt, 'remember everything I have ever told you about Charlotte. You've already seen what Seona is capable of. Charlotte occupies another level. Be wary. Be careful. And be strong.'

She nodded and left. He wondered if he should have reminded her about the restraint, but then pulled himself up – the very fact that he wondered if he should have reminded her made him ponder even more if her tenure was perhaps indeed coming to an unfortunate end.

Time would tell. Time. The huge hourglass in his mind's eye continued to bleed sand, and he knew in his heart that there really wasn't very much of it left at all.

Seona knew she had to keep going, but the fatigue was smothering her.

Level three had been ready for her, and there had been no opportunity to assert herself. Three men, three women, uniformed and utterly silent – they'd taken her roughly, applying the gag before she'd even had a chance to challenge them.

Dark Eyes' fingerprints were all over the scenario, and the House where she'd been trained so long ago kept recurring in her mind. Something about the smell and texture of the clothing worn by the women recalled the austere outfits she'd been forced to wear all those years ago. The men wore plain suits with collarless white shirts, and all had their dark hair firmly gelled back. And they were all so serious, studious about their business as they used her, working silently to shift her limbs according to some tacit agreement.

More than ever before, the huge angled mirror occupying the centre of the room's main wall distracted her. The Librarian had disappeared, but it was impossible not to believe that someone was behind the enormous reflective pane, watching as she was probed and spanked, turned and posed like some doll. Perhaps Charlotte had arrived, and perhaps she too was watching.

She closed her eyes again and let the hands move her, raise her joined legs. One of the men had already been inside her pussy, only briefly, but perhaps it was the same man who now fingered her behind, brusquely reaming her as the women held her down, female lips and tongues working hard on both of her nipples as she was shifted further up the low padded dais, her head arching further back, the gag suddenly pulled free of her, her mouth remaining open to accept the two cock-heads pushing at her tongue and lips.

Although they'd clearly been instructed not to speak, the rhythmic breathing of the gang told her what she needed to know, and the lengthy gasp from the man at her behind as he sank into her pussy again told her that he would probably be first to go. The sudden charge at her clitoris was shockingly strong and effective – fleeting pain of nibbling teeth interspersed with the soft calming tongue, and that surely was the third woman, head pressing down hard on her sex as the man deliberately worked in and out of her.

The scent of the females was dizzyingly medicinal, virtually disinfectant – essence of carbolic blended with male sweat, the warmth of her own saliva being spread on her cheeks and nose by the cocks being smeared and tapped against her forehead and neck before they moved away. Then one of the women was licking at her face, not kissing but lapping at her like some dog tracing the movement of the men, Seona's face cupped and caressed as the tongue lashed her nose and teeth, the other woman now working on her neck, nuzzling deep and dark and taking the flesh between strong teeth. As her hands were released, cock filled both palms, and she gripped hard, rubbing the shafts in tandem.

If the three women had been revealed to be sisters Seona would not have been surprised – no doubt the voluminous blonde curls were hairpieces, but the severity of their make-up lent them a sinister similarity. Without their pale green blouses and smart little skirts and scarlet lipstick it would probably be impossible to identify them again.

The man occupying her pussy started to quicken, pulling his cock from her and holding the thick base hard against her distended lips as the woman's face moved away, perhaps to suck him. He pushed her joined ankles even further, forcing her behind higher. He was going to bugger her, nothing surer, and she relaxed herself in readiness as the fingers circled again, not invading but merely easing the tightness.

He did not enter as expected, but kept rubbing firmly up and down as the women shifted again, leaving her head to hang over the edge of the platform, her arms now starting to ache with the effort of wanking the two cocks as they moved closer, poking towards her breasts. She flicked at her hardened breast-tips with the smooth glans-flesh, her legs now being lowered again as she was mounted by one of the women, long soft nipples being presented to her lips in turn. The men backed away, leaving her hands free once again, and she immediately cupped the breasts, opening her eyes to see the creamy pink-tipped orbs as she lapped at them, sucking hard to engorge the buds, and the sensation of her shaven pussy being covered by the woman's own thick pubic hair was momentarily confusing, accompanied by the insertion of something slender and cool into her pussy. If it was a dildo it was a small one, but she bucked against it anyway, feeling it curve and move inside her as the woman established a slow steady rhythm, the fingers of another working between the pubic mounds to flick at the wetly nudging clitorises.

She caught a glimpse of the scenario in the distant angled mirror as her head was moved again to take

one of the cocks – closing her eyes didn't help dispel
the garishly coloured scene; the woman on top of her,
her own blue-latexed legs being supported by the man
whose cock-head was being bent and crammed into
the blonde's broad behind, the whiteness of the
dildo-strapping brilliant against her lightly tanned
skin as she fucked Seona in time with the man's
urgings. The other man, shaft in hand, smoothing
Seona's hair as he pushed deeper into her mouth, and
on either side of her, crouching and delving beneath
the bodies to massage the bucking flesh, the two other
women, skirts hiked up about their waists, blouses
open, one of them sucking hard on the other standing
man.

The dull click of heels signalled the shifting of one
of the women, and her breathing neared, short
shallow gasps pausing as the thighs nuzzled her head,
the angle of the cock in her mouth shifting as the man
made space for the blonde to straddle Seona's face.
She stretched her neck back further and raised her
hands behind her to seize the broad behind, the
suspender belts allowing her to accurately assess the
geometry of the approaching pussy as it neared her
face. The hot glans was pulled from her mouth again
and she stuck her tongue out, scenting the nearing
sex. Her tip found the smoothness of swollen labia,
already wet and tenderly brought to her face with
breathless anticipation.

Seona's tongue strained, her neck aching as she
forced her face high and hard into the lightly-haired
softness, her nose buried in the well of the opening as
she tongue-stabbed the woman's flanging lips, the
bold clitoris hard and gyrating erratically as a cock
entered her from behind, shifting Seona again as the
space became more crammed. His scent wafted
stronger now, mingling with the aromatic saltiness of

the woman as Seona endeavoured to maintain contact, his hairiness brushing her forehead as he started to dictate the pace of the fucking, the broad length sliding in and out with increasing urgency.

The woman atop her withdrew and the relative coolness of the air washed across her body as she was moved again, hands hauling at her. She kept her face at the woman's sex as long as possible, briefly opening her eyes to see the hard dick now buried deeply in the pussy, the clitoris prominent thanks to her attention.

She was on her knees and the man was now going to enter her anally. One of the women was snaking beneath her, hands already pulling hard at her nipples as the standing man raised the woman, hands strongly supporting her beige-stockinged thighs as he raised her, still impaled on his dick, shifting forwards to bring her within distance of Seona's mouth. With the pussy accessible again, Seona lunged at it with her tongue, sucking hard on the tiny erection as another mouth closed about her nipple, the suction painfully hard, bunched fingers pushing into her pussy as the hands steadied her raised backside and started to feed the solid cock into her behind.

The entry was easy, and completed in one careful but firm thrust, the hardness of the dick already being tested through her passages by invading fingers, slender and probing and undoubtedly female, and Seona had to jerk back only the once for the cock to become completely buried in her arse, her pussy simultaneously capturing the completeness of the small hand, only brief pain preceding her strong clamping about the wrist.

Buggered and fisted at the same time? She couldn't recall the last time, and the mere notion was so filthy that the telltale flowering of orgasm sparked in her belly. But she was damned if she was going to succumb yet. She would see them off, each and every one of them. She hadn't come this far for nothing, and they would surely discard her as nothing if she couldn't handle a straightforward gangbang. The energy seemed to resurge, bolster as she brought one hand to her behind, circling the slender hardness sliding in and out of her bum, the other raised before her to flick and pull at the purple clitoris, and they were on their way now; she knew her patient submission was finally paying off.

'I'm still here, you bastards!' she exhorted as she bucked against the cock and fist pushing into her, snaking her hand beneath the woman's besieged pussy to grip the heavy hairy bollocks pummelling into the sex only inches in front of her. She squeezed hard, heard the man's squeaky grunt as he redoubled his efforts. She could sense their unanimous need to cry out, to reply to her challenge, but it was clear now that they were forbidden, and the intensity of their attention seemed to be suddenly magnified, a new urgency evident as she flung down the gauntlet.

She gripped the bulging clitoris between thumb and forefinger and held firm despite the squealing of the woman who was powerless to stop the man's desperate fucking. The woman below her was trapped, her mouth and fingers working at Seona's breasts with almost rabid fury as the other fingers caressed her packed sex, helping the others fuck deeper and harder.

'Come on!' Seona screamed, pushing her own fingers hard at her behind to slip in aside the man's cock, 'you can't do it, you bastards can't even –'

Her defiance was interrupted by the blast of come which had found its way into her mouth, and she swallowed hard, looking up to see the cock spitting at her, the cock-eye distended as it discharged, the

188

woman's pussy still gaping wide, the clit jerking madly into the air as Seona gaped, the swollen bud still in her pinching grip as she recaptured the cock-head and sucked it deep into her mouth, teeth gripping the jerking shaft to deny his withdrawal.

It was his cry which issued first, and the woman he'd been fucking followed quickly, her own fingers frantically helping Seona's to beat out the rhythm of her orgasm as she spurted her own clear fluid over the fingers and mouth-clamped cock. Seona released the pulsing cock-head, still bubbling the vestiges of his come, and it was a swift movement of fingers which allowed her to grip him low and hard and dent the wilting as she stuffed his shaft back inside the climaxing woman.

The man staggered back, releasing the woman as he retreated, and she came back to ground, her stockinged feet wide apart, fingers still trying to keep him inside as she reached her own peak, fingers working furiously at the clit which Seona had sucked into such fullness.

They were nearly there. The cock was being hammered into her behind with such pace now that he couldn't possibly last too much longer, and his puffing was now audible, became her focus as she bucked back still further, fingers closing tight about him as she shortened his access, compressed his solidity more than her backside could. His hands came to her buttocks, one trying to shift her fingers away as he sought the depth again, but she denied him, allowing now only his cock-head to enter her backside, the grip so secure that he'd have to strike her with severe force to remove her barrier. The woman's hand expanded within Seona, filling the space his cock had been enjoying, and Seona knew she had him then as he attempted to withdraw – she raised herself on one arm to ease the pressure on her shoulder and squeezed so hard on the slender cock that the man roared, slapping at her arse like a surrendering wrestler. Seona ignored the pain and held him in place, wiggling her backside from side to side so rapidly that the woman's fist started to slip back out, further distending her pussy against the occupied anus, his come now all but inevitable.

With the man in front of her taken care of and the second now raging towards his own climax at her backside, the third had to be tackled, and she glanced around to see him rubbing at himself, eyes fixed on Seona's behind. She leaned back and grabbed him, tightening her fingers about his and pulling him towards her. He let go of his cock, allowing her to sink her fingernails deep into the shaft, and he was ejaculating even before she managed to haul the thing anywhere near her face, the discharge jetting beneath her. Seona maintained her hold on it and directed his come at the head of the woman below her, the one sucking on her breasts. She heard the gagging of the girl as the thick stream found its target, the man shuffling nearer to push his dick below Seona's chest as he released a high long moan of relief.

The involuntary sound the man released seemed to ignite the colleague working at her behind – his dick thickened within her, ready to erupt, and when he did start to come she was sure to pull him away, still gripping him so hard that his sperm could not emerge despite the swelling of his veins and the firm thrusting which he perhaps hoped would get him back inside. Seona sat up, turned to see the blonde whose fist was still inside her, face now looking up at her in disbelief.

'I told you, bitch,' Seona snarled, 'I'm still here.'

As the blonde attempted to withdraw her hand, the panic fleeting across her face, Seona clamped her muscles about the slender wrist and pointed the bloated cock at the woman's perfectly made-up face. The spunk erupted in a solid white column which made the blonde screw her eyes shut instinctively, the thick discharge adhering to her painted face like some malevolent worm, her tightened lips receiving the second spurt as Seona relaxed and pulled away, using her own hand to grip the woman's wet wrist and draw it from her pussy.

The man sank to the floor, hand massaging his cock as the woman too backed away, wiping the creaminess off her face, the sperm coating her fingernails as she scooped it from her eyes and nostrils.

'Right,' Seona said as she smoothed her holes closed, looking down beneath her at the woman who'd been biting her breasts, 'I guess that just leaves you.'

Seona reached for the woman's hair, but the blonde slipped off the platform, her hands already drawing the blouse back across her bra-bound breasts as she sought the protection of the couple who'd first climaxed.

The mirror beckoned again, and Seona turned to see herself, kneeling on the platform, now unchallenged and surrounded by the exhausted bodies. The smells were intoxicating and the thick silence punctuated by groans and high-pitched moans was the soundtrack of victory.

Surely, now, she'd done enough.

She sat, swung her legs off the platform, and surveyed her body: semen coated her thighs, fringing the latex stockings, several drips had even found her right shoe and slowly snaked down the gleaming black leather. Her breasts were reddened and marked with the tracks of fingernails and teeth, her hands soaked with the juices of all.

What on earth might she find at level four? She shook her head at the distant reflection of the strong woman in the mirror as if it was a stranger, and reminded herself what she was doing and why.

'I'm still here,' she said to the reflection, and was pleased to see that the woman nodded back at her.

Charlotte paced towards the shutter again, just for the hell of it. The two blond men shuffled, tightened their clasped hands and feigned indifference as she stared at them.

They'd already been waiting for more than half an hour. Although the food and drink provided had been appreciated, she was still furious and didn't care how much she let it show. The journalist had eaten, but was now dozing on the matted flooring, a small cushion under his head as he snored lightly. He'd weakened since their arrival, the cumulative effects of the beating and the long journey finally taking a toll which he could no longer fight.

But Charlotte had plenty of fight left, and the awful suspicion that Seona may somehow have betrayed her only served to magnify the rage. There had always been that deep respect for Dark Eyes despite the sordid nature of his business and his grandiose narcissism, but whatever she owed him had been repaid many times over and she knew now that if she set eyes on him she would surely attack.

She returned to the low wicker seat and perched on its edge. Imogen was quiet. Too quiet. She'd been remarkably calm throughout the journey, just as she'd previously maintained a steady silence during the interrogation of the journalist. Now, as she nibbled one of the small spicy crackers and gazed towards the men who'd fucked her the previous evening, she appeared distant, almost resigned to whatever might happen. Perhaps she was reflecting on the unhappy marriage she would be flying back to, or maybe ruing the day she'd ever set eyes on Charlotte to begin with. Whatever the reason, Charlotte's gentle hand on her lap didn't seem to break her reverie at all, her hand coming up to cover Charlotte's as she continued staring into the space where the men happened to be standing.

The festering anger threatened to become a tearful breakdown, and Charlotte stood again, nervously walking off the urge to slump into despair. They'd all been so damaged by Kayla, by the subterfuge, the deceit, the constant fear of disclosure. And that bastard Dark Eyes had capitalised on that damage, seemed hellbent on maintaining the hold he'd once had on them.

Well, no more.

The sliding of the shutter was slow, almost hesitant, but when Charlotte turned she saw the Librarian enter and knew that the fight was just about to begin.

The woman was barely recognisable as the rather cool and self-assured character who'd so rudely invaded their apartment the previous night – her posture was rigid, shoulders tense and reddened eyes wide as she stepped into the room. She had been crying, and the rather hastily applied make-up couldn't conceal the fact.

The top she wore was jet black and appeared to be made of solid leather – although it left her belly bare, it couldn't possibly be comfortable, and the compression of her large breasts would have been reason enough for her apparent discomfort, but Charlotte felt a genuine pang of pity when she saw the way the woman's sex had been concealed. The chastity belt – for there was no other way to describe the thing – was made of similar leather to the high-necked top, but the ugly thick belt which looped through the waist-hoops and was secured with a small shining steel padlock had to be unbearably irritating. The thick edging, heavily stitched and gnarled with past use had presumably belonged to another – it had not yet warmed and moulded to the Librarian's shape, and her inner thighs were already grazed red. No wonder she didn't look happy.

'You will get ready now,' she said flatly, her voice tired. Charlotte fought down the urge to feel sorry for her.

'No. You will tell me where my friend is,' Charlotte said strongly, arms folded once again. The men stirred nervously and Charlotte heard the wickerwork creak as Imogen shifted forwards in the seat.

The Librarian raised an open palm, shaking her head with closed eyes as if another word uttered would rob her of the will to live.

'Please listen to me very carefully,' she said. 'I have no interest in your predicament. He wanted you to come here. You didn't have to. Now? You are here. I won't ask you why. Please just accept that things have been arranged as they are and have been set for a long time. Your resistance is utterly futile because there is nothing for you to push against. You are free to leave at any time. But if you do decide to stay, know that you will not be begged and implored to follow the most basic of instructions. Look at yourself.' She gestured at Charlotte and Imogen with contempt, scowling as she raised her face and sniffed in deeply.

'I can smell you from here,' she said, so matter-of-factly that Charlotte felt her cheeks colour. 'You will get ready,' she continued, 'and then it will be your decision whether you stay or go. You could do worse than to take advantage of the offer to refresh yourselves. It would be most impolite not to, and you know as well as I do that if there is anything which enrages him, it is bad manners.'

In this last respect she was certainly accurate, and Charlotte looked to the flooring at the Librarian's feet – just a fleeting acknowledgment, an apology of sorts, but she could tell from the Librarian's eyes that it had been recognised.

'Just one thing,' Charlotte asked. The Librarian remained impassive, now staring at the seated Imogen as if scandalised that the woman had the temerity not to stand in her company.

'Is she all right?' Charlotte enquired tentatively. This woman didn't have to tell her a thing. The Librarian's gaze returned to meet Charlotte's waiting eyes.

'The sooner you clean yourselves, the sooner you will find out.'

Charlotte felt her jaw twitch as the clearly unhappy woman turned and left the room. She brought her hands behind her back and started unbuttoning her dress.

Seona stood as still as she could, but the adrenalin was dissipating, exhaustion pulled at her knees and back and she yearned rest.

Dark Eyes was moving in the dimness at the far end of the room. He'd remained silent when the Librarian left them alone and she'd resisted the urge to speak, to indulge in any niceties. Their contact had been fleeting – the occasional call from him had maintained her interest, and she'd eventually agreed to the elaborate operation to bring Charlotte back to him. But she knew he was capable of deceit, every bit as capable as she was. There could still be a sting, and the possibility of it kept her alert even if her body was wilting.

'Does she suspect?' he asked. No hello, no how-have-you-been. Charlotte first. Charlotte always.

'Now? Perhaps,' Seona replied, surprised at the strength of her own voice.

He moved nearer, was wearing a gown lightly tied at the waist. He looked thinner than she remembered him – the hair was as perfectly groomed as ever but had certainly receded a little, and the eyes were still as penetrating and sharp but were loaded with a sadness she'd never noticed before.

'Thank you for doing this,' he said. 'I know it can't have been easy.'

'It wasn't,' she replied, 'but I wouldn't be doing it if it wasn't for the best.'

He smiled and turned from her, an extended arm indicating the vacant seat. She moved towards it, her knees buckling slightly, reaching for the slender armrest for support as she eased herself into the chair, savouring the relief as she sat back fully, the wickerwork creaking softly under her weight. The glass of iced water on the little table to her right shifted, the ice tinkling as she reached for it.

'Let's not waste time on word games. You did it for yourself, just as I did. You always wanted to be Kayla. You would never have tolerated what you did if you hadn't felt that the chance would come, that your patience and devotion would be rewarded in time.'

She sipped the water, felt it track a cool path down her chest.

'Unfortunately, I don't have the luxury of time to spare,' he continued, 'so it won't be up to me. The decision has already been made and Kayla is in place. She needs an assistant, someone experienced. The role is yours for the asking, but you will have to ask her directly.'

'And if I decline to forward myself for the position?'

He neared her again, gathering the robe about him as he sat in the identical seat opposite.

'Then I will have no further use for you.'

The anger welled in her chest, tears nipped at her eyes.

'You never did have any real use for any of us,' she said, voice cracking as she avoided his eyes. 'We were always nothing more than toys for you to play with when you were bored. And you've always been bored, haven't you?'

Dark Eyes lowered his face to stare at the cupped hands in his lap and she could see now that he looked old and tired as he shook his head and idly smoothed fingertips against their opposite numbers.

'What I told you was not for effect. I am dying. Maybe three months, six months, whatever. Maybe tomorrow. You have another three, four decades. All that we share, all we ever had in common is the here and now. There is nothing else. Bored? Yes, I was bored, always bored after she died. She was your age. The most exciting woman I ever met, and she was my wife. You cannot imagine what that is like. Men spend lifetimes fantasising about such women, such love, but very few ever find the chance to experience it. I did. And not a moment has passed since her death when I haven't longed to recapture that excitement, that satisfaction. Fantasy simply is not enough when the flesh and blood reality is attainable.

'You should know that by now. I know of your husband, your Blair. A wealthy son from a well-to-do family. He is acceptable, eminently acceptable. But he will never truly satisfy you, Seona, whether or not you choose to admit it. You have given and received

197

rapture that he could not imagine in his small, acceptable world. You would not be here if you, too, were not bored to the point of madness, and the same applies to Charlotte and Imogen. Noone forced you to come here, noone compelled you to do what you have just done.'

She sniffed, still determined that the tears would not well, but she knew he was right. The smell of the people she'd just fucked rose from her own body, strong and suddenly obnoxious.

'You dare to make so many assumptions,' she said, meeting his eyes for the first time, the surprise sparkling in them as she sat forwards to emphasise the severity of her challenge. 'The loss of your first love gives you no right to condemn the rest of us, boring or otherwise. It's not for you to say who is acceptable to another. Some of us like being acceptable.'

The amusement caused by her outburst appeared to quickly diminish, and he stood, hands held behind his back as he stepped across the gap separating them. He had never struck her, but she raised her face in anticipation, closed her eyes and waited, resolved that she would not cower. But the blow did not come.

'The women will take you to Kayla, or take you away from here. The decision is yours.'

He walked away, was briefly bathed in soft blue light as he parted the shutter to the study. Then his shadow was drawn into darkness, the faintly glowing paper door briefly bearing his silhouette before he was gone.

Silence, thick and heavy, filled the room as she lowered her head onto folded arms and quietly sobbed, but the self-pity didn't last long.

She knew what she had to do, knew that she'd left herself no real choice.

Kayla would be waiting.

Nine

Imogen was unhappy with the outfit. She didn't like the way her breasts were forced into the tough leather cups of the corset, and her waist was drawn in to such a degree that she simply couldn't breathe properly.

Charlotte's flesh was still tingling after the powerful shower and rough cleansing routine that reminded her so much of the early years, their shared time at the House when Dark Eyes and his strange plans had seemed so mysterious and alluring. But that had been then, and she was not about to allow nostalgia, however pleasant, to temper the rage she felt. She didn't need to see him to know that he had diminished in the intervening years – in her mind's eye he was a small and unhappy man now, just as he surely had been back then too.

The quiet persistence of the little Oriental women attending to them was irking Imogen, and she was getting impatient. Charlotte closed her eyes and tried to enjoy the brushing of her hair, but the strokes were so hard that her scalp ached, and she too was finding it difficult to get used to the outfit, so tight and unforgiving about her torso.

'It'll be over soon,' Charlotte said, but she knew the self-assurance in her tone would not fool Imogen. They hadn't even discussed it, but it was clear that they'd been duped and Seona had surely had more than a little foreknowledge.

'The sooner the better,' Imogen added before squealing, her hair being tightly clasped and pulled high as the broad tape was secured to form a slender column from which her locks rose like spurting water. 'He's gone too far this time. If I get my hands on him he'll wish he'd never been born.'

Charlotte weighed Imogen's words. Perhaps that was his problem after all. He couldn't bear normal life, had never accepted it, always felt he was destined for greater things than mere mortals had to endure.

The Librarian entered again, as anxious as ever to assess progress, watching silently from behind them as the women worked on the final touches. Charlotte stared hard at the woman, tried to imagine what background she had come from, how he'd managed to draw her into his insane world. Her expression was so forlorn, so worried beneath her thick make-up – what promises had he made to her? The temptation to ask was strong, but explanations could wait – the journalist would be more than interested, would make sure everything was properly documented, correctly verified. No doubt about it now – Charlotte would make sure that the bastard was finally exposed, his madcap schemes given the glaring publicity he'd always feared so much. There would be pain for all of them, that much was certain, but it simply had to be done.

The Librarian neared, and Charlotte tensed. The woman's every move seemed loaded, menacing, as though she might explode into hysterics at any moment, but something in her eyes was searching Charlotte's in the smeared mirror, and when she spoke her tone was heavy with emotion, throat betraying her nervous, fragile state.

'I must ask that you forgive the manner of your being brought here. It happened as it had to.'

Charlotte did not answer, but neither did she avert her eyes from the Librarian's hard gaze.

'I understand the desire for revenge. Believe me, noone feels it more keenly than me. But he is weak now. Weak and tired. He would not send a polite invitation for your presence, and you would not expect it. He must maintain the charade as long as possible, and this is the final act. Please indulge him this one last time.'

'Indulgence,' Charlotte said quietly, turning the word in her mouth, wondering what it meant.

'He deserves nothing,' Imogen piped up, brushing away the hands of the woman working on her lips. 'Why should he expect anything from us?'

'You're right,' the Librarian replied, hands spanning the thick belt which protected her sex from attention, 'he deserves nothing. And nothing is what you may choose to give him now. You know that would be an effective revenge. A quiet departure now would be even more painful for him, if that is what you want. But your friend will not follow. She has chosen to stay. If you wish to see her then you will have to see him.'

Charlotte shifted forwards in the stool, found the floor with the tightly fitting boots and stood to face the Librarian. The older woman clasped her hands in front of the thick leather harness as if embarrassed by it, but her eyes showed no fear.

'Take me to them,' Charlotte said. The Librarian shook her head.

'You must see what he has done, and you must satisfy him that you are worthy of meeting Kayla.'

Imogen got to her feet, her shoulder practically touching Charlotte's as they faced the defiant woman.

Imogen's gloved hand was raised, the finger pointing straight at the Librarian's face.

'I'm tired of these games. Has he told you who we are, what we've done? You talk of being worthy to meet some girl who isn't fit to tie our laces?'

'I know well what you've done, the both of you,' she replied, the smile returning, 'but as I mentioned, there is the question of indulgence.'

Charlotte glanced down at the heavy leather belt-work about the older woman's pussy.

'Something you've been denied,' she said, and the woman nodded as she replied.

'As he has denied himself for these past days. Restraint is so much more difficult for those who cannot bear it.'

Charlotte looked up to Imogen, but there was little trace of pity there.

'No more tricks,' Charlotte said, 'and no more delays. Take us now.'

The Librarian backed off several steps, turned and left, the little escorts scuttling ahead to open the doorway for her. Imogen strode forward purposefully, and Charlotte watched her friend, transformed now in the bondage gear, her fingers already tensing and stretching within the tight black rubber. Someone was going to suffer, and soon.

Seona tried to still her breathing, but the blindfold only heightened the intensity of every sound.

He'd returned silently, held the broad black band before her, and she'd accepted it, affixed it herself. He'd taken her by the arm and led her for what felt like an age, the echo of her shoes reverberating along the narrow spaces as she was taken to await Kayla.

Perhaps minutes had passed since he'd left her standing there, but she couldn't be sure. The air was cleaner, fresher, but still oppressively warm, and she had the sense that the room was somewhat smaller than those she'd seen previously. If they were indeed on the topmost level of the Pagoda then it would make sense.

Her head moved instinctively, reacting to a sudden shifting over to her right, cloth against cloth, conceivably nothing more than wind moving drapery, but she'd yet to see an open window anywhere in the building and no breeze could be detected. Someone was there. She wanted to call out, confirm the presence, but knew she would just have to wait.

The sound came again, was followed by something approaching across the floor towards her feet. The fear that it may be some kind of creature was soon dispelled as the object gently bumped against her foot and came to rest, the soft female footsteps slowly following the path the object had taken.

She suspended her breath completely, fear gripping her belly. She tightened her grip on the hard-backed chair that stood before her as the woman neared, and she felt the chair tremble as the person touched it, felt the fingers graze against her shoe as the object was retrieved.

The fleshy tearing sound and the sharp tang of orange accompanied the sudden cold splash of juice on her breasts, and she leaned back, fearful as the pulpy coolness was pressed against her breastbone, pushed to expel more of the citric fluid which poured down her torso, running along the leather belts, drips finding her thighs and belly. She waited for tongue or fingers to follow, but instead the woman moved slowly behind her, and she could feel the eyes weighing her up, assessing the state she was in after the business downstairs.

Small hands came to her buttocks, gently palming them, spanning the deep leathered creases where the belts depressed her taut flesh and the drying discharge of the men and women was stickily warm. Seona leaned on the chair-back, sticking her backside out slightly as the inspection continued, the woman now crouching, running her hands down Seona's thighs, gently fondling her calves and straining ankles. The hands returned up her body, lingering at her waist, a solitary finger tracing the gentle curvature of her spine, both hands coming to rest on her shoulders before moving in front of her.

Seona gasped as her nipples were firmly pinched and held fast against her instinctive jerk – the woman made a sound which was laden with warning and Seona bit into her bottom lip, forced herself to take the steady pain as the woman moved against her, soft breast-peaks nudging against her back, a cool light gown brushing against her legs. The pressure on her nipples was momentarily released before strong fingers squeezed again and the blackness behind the blindfold started to sparkle and fill with shifting kaleidoscopic colours.

And then she was gone. Seona exhaled noisily, gulped in some new air. She was close to collapse and knew she wouldn't be able to take much more, and her arms started to shake as the footsteps returned, faster than before.

The fingers worked swiftly, pulling at the straps, releasing the intricate body harness, and Seona allowed her limbs to be gently manipulated, moved as the strapping was unhitched. The blindfold was peeled away from its self-adhesive patch and left limply clinging to Seona's face as a cool damp cloth was wiped across her neck and shoulders. Seona raised her hands slowly, wary of reprimand, but none came and she removed the blindfold.

The room was larger than Seona had sensed, but the floor-to-ceiling drapes which concealed much of the room's perimeter compounded the claustrophobic atmosphere. Several of the hanging cloths were virtually see-through, but the dim light gave few clues as to what lay beyond the warm space. The floor was covered with enormous cushions fashioned from a variety of materials, and there was not a stick of furniture to be seen. It was impossible to describe the space as a bedroom, but neither could she think of any other function for it.

The woman moved around to face Seona. She was short, the hair was quite obviously a brand-new version of the classic Kayla wig, and the face below it was utterly entrancing. Seona knew she was staring but was too tired to be wary any more, had no fear now that she could see the eyes of the young woman who'd been chosen to replace Charlotte. Like Charlotte, like Imogen, she was just a woman, but she was young and she was Kayla – as young as they had been when they contested the title so many years ago.

The woman refolded the small white cloth as she looked up into Seona's face, smiling to reveal her beautiful teeth, her lips exquisite and full, naturally reddened like her cheeks.

'I've been waiting for you,' Kayla said, raising the cloth to Seona's face, gently wiping it along the curve of her jaw, opening the coolness to cup her cheek. Seona closed her eyes and savoured the kindness of the welcome, relieved that the initial assessment she'd been subjected to was, apparently, over.

'Would you like to kiss me?' asked Kayla, and Seona kept her eyes shut as she opened her arms and drew the smaller woman to her, finding her mouth without sight, forcing no move, allowing their lips to join softly.

Bringing her hands to the woman's waist, fingers trembling lightly in anticipation, she yielded to the increasing strength of the kiss as she felt the smooth warm flesh shift closer to her. Something was strange, disconcerting, disturbing beneath her fingers, and she stroked lightly as she opened her eyes. She felt sure the woman was entirely bare beneath the thin cotton robe, but the texture of her?

Seona had never experienced flesh like it before. Kayla's skin was covered with hair so fine, so tightly compacted that it could quite easily have been suede. It was no mistake, no blemish or figment of her exhausted imagination. Seona moved her hands higher, smoothing up to grip the slender shoulders, the sensation against her fingertips utterly fascinating, and her astonishment had to be evident in her eyes as Kayla pulled back, smiling again as she fingered a stray wisp of blonde hair away from her face.

'There is a little time for you now to sleep. So –' she stepped back, drawing the robe about her again as she indicated the strewn cushions, 'I will wake you when the time has come.'

Seona watched as Kayla walked away, barefoot and petite, her tiny waist accentuated as she tied the belt about her robe and parted the drapes.

Within a minute, curled on the floor, her pained and stretched body now cushioned and a thin cotton sheet drawn over her, Seona was sound asleep.

Charlotte couldn't help being impressed.

The idea was simple enough, but the execution was brilliant. The building was as intriguing as it was practical, and his interest in all things Oriental had been beautifully realised.

The Librarian did not accompany them into the viewing rooms, but stayed outside with the escorts as they worked their way up the levels.

Level one was silent, but the Librarian described the nature of its functions. The second level was busier, and Imogen had appeared rather taken with the two young Latin American chaps who were strenuously pleasing the middle-aged black woman with their fingers, teasing her as she tried to pin them down with her arms and mouth. One other second level room was occupied, but the participants, three women and two men, were sprawled, chests heaving, limbs entwined, the peak of their joint pleasure clearly achieved just before the unseen viewers entered the concealed room.

The level three activity was altogether more frenetic, the first room hosting what appeared to be a wild orgy, twenty or more participants writhing in a seemingly random heap, their liberally oiled bodies slipping and sliding like fish in a box – there was no discernible pattern to the couplings, noone in charge, no power struggles in evidence. It was simply a massive screwing session, and everyone involved seemed to be thoroughly enjoying themselves. It was interesting, but couldn't be construed as much of a challenge, and they soon lost interest.

The second room they were shown appeared to have a similarly stultifying effect on Imogen, but Charlotte persuaded Imogen to stay as she watched the young black woman use her strap-on to fearsome effect on the two older white men, one of whom had already entered the other. She was an intimidating and physically impressive character, and Charlotte felt more 'than ever the passage of the years, she recalled when she'd taken her own body so much for granted, never anticipated how the years would steal her stamina. If anything, she would soon be faced with a scenario more challenging than the one being dominated by the black woman as she straddled the men and sank her artificial cock in between their joined lips, forcing them in turn to accept as much of the thick pliable plastic as they could manage.

Imogen was not as taken with the scene as Charlotte. She eventually left, and Charlotte reluctantly followed, the stark imagery she'd just witnessed still tumbling in her mind as she followed her friend up the broad wooden steps to the fourth floor of the Pagoda.

The body language of the Librarian had changed again as they advanced down the corridor – she appeared much more hesitant, was virtually tiptoeing in her boots as she entered the doorway opened by the escort. After a few seconds she re-emerged and stepped back, indicating that Charlotte and Imogen should enter. Imogen went first. The Librarian avoided Charlotte's eyes again. They had to be getting close to them now. It seemed unbelievable that the three of them – Seona, Dark Eyes and Kayla – would be in the same room at once, but perhaps that was the tactic, to intimidate them with a show of unity and strength before Charlotte even had the chance to confirm Seona's treachery.

It would be tough indeed, but as soon as she entered the viewing room and saw what was happening beneath the shifting pastel-tinted lighting, she realised what the Librarian had meant when she mentioned proving themselves worthy.

The three women were awesome enough – in their heels they were all as tall as the shortest of the men, and they were truly frightening. Charlotte's gut reaction was that the men were surely troops, perhaps even mercenaries of some kind. Their bodies were not those of sculpted body-builders and showed no signs of pampering, each was, to a greater or lesser degree, hairy. The youngest was perhaps in his early twenties, but the eldest was, if anything, touching forty. It was difficult to tell in the constantly shifting light that seemed to soften their features, but they were certainly not shrinking violets or hired models. These men were fighters.

Imogen turned to Charlotte, and the concern was clear on her face.

'Recognise anyone?' she asked, and Charlotte shook her head even as she scanned the women, who were all peering at the mirror, occasionally touching up their hair but clearly aware that they were being watched. The men, too, stared at the mirror defiantly, unsmilingly, as if disgusted that they'd already been kept waiting so long.

Imogen's hand tightened on Charlotte's arm. 'I don't like it.'

Charlotte nodded. She didn't like it either, but it was clear, turning to see the Librarian standing in the open doorway, that if the group was not confronted then there would be no meeting with Dark Eyes and Seona might well escape retribution for her betrayal.

'Who are these people?' Charlotte asked. The Librarian leaned back, said something to the escorts, and she waited until their footsteps had faded before speaking.

'They met a week ago. In Munich. They're all friends of Dark Eyes. I don't know any of them. They've been here for three days, waiting.'

The Librarian looked down at the heavy leather clamped about her sex.

'I've only had this on for a couple of hours. Can't imagine how they must feel.'

Charlotte looked back at the figures moving silently behind the glass. No wonder they all looked so miserable. The plain blue gowns they all wore bulged about the hips. Of course. They'd been starved of contact since their arrival. It would be like throwing meat to lions.

'You can't expect us to go in there,' Charlotte said, turning to face the Librarian.

209

'I expect nothing. I do as I'm told. I'll be there with you, if that's any consolation. Believe me, the sooner this is over with the sooner I can get this damn thing off. They know the rules, and they know he'll be watching. I'm afraid that's the only reassurance I can give.'

'We'll need something. We can't go in there empty-handed. I presume you have suitable equipment?' Charlotte said, the fear subsiding as she scanned the figures again. If they were so desperate then they'd need serious discipline.

'Of course. The girls are fetching a selection for you right now.'

Charlotte approached the gláss, stared hard at the people, bored and unimaginably frustrated, their expressions displaying nothing but gloom. It would be like popping the cork of a shaken champagne bottle, but only if she got it right from the very beginning.

The bunch of canes and crops brought in by the women was impressive in range, and Imogen made her selection first – the slender hooped cane was an unvarnished and wickedly thin instrument, but Charlotte selected an old and well-used leather crop. The Librarian herself had no hesitation in picking a thick-handled cat-o'-nine-tails, which appeared new but had been lightly oiled to lend suppleness to the rather unwieldy bunch of slender straps emerging from the stump of the foot-long steel-studded stick.

The Librarian's fingers were turning the padlock on her belt as she stared through the glass, and her nipples were starting to make their presence obvious even through the thick leather vest. The poor soul had to be utterly choking to get the ugly underwear off, but Charlotte knew that when she did so she would make up for it. In the meantime, she could be a valuable ally, and it was best to keep her well on-side.

'If we go in there,' Charlotte said, slowly and clearly as the Librarian looked to her, 'you promise to help?'

The Librarian nodded and her eyes were fastened on Charlotte's as she replied. 'Despite what you may think, my responsibility is to make sure you get to him safe and sound. If I don't then my life won't be worth living. I love him, and that's why I do as he says. You will come to no harm.'

'Fine,' Charlotte said, nodding to Imogen who returned the gesture. 'Let's do it, then.'

The Librarian led the way, and once again the long walk along the corridor seemed to bear no relation to the proximity of the room. Imogen was ahead of her, flexing the cane between both gloved hands as if desperate to get started.

Charlotte tried to calm her breathing as they waited outside the door. The Librarian made sure that the escorts were positioned on either side of the entrance, turned to check all was ready before lifting the little silver key before Charlotte's face.

'It's up to you when to release them,' she said quietly as Charlotte nodded, 'and be very wary of the women. They are strong.'

Charlotte slipped the key under the glove where it was tight about her left forearm as she searched the Librarian's eyes for any flicker of betrayal or fear. There was none. Despite herself, despite all that had happened, Charlotte knew she now had no option but to trust the older woman.

The Librarian looked at Imogen, who in turn looked at Charlotte. Charlotte nodded – the Librarian turned to face the shutter, then the escorts dramatically drew it open and they marched inside.

If it had been possible to bottle the air, Charlotte would've done so. She'd never experienced such tension. The men were all standing, but seemed frozen as Charlotte followed the Librarian and Imogen into the circular room.

The women got to their feet, the tallest of them already unlooping the robe-belt, allowing it to fall open to expose a well-developed torso, and this woman was the first to make any sort of advance, stepping forwards two paces as her colleagues took up their positions behind her, one either side. She was the boss.

The eldest man advanced, his colleagues adopting similar positions behind him as Charlotte felt Imogen and the Librarian backing her up.

The shutter closed softly as Charlotte slapped the riding crop into her open-gloved palm. The key felt as if it was burning a hole in her forearm.

'I hear you've been waiting for us,' Charlotte said quietly, and the tallest woman peeled off her robe to reveal the oiled body, the awful thickness of the tight belt trapping her sex. It was identical to the model worn by the Librarian, a similarly small padlock glinting at the left hip where the vicious belt had been tightly secured. The woman shook her loose dark shoulder-length hair, draped the robe over her forearm, folded it again and twisted it into a slender bundle before hurling it across the room to land at Charlotte's feet.

'Get this thing off me,' the woman said. Charlotte held her stare as the men shifted forwards, following their leader step for step as he too disrobed, passing the gown back to be taken by a younger colleague.

'Me too,' he said.

'Stop,' Charlotte ordered, raising her crop vertically.

They did so. She could feel their eyes burning into her, searching for weakness as she spoke.

'One of us may be able to release you, but until I decide who can do it and when, you will all do exactly as you are told.'

The leading man looked across to his female counterpart as he looped his thumbs inside the broad leather spanning his belly.

Charlotte advanced. Her heart was racing, the adrenalin not channelling as efficiently as it used to – she was out of practice and knew it – all the more important now to maintain the illusion of control. The Librarian and Imogen stayed close.

And then, just as she was ready to demand obedience from the respective leaders, the control slipped. Something moved above her, above the angled pane they'd viewed the room from. It was nothing more than a glimmer of light as something was shifted, a reflection of light above the drapes, and she was only beginning to wonder if there was yet another viewing room situated above them when the men and women all moved together, falling upon them with a fury which was utterly terrifying.

Charlotte was on her back before she knew what was happening, the tallest of the women grasping for her hair, large oiled breasts shivering and waving only inches from her as the open palm came across her face once, twice, and then a third blow so stinging that she closed her eyes and cowered.

'Where's the key?' shouted one of the men, and Charlotte opened her eyes to see that the Librarian was fending off the main man with vicious swipes of the whip, the flailing bunch of leather straps finding his shoulders and neck as he tried to near her. Imogen was also on the floor, a robed man pinning her down as the small blonde woman palmed her outfit, searching roughly as Imogen kicked and yelped with rage.

One of the men was hauling at Charlotte's boot, fingers trying to force her toes to point, another hand yanking the knee-high opening. The woman on top of her was rabid, unhinged, fingers clawing at her hair as if she believed the key might be hidden there. Charlotte pulled back her leg and kicked out, a sharp gasp accompanying the contact she'd made with her heel. With her legs free she raised them, kicking higher again to bring one booted calf around the woman's neck, and then, with one arm hammering onto the floor to provide the required leverage, she released a scream, twisted her torso and spun the hysterical female away from her, following up with a severe crack of the crop against the back of her bare thigh.

The woman curled away on the floor as Charlotte stood, already advancing to threaten the gasping man who was clutching at his diaphragm, the raised red welt already showing where her heel had caught him.

Imogen was utterly trapped, the man engrossed in trying to remove her breasts from the tight broad leather brassiere as the girl held her arms down. Charlotte had to take only three steps to be within good striking range, and the crop came down hard on the man's back before she landed another two fierce blows on his calves. He rose as if to challenge her, but, stooping to retrieve Imogen's cane, she now had two weapons and he was bare-handed and backed off, palms raised as he whimpered.

The Librarian needed no such assistance, the head man having retreated with the third woman staying close behind him, and it was he who then spoke on behalf of the group.

'Please get us out of these fucking belts! Please!'

Charlotte puffed heavily, waiting for Imogen to get to her feet, and when she did so she passed her the cane and crop, delved into the glove and quickly located the key. She raised it, smiling, allowing it to glint in the dim light. One of the women cried out in desperation, started to sob, and the head man moved instantly towards her, arms already rising, eyes crazily wide.

Charlotte popped the key into her mouth, nestled it between her teeth and cheek. He stopped in his tracks, a smile of disbelief coming to his lips as she spoke.

'We do it my way or not at all,' Charlotte said, and he retreated, palms raised.

With Imogen and the Librarian back behind her, Charlotte retrieved her crop and tapped it on her boot as the group was herded back towards the huge mirror. Seeing them at close range now, their expressions as pitiful as their limbs were tense, it was possible to feel sympathy, but she knew that control might easily slip away again if she showed the slightest weakness. The ringleaders would have to be made an example of.

'You,' Charlotte said, pointing her crop at the tallest woman. 'Come here.'

The woman was perhaps the same age as Charlotte and was entirely bare apart from the thick belt. Her breasts, oiled and heavy, swayed as she paced across the space. Charlotte passed the crop back to Imogen, slipped off both gloves and took the little key from her mouth.

'Your punishment will serve as an example,' she said as she stepped forwards to grip the little padlock, the saliva-coated key easily slipping in, the lock unspringing with a click which made the woman gasp.

'Take it off, face your friends and bend over,' Charlotte ordered. The woman did it quickly, pulling it away from her sex impatiently, and the Librarian's arm extended to take the contraption away from her as the woman turned, parting her legs but keeping them straight as she stooped to grip her ankles.

Imogen needed no spurring and was soon lashing at the proffered buttocks, the sharp reports of the cane echoing about the room as Charlotte watched the scenario mirrored behind the quiet captives.

The woman did well, didn't make a sound until Imogen lowered the centre of her attention, the cane cracking across the thigh-tops as the Librarian joined in with the bunched lash, the two of them alternating their strokes as the woman started to pant with every blow.

'You next,' Charlotte commanded, indicating the eldest, lightly bearded man, and he advanced rather more cautiously than the woman had done, his eyes fixed on his colleague's reddened buttocks as he followed a wide berth past Imogen's swingeing cane. Charlotte unlocked him, the belt was angrily hauled away from him and his cock sprang up, already fully erect and painfully red. His scent rose to her, salty and warm, and she brought the tip of the crop to his cock-head, pressing against it to measure the solidity of the erection as he grimaced, eyes closed.

'Get over there and fuck her,' Charlotte said before flicking the crop-end against his shaft. He winced, backing off, then moved towards the woman, his hand pulling at his compressed balls as he reached her.

Imogen and the Librarian gave him enough time to push his cock into the woman's pussy, then resumed the lashing, this time targeting the smaller tight male buttocks. He seemed oblivious to the blows – even as

216

they quickened and intensified – but became notice-ably more powerful. His hands had the woman firmly gripped by the hips and his come was fast, frantic and fully discharged into the thrashed behind as his own was further punished. His thrusts toppled the woman, and he came to the floor still on top of her, cock firmly embedded and still jerking as she bucked madly against him, his emerging discharge forming a slender white ring about the juncture of shaft and swollen cunt.

Imogen seemed keen to continue her assault, particularly now that the man's scrotum was visible, but Charlotte reined her in, raising a hand to indicate that she should back off. The others watched in complete silence as their colleagues writhed and groaned, the pain of the punishment now starting to hit hard, but the small blonde woman seemed re-moved, eyes glazed and semi-closed as she roughly pulled at her own nipples, tongue forced down hard in a futile attempt to suck away the frustration. She was getting close, and it made sense to leave those with most self-control until last. The blonde didn't even realise that Charlotte had summoned her – she had to be reminded by the man next to her, but then she moved swiftly, hopping over the spread legs of her prone colleagues, fingers already pulling at the tiny padlock.

'I want her,' Imogen said quietly as Charlotte pulled the padlock from the belt, and there seemed no good reason why not, especially if she could kill two birds with the one stone. Charlotte pointed at the youngest of the men, a broad-shouldered crop-haired youth who appeared utterly bemused with the whole scenario and had, notably, not lent his support to the attempted mutiny. His apparent calmness could, of course, have been due to mild shock, but he stayed still and steady as Charlotte freed him from the sweat-stained leather jockstrap.

'The quicker the better,' Charlotte reminded Imogen, but her friend was already working on the blonde, forcing her to stand with hands on her head, feet spaced widely as she caned her arse.

The remaining two standing at the mirror appeared to be the coolest of all – he was in superb condition and had clearly seen a lot of action in his life. The series of pale long scars which marked his chest and abdomen were the result of more than some kinky game, and his nose looked as if it had been badly broken more than once. His eyes were pale and alert as he watched his colleagues.

And something about the young pale-skinned woman now standing alongside him reminded Charlotte of Tara, the virgin she'd enjoyed in her bathroom what now seemed like a lifetime ago. She wore little make up but the high heels helped to lengthen her rather stocky, powerful legs and her see-through nylon black bra firmly elevated her broad, hugely nippled tits. She, too, appeared calmer than her friends. The quiet ones were always the worst.

The couple on the floor had moved, the woman on her back as the man sucked on her breasts, his cock filling and stiffening again as her fingers worked him back to erection. They could safely be ignored for now. Imogen was happily directing the fair-haired youth as he knelt, tongue lapping at the blonde's sex as the lashing was alternated between them both. She was in control.

So, just this final pair to take care of.

The Librarian accepted the key from Charlotte and set about freeing the man as Charlotte summoned the woman. She strolled across so casually that Charlotte smacked the crop on her boot as a warning, but the young strawberry blonde didn't appear the slightest bit fazed, merely completed traversing the floor as if she was doing a slow-motion rehearsal for a catwalk appearance, a smile dancing about her expression as she held Charlotte's stern stare.

'Do you find something amusing?' Charlotte said, gently tapping the crop into her bare palm. The girl stared on, even daring to jut her chin proudly as she broadened the grin and placed her hands on her hips, one foot moving forwards as she struck a pose, maddeningly defiant.

'As a matter of fact,' the girl replied, her accent English and every bit as cultured as Charlotte's, 'I do. I find you amusing.'

Charlotte brought the crop down hard across the girl's thigh, and although she winced, her eyes closing as she frowned, containing the need to cry out, the smile did not entirely disappear.

'Perhaps getting your friend's cock in your mouth will wipe that smile away,' Charlotte warned, tensing the crop again as the Librarian raised her lash, prompting the man to move closer to them.

'Maybe so,' replied the girl, turning to see the man advance, his bloated dick obscenely thick, although it had yet to reach anywhere near full erection, 'but unfortunately I don't have a clitoris halfway down my throat. If you'll remember, the point of this place is challenge, progress. Noone has progressed past me because I can't come. I never have. Noone's ever tried to bring me off harder than I've tried myself, and if I can't do it I very much doubt that you and your little friends can.'

'Your gratification is the least of my worries right now,' Charlotte snapped, 'so get on your knees and suck him until I tell you to do otherwise.'

The girl slipped off her robe and knelt, smoothing

her breasts high, adjusting the black nylon to symmetrically frame her cleavage.

'And you can take that off,' Charlotte added sternly. The girl's smile vanished, her eyes flashing defiance, but she raised her hands behind her, unclipped the bra and peeled it off, looking down at her own nipples as they were exposed. She kept her eyes on Charlotte even as she reached up to take the monstrous penis in her palm, and she gently squeezed it, bloating the broad head further as her smile returned. She opened her mouth, tensed her jaw and forced her throat to bulge in preparation, and then, with eyes still locked on Charlotte's she pulled him nearer, raised her face and took the huge sweat-coated cock entirely into her face with one lunging movement which made Charlotte wince with sympathy.

The man gripped the girl's head, his face contorted with bestial lust as he pressed into her, but then the Librarian's lash came hard across his bare back and he raised his hands as directed, knotting his fingers behind his neck, arm muscles flexing tightly about his trapped head as he tottered under the strength of the girl's assault.

Charlotte turned to see Imogen urging the crop-haired youth to speed up his thrusts – he'd mounted the kneeling girl from behind and was eagerly fucking her as Imogen carried on caning him fiercely, the parallel bands raised and glowing scarlet on his thighs and buttocks. They would soon be finished there too, but the smug smile of the strawberry blonde was still irking her, hovering in her memory as she turned to see the man's erection complete, the girl unable to take much of him now that he'd swelled to a magnificently straight and wrist-thick fullness.

'Lie down,' she ordered, and the girl looked up quizzically, her lips still encircling the huge dick-head as Charlotte brought the crop across his belly. 'Lie down now!' she screamed, and the man lowered himself unsteadily, hands reaching the floor for support as the girl released him.

'Hurry up and get on it,' Charlotte snarled, further enraged to see that the dismissive expression was back on the girl's face. 'We'll see if you can come or not.'

The girl stood, straddled the man, parted her legs and squatted straight down onto the thick staff, the Librarian bending to steady the shaft as he resumed the position, hands folded behind his head. Charlotte could see now that the girl's sex was lightly haired, but the apparent ease with which she had taken the broad length suggested that her pussy was not quite as tight as her stature suggested it should be. Charlotte stepped between the man's legs, and used her boot-toe to further part the girl's legs while pressing on her back with the crop to make her bend and lie face down on the man's chest.

Her pussy was now completely full with the breadth of him, but her arse appeared tight and dry.

'Wet her at the back,' Charlotte said, and the Librarian bent, palming at the parted buttocks, wetting her fingers in her own mouth before starting to ream the brown spot just an inch from the broad thrusting cock.

'Get her nice and wide for me,' Charlotte ordered, before turning her attention to how Imogen's charges were faring.

Imogen was panting, sweat glistening on her cleavage as she admired the man's efforts, the blonde now on her back, her legs wrapped around his back as he lifted her, pulling her onto him.

'Time to finish them,' Charlotte snapped with obvious impatience. Imogen knelt behind the man and her gloved hand located his testicles, bunched them together and pulled them up his bucking arse-cleft as Charlotte reached down his belly, fingers quickly working through his thick hair to locate the point where his shaft met the girl's parted lips. Pressing hard into the upper base of his cock and angling her fingers just so, she felt the swollen bud of the woman graze her fingers, and adjusted accordingly, bringing two fingers to form a tight channel along which the clitoris would be brought by the man's accelerating thrusts. And Imogen's severe ball-massage soon had the desired effect, the man undoubtedly realising that the quicker they both climaxed, the sooner it would be over. His face reddened, teeth biting into his bottom lip as he screwed his eyes firmly shut and hammered his way towards a peak, the girl now squealing as Charlotte's stiffened fingers pressed hard against her sex, never allowing the pressure to fully ease, and the woman continued to help Charlotte press upon the same point even as the man withdrew under Imogen's insistence, his cock erupting his offering onto the floor beneath him as his testes were squeezed firmly.

Charlotte bent to finish the blonde off, her fingers rapidly describing a circle on the girl's sex as she bucked wildly, open palms slapping the floor when the peak was reached. Charlotte roughly inserted her already damp fingers into the widened pussy to further coat the digits fully, then stood to see that the Librarian had done a fine job or reaming the insolent English girl and had already managed to get three bunched fingers into the tight arsehole.

'OK, just you two,' Charlotte said as she swiftly returned, wasting no time on preliminaries as the Librarian pulled her fingers away from the puckered and slackening hole.

'Suck her tits,' Charlotte said, and the Librarian needed no second bidding, stretching herself alongside the couple before reaching up to grab the nearest peachy breast, hand reaching across to cup and pull at the other as she took the crimson nipple between her teeth and commenced nibbling. The girl responded immediately, pulling the Librarian's head closer as Charlotte assessed the size of the cock now being ridden by her.

'So, you've never had a come?' Charlotte said, but the girl merely continued fucking as Charlotte placed a hand firmly on the small of the girl's back and started to press her fingers into the backside. The girl did not object, nor did she appear to alter her rhythm, steadily riding on the broad shaft as Charlotte started to push harder, a mild cramp already seizing her fingers as the anus clamped about them.

'Well, don't say we didn't try for you, dear,' Charlotte snarled before redoubling her effort, and the girl started to go faster, the Librarian also assisting in pushing the girl's backside further onto the conjoined digits as she realised what Charlotte was trying to do.

'Lube!' Charlotte cried, and it was Imogen who located some, a small bottle of viscous fluid which she steadily dripped onto Charlotte's joined fingers as the pace of the fucking increased, the girl now riding the massive dick at a pace which was surely going to finish him off soon. Charlotte twisted her wrist, ignored the building pain in her fingers, and felt the tremor of the girl's scream shudder throughout her body as her anus widened to take Charlotte's hand.

'Never say never!' Charlotte shouted as she felt the girl's sphincter widen and gape and finally close about her entire hand. The man grunted, perhaps realising what was happening as the Librarian panted, still desperately licking and pulling at the girl's breasts, but Charlotte took in a deep breath and concentrated on fucking the tight arse with her fist, pounding in tandem with the man as the girl's frantic reaction sent him over the edge. The Librarian's fevered sucking and licking became more frenetic as the girl writhed and bucked, screaming again as Charlotte pulled as hard as she pushed, the anus tight about her wrist.

'There's a first time for everything, dear,' Charlotte laughed, watching as the girl forced her torso up, breasts swinging wildly as the Librarian, and now Imogen, sucked and pinched at them. Charlotte felt the man's cock swell even further in the packed pussy before the telltale shuddering of his orgasm conveyed itself though the fleshy barrier and Charlotte smacked the girl's arse-cheek hard with her free hand, then again and, harder, yet again before carefully but resolutely pulling her bunched fingers, squeezing them tight together, attempting withdrawal. The girl howled, pulling herself away from the cock, but the hand was still in her backside as the orgasm tore through her, her whole body shaking and spasming so hard that, with a roar, she pulled fully clear of Charlotte, dropping her fingers to paw at her own clit as she shrieked the pulse of her climax, the man's cock spurting his final discharge across her gaping holes as she slumped over him.

The beautiful trembling of the girl's flesh was inspiring, maddening as Charlotte bent to slap again at the taunted flesh with the hand that had just been so deeply inside her, fingermarks becoming clearer on the broad pale buttocks.

'There we are, dear,' she said sarcastically, 'now, I know your personal circumstances are somewhat unusual, but that's all you have to remember next time you want to know what an orgasm feels like. You just ask someone to put an inordinately large penis inside your pussy, and then, when you've been on that for a little while, you ask someone else who has small hands to stick one of them up your arse. Couldn't be simpler.'

Charlotte stood, the sweat now starting to bead on her forehead and chest as she realised she was getting insanely aroused. It had taken a little longer than she'd thought, but there could be no more tricks now, no more procrastination.

She had to get her hands on that bastard Dark Eyes, and Seona would be next. After all that she'd done for them, in so many different ways, the notion that they could conspire to have her end up in the back of nowhere with her hand up some insolent bitch's arse was merely fanning the flames.

No more room for careful consideration of other folk's problems or concerns, and no more trusting to anyone else to secure an end to this madness. She alone was capable of taking him on, and everyone, including him, knew it full well. That's why he'd gone to such trouble to have her brought here in the first place.

Well, if he really wanted to take her on, she was ready for him.

It was showdown time.

Ten

If the Librarian had not been so helpful in quelling the mutinous behaviour of the level four group then Charlotte would not have believed it was anything but a straightforward set-up.

'I have to leave you,' she said, fingers nervously rimming the leather belts still strapping her sex beyond her touch, 'so please refresh now, while you have the chance. Take whatever you think you may need. Only minutes now. I promise.'

Her anxiety was understandable, and if she was anywhere near as aroused as Charlotte then she'd have that contraption off at the very first opportunity. Imogen, too, was well and truly warmed up, and she was drinking the fruit juice supplied as if merely refuelling.

The Librarian left quickly, but the two Oriental women were in position as always, the friendlier one smiling in at Charlotte before she closed the shutter. Charlotte scanned the tiny room – racks of costumes neatly hung and all individually covered with transparent plastic dust shields, and tall thin glass cabinets holding punishment instruments as well as the usual array of toys and exotic lingerie.

None of it would be needed now.

Charlotte had control of her hands, a clear mind and an overwhelming curiosity – Dark Eyes might well have other tricks up his sleeve, but she was not leaving now, not until she got the explanations she needed, from Seona as well as him.

'Before we see them,' Charlotte started, 'do you have anything to tell me?'

Imogen stared hard at Charlotte, licked her lips and sipped again at the orange juice. Charlotte crossed to the little wash basin and adjusted the water to a steady slow trickle before wetting her fingers, gently cleansing herself as she spoke.

'Do you trust me?' Charlotte asked then, avoiding Imogen's gaze, and the answer came back immediately.

'Yes. I do. After what's happened between us, after, well, you know what, I would've thought that question might be more apt coming from me,' Imogen said, the relief clear in her voice.

'I do trust you, dear, especially after what happened, but this is our last chance to know for sure. It could be we have noone left to trust but one another.'

Imogen nodded sadly, and Charlotte crossed to hug her, hold her close.

The kiss should have been brief, tense, but Charlotte knew her stern-faced friend needed it, always hid so much of her fear behind the facade she'd built brick by brick over so many years, so she maintained the contact, waited until the firm lips yielded and opened to allow her tongue to probe reassuringly.

The embrace was warm and they stood together, swaying gently in the candle-scented air, and she wished that Seona could be with them as they had been only a few nights previously. It had been so simple then.

Why had the years shattered their friendships, played so many games with them? Seona was somewhere in the building, perhaps waiting to see them, and she was surely confused, afraid, if not just downright treacherous. It was impossible to believe that the ruse had been so premeditated. They had learned the carnal arts together, watched one another strain with strange men and women, with instruments and machinery which tested their bodies to the limits of endurance, the borders between pain and pleasure traversed time and time again. They had shared those experiences, and to find now that they had drifted apart was utterly draining, deflating.

And yet, they were where they were. In a Pagoda built by a self-styled guru in the middle of nowhere, with no defence, no excuse and no clear reason should anything go wrong. She had never fully understood the concept of kismet, but now seemed as good a time as any to start giving it some credence.

And perhaps the concept of fate was enough then to bring her face down to Imogen's neck, to make her bite gently into the flesh as her own buttocks were kneaded firmly. They could do it to one another so swiftly, the buttons could be pressed so precisely that yes, it would be possible to bring one another off in minutes, perhaps even seconds, but she knew that Imogen knew there would be no satisfaction until the chore had been completed, the task put to bed.

And yet, the momentary suspension of one's flesh in the hands of another was so affirming, so positive, that she could not help but yield, and she brought her own hand back behind her to encourage Imogen's hard fondling, working harder with her own fingers to tease more of the breast-flesh from the stout leatherette holders. It could easily happen now, right now on the floor of this tiny room, and Dark Eyes, Seona, the Librarian and the rest of the world be damned.

Charlotte dropped her hand to Imogen's crotch and roughly grabbed her pouting sex, gasping into her friend's neck as she returned the gesture, both hands now working hard at their openings, fingers probing and parting. Their combined scent rose to her, strong and reeking of need, but there was a distant noise disturbing her, a gentle but persistent rhythm which didn't coincide with the pulse of Imogen's fingers.

It was a rapping at the door.

The shutter drew open slowly, and the time had come. Charlotte drew in a deep breath and caressed her friend's cheek, allowing her fingers to linger as Imogen closed her eyes and steeled herself, pursing her lips and frowning deeply, mentally psyching herself as she always did at moments of great stress.

Charlotte went first, and the walk, for once, was short – the shutter directly opposite the little room was open, and there at the far end of it, seated on a plain hard-backed chair, sat Dark Eyes.

She stopped at the doorway, Imogen just behind her. She'd imagined that she would surely go for him – at the very least she'd anticipated that he would receive a barrage of expletives such as he'd never experienced before.

But she felt nothing. Nothing at all. He was smiling, hands clasped together in his lap. The black silk robe was of precisely the same style as those he'd worn so many years ago. For all she knew it could have been exactly the same one.

She stepped forwards, and Seona came into view, also seated, to Dark Eyes' extreme left. There, on his right hand, the woman who had to be Kayla. At first sight she seemed plain, unremarkable, the fringe of the blonde wig closely shielding her eyes. About ten feet separated each of them, and the massive purple drapes that had been drawn across the wall and which continued at a gentle curve below the chairs to cover most of the floor space created a surreal sensation of the characters being somehow afloat or airborne, gently hovering in the deep solid colour.

The Librarian appeared from a door in the right-hand wall – she'd donned a simple pale blue robe and looked transformed again, probably because she'd finally been permitted to remove the hated belt. She moved across to join Seona, standing behind her, one hand placed on her scarlet-robed shoulder as Dark eyes stood, extending his open hands as if ready to receive Charlotte into his embrace.

She stayed stock-still, moving only her eyes – the character purporting to be Kayla was wearing a gown of startling white with some faint pale-blue pattern which caused the garment to virtually glow against the richly purple backdrop, and the petite woman appeared calm, her posture relaxed.

'Charlotte?' he said, as if testing that her presence was real. She turned to quickly check that Imogen was all right, and found that her friend's eyes had already brimmed with glistening tears and were focused on Seona.

She turned to face him again. The fury had died, but been replaced by something else, something more painful. The man was the same, had worn better than she expected, but the theatricality of the setting he'd created, the posing of these women who'd served him, followed his orders, attended to his needs through so many years? It was suddenly absurd and sad, and she knew that she and Imogen were every part as integral to the facade as he was.

'What do you want from us?' Charlotte asked, surprised that her voice now sounded so small and weak in the cavernous, shapeless room. He extended his arms again, tilted his head and smiled.

'What did I ever want? You,' he said.

Charlotte felt the weakness in her knees, the trembling of her thighs as the adrenalin started to course yet again. He was doing it. The hypnotic voice, the gentle movements, the avuncular tone he'd always adopted with them hadn't changed a bit. She stepped nearer, Imogen now right beside her, sniffing as she wept.

'I've been waiting so long,' he said, and the self-pity in his voice was perhaps genuine, but Charlotte was not hearing him now, was watching his lips move but ignoring the sounds he made. His eyes were absorbing, mesmerising, she had to get closer. Another two, three steps. He was less than ten feet away, so close now she could hear the gentle rasping of his breath as he inhaled hugely, eyes closed. Kayla crossed her legs, drawing Charlotte's attention, and she could see, so much closer now, how radiantly beautiful the young woman was, surely more beautiful than any of them had ever been? Perhaps not. Perhaps she, too, had possessed that aura. Her eyes were bright and clear, but Charlotte sensed the turbulence within the woman, the awful potential which lay in her – had he seen that quality in her also, so many years ago?

His hands were trembling slightly as he lowered them, and the welcoming smile faded as he realised she was not going to embrace him as he wished. Seona was sitting at the very edge of her chair, the Librarian's hand still placed on her shoulder, and when Charlotte caught her eye she looked down at the hands cupped in her lap. No need to even ask her now if the betrayal Charlotte feared was just some awful product of paranoia – why she'd done it was another matter, and one which could not be attended to right now.

He stepped forwards. Charlotte stood her ground, hands by her sides, Imogen still very close.

'You don't want me,' Charlotte said, unafraid now to stare right into the deep dark pupils – if anything she was now eager to see just how far he'd be prepared to go before accepting that she was not going to fall at his feet.

'I do, and you'll never know how much,' he replied, fingers slowly untying the robe-belt.

Charlotte avoided the temptation to look down, knew that he was going to open the robe. Imogen was now leaning on her, perhaps even hiding behind her, but Charlotte could not turn to assure her, dared not lose contact with his eyes.

No, she'd never been a prostitute, but only because he'd assured her so. She'd never been a pervert, but only because his tastes had made her extremes seem normal. The bastard held every memory of her prowess and progress within those dark, bottomless eyes and she could now, in all honesty and nakedness, acknowledge every single one of them. He had buggered her and seen her buggered, seen her punish and be punished in ways that most people would never dream, and yet, facing him now, she knew that she had worn the intervening years so much better than him, and he was now frail, weak and ready to fall, simply because he didn't know how strong she'd become.

Yes, she was stronger now, stronger than him, perhaps even stronger than he'd ever been, and with every passing fraction of a second she felt his power over her diminish.

He allowed the robe to fall open, and she was aware of his nakedness, the darkness at the edge of her vision where his pubic hair was, the flickering suggestion of a pale line below, but still she didn't take her stare away from the eyes she'd never been able to fully remember nor totally forget. He was close enough now that he could touch her if he wished, but she knew he wouldn't dare. Not now. Not until she looked away. Then, she knew, her challenge would have failed.

He glanced down, his eyes fixed on her feet, her boots, her thighs, so obviously coated and smeared with the discharge of others, her corseted waist, the flanging hips and smoothness of her hips, the raised breasts, tender and reddened and damp with perspiration. She could hear his breath quicken as he drank in her hair, the loose wisps about her ears and nape, the curve of her jaw-line, the colouring on her cheeks and eyes. Finally his eyes returned to look into hers, and she knew she had him.

The shudder which raced up her spine was a visceral signal that she was winning – he was losing control, the primal lust overriding any restraint he may have been capable of. He glanced down again, then looked back to her with the self-satisfaction she remembered witnessing so long ago. His cock must have been growing, swelling, but still she would not look down. He was enjoying the process more than enough for both of them, so she continued holding the steady examination of his eyes as he scanned her, waiting for him, daring him to look back at her again.

When he did, his breath now rasping louder and faster, she knew she had him. The pupils had dilated so fully that he appeared deranged, possessed, but she knew now how simple the explanation was.

'I want you,' he whispered, and she nodded slowly.

'Yes, I know.'

He smiled again as he stepped closer. The nudge at her bare belly was the head of his cock, already damp with pre-come, and the weight of it rested against her. He was waiting for her to do something, the next move would have to be hers.

'I'll do something to you,' she smiled, straining not to blink lest the spell be broken. She had him, and he didn't know it, was clueless – the excitement was emanating from him like static.

'Right now,' she continued, still quiet but loud enough for all to hear. 'I'll do it right now in front of all these people.'

He seemed to lurch slightly then, his dick pressing, sliding up to nudge the lower flange of her corset.

'I'll fuck you in a way you've never been fucked before, in a way you've never even imagined,' she said, her own voice wavering slightly as the tension built – she knew now what she had to do and how to do it, but if she lost control of his eyes for a second it would crash about her and the chance would be lost.

She brought her right hand in front of her, raising it to the base of his cock. With forefinger alone she pressed lightly against him, eyes still locked on his as she drew the digit slowly, then slower still as she progressed up the hardened central vein, lingering as she neared the peak of it.

'Would you like that? To be well and truly fucked as you never have been before?'

His eyes were glazing, coated and dulled as he nodded.

'Yes Charlotte, yes,' he gasped.

'Very well,' she replied, moving her face closer, closer again so that he was only inches from her.

'Fuck you,' she said, gently tapping at his solid cock-head with her finger as if flicking a stray hair from her face, before slowly pulling back her head and then turning away.

She heard the rasping grunt from him as she walked away, the embryonic roar strangled and choked in his throat. He was watching her leave, seeing her walk away from his power once and for all.

234

She turned at the door – he was on his knees, face raised to the ceiling, arms supporting his slender frame as his cock ejaculated strongly, the whiteness curling and curving in the air before affixing itself to the purple drapery and his own belly in turn, waving and spasming as it spat its final bursts.

He slumped back, eyes shutting as the Librarian rushed to tend to him. His hands came to his chest and he started to curl into a ball as the robe was used to cover him again, but Charlotte wasn't waiting any longer. She knew what she had to do next.

Crossing to the small blonde-wigged figure, she extended her hand.

'Your name is not Kayla. Your name is Kristina Maria Prystnykz. This is no place for you. Come with me. I will take you to England. You will be very well taken care of.'

The young woman gawped at the scene before her, the fallen Master who'd also made promises, the Librarian who'd sworn to defend her, protect her if anything happened to him.

'I don't know, I can't –' she stammered, but Charlotte grabbed her hand and hauled her from the seat, dragged her, still protesting, to where the Librarian was smoothing Dark Eyes' brow.

'I'm taking her with me,' Charlotte said, 'and you can't stop me. She's coming back home with me. I've a publishing deal set up for her and a friend. Should be quite a story. I'll be sure to send you a copy.'

The Librarian looked up, and there was no anger, no malice whatever – Charlotte could hardly believe that the woman was smiling.

'Your friend will be staying?' she asked, and Charlotte looked across to where Seona's head was buried in her hands as she sobbed.

'I guess so. If I'm not mistaken you're short of

someone to play Kayla and she seems rather keen. Aren't you, dear?'

Seona looked up, tears sheening her cheeks as she sniffed, 'I'm so sorry.'

Imogen started sobbing again. Charlotte led Kristina over to where Seona was still perched on the seat, and her friend cowered back, hands raised to her face as they neared.

'No need to be sorry, darling,' Charlotte soothed, the anger now calmed, the atmosphere suddenly normalised since Dark Eyes had collapsed, 'what goes around comes around. You're due a shot at it. You've had a miserable enough time at home with that buffoon of a husband. Stay here awhile and enjoy yourself. Seems a busy enough little place, I'm sure you'll have your hands full.'

Seona gazed up, her expression disbelieving, but Charlotte bolstered the smile and extended a hand to gently cup her friend's cheek.

'Come back home when you're ready,' she said before bending to kiss the crown of Seona's head.

'Oh!' Charlotte exclaimed as she turned, Kayla's hand still in hers, 'That reminds me. You'll be needing this.'

Charlotte raised her hands to claim the wig from Katrina, but it was Kayla who spoke as she backed off, her fingers already clamping the platinum hairpiece to her scalp.

'Leave it. It's mine. You don't know what I had to do to get this. I'm not giving it to anyone else. Ever!'

Charlotte felt the energy sap from her, despair clawing at her belly. She was getting so tired, so fucking tired, but she knew she couldn't leave her, not knowing what she knew now – would it be ten, fifteen years before this beautiful young girl finally realised what she was doing? It would be a crime to leave her, pure and simple.

'Please,' Charlotte pleaded, 'please don't be fooled, my dear. This man here, this place, this, this –' She gestured with open arms at the fake opulence, the utter sterility of it all, but she knew that the girl was seeing only freedom and power, the chance of a new life.

'You know that I've done this,' she said then, speaking quietly, although the others could hear in the deathly stillness of the room. 'I've done it and so has she. It's fun, yes, but the fun wears off and you want other things, you want normality. You'll never have that here. Never.'

'But I am Kayla,' the girl replied, fingers slowly descending from her scalp as she tried to straighten her posture, raise her chin. Charlotte shook her head, fought back the tears.

'No you're not, my dear,' she said softly, 'you are Katrina. You've done well, but there's nothing else to prove. Katrina can have a good life, Katrina can be free, have money and fun, all of those things. Perhaps, who knows, perhaps even love? But Kayla gets none of those things, not ever.'

As Katrina lowered her eyes and stood still, Charlotte stepped nearer and slowly, carefully removed the blonde hairpiece. She turned and placed it on Seona's head, tugging it roughly into place before standing back to admire it.

'Fits a treat,' she said merrily as she grabbed the girl's hand. 'Now, if you'll all excuse us, we really have to be getting home.'

Epilogue

Charlotte closed the book gently and passed it over the table to Imogen.

'If there's one thing I can't stand it's sloppy grammar. I know it's an advance copy, but really darling, you have to wonder what the world's coming to when simple dialogue can't be accurately transcribed.'

Imogen raised the hardback up and gazed at the picture on the back wistfully.

'She is gorgeous, though, isn't she?'

'Thoroughly,' Charlotte agreed, raising the napkin to her lips, gently pressing, 'but look, we really ought to get going, it'll be starting soon.'

'If only, if only –' Imogen sighed, and Charlotte frowned as the waiter neared with the coffees.

'If only what?' Charlotte whispered, exasperated. Imogen had only had three glasses of wine, but already she was getting frisky. It was going to be one of those nights.

'If only we'd had the foresight to do the same. I mean, can you imagine it? The adulation, the constant flash of cameras? The acclaim from critics worldwide? And the fan mail? I mean, good God, what must that be like?'

Charlotte suppressed the smile. Imogen had just agreed the divorce settlement, and her dearest old

Bobbo had finally agreed an eight-figure full-and-final hard-dollar payoff. What else she could find room to fantasise about was beyond reasoning, but there she sat, dreamy-eyed and pining for something she would never have.

'The whole idea is ghastly,' Charlotte cautioned in her sternest tone, 'and you're just upsetting yourself thinking about it.'

'You know as well as I do that we got up to some tricks in our time. I'm sure we could fill a volume or two.'

Charlotte sipped at the coffee and smiled, nodding.

'Absolutely. But some things are better left unsaid, correct grammar or otherwise.'

Imogen looked to the window, to the pulsing night-time London traffic sloshing its way through the pounding August shower, and Charlotte followed her gaze to watch the rushing bodies, the raised umbrellas swaying over their owners as they headed home. It would be dark soon and Kristina's book launch would start within the hour. It was indeed surreal, but stranger things had happened and would surely happen again. Life went on, surprising and appalling and wonderful by turns. Tonight happened to be one of the wonderful junctures, an evening when memories and dreams could happily collide in something realised, tangible – friends new and old could be remembered in celebration.

'Got a postcard from Seona this morning,' Charlotte said, her chin resting on a raised palm as they continued to study the passing human flow. 'She's in Toronto.'

'How horribly boring,' Imogen replied, and Charlotte focused on her friend's reflection in the window, returning the smile. 'God only knows where she'll end up next.'

'She's enjoying herself, that's the main thing,' Charlotte said, but Imogen was already laughing, replacing the coffee cup on its saucer before clapping her hands lightly together.

'And what does Blair make of all this?' she demanded, impatient. Charlotte waited, adopting a suitable expression of puffed-up gravitas before imitating his voice. 'Well, Charlotte dear, you have to understand that Seona is an independent character, very strong-willed you know, and if she wants to embark on a round-the-world tour at the drop of a hat, who am I to stop her?'

They were still laughing when the waiter brought the bill.

Kristina looked fantastic, although curiously tiny behind the piles of books that had been stacked on the table. The congo-line of customers snaked all the way through the store, but Charlotte and Imogen stayed well back, watching her sign and smile and pose for the cameras as Anton also looked on.

'How long to go now?' Charlotte asked. He nodded as he swallowed the wine, raising four fingers.

'Only a month to go now, God willing, we will have a baby. All she talks about is babies, baby this, baby that.'

'Sweet,' Charlotte said as Imogen grimaced.

'Beastly business altogether. Have you chosen a name yet?'

He looked to Imogen, then back at Charlotte warily, as though expecting a cruel joke.

'Well, no, we haven't decided yet. We don't want to, what is it now, we don't want to tempt fate.'

'Quite right too,' Charlotte agreed, 'but whatever happens, be sure to come and visit your Auntie Kaylas every now and then. You're just down the road for heaven's sake, and a beautiful house it is too, so there's no excuse.'

He nodded, blushing, shaking his head at the memories, the curious circumstances of their meeting.

'You know, if you hadn't jumped on top of me in that apartment, if you hadn't interrogated me –'

Charlotte placed a hand on his arm to stop him.

'I did, we did, you wrote it all down, changed the names. So what? It's all flatly unbelievable anyway, and that's precisely why it works so well as fiction. Besides, you couldn't have a more beautiful author to ghost for.'

'I guess,' he said, smiling and still shaking his head as if unbelieving that it really was happening.

They watched in silence as Kristina had a word with her agent – the middle-aged woman helped her get out of the seat and escorted her to the reserved area where her husband and friends were waiting. She kissed all of them in turn, leaving her husband until last, but she kept a tight grip on his hands as she stood.

'Thank you,' Charlotte said, raising her glass to Katrina as the others followed. The young pregnant woman looked confused, embarrassed.

'Thank you for what?' she asked. Charlotte took her hand and squeezed it gently.

'For years I was that woman, and I know it was real. I was real. But no one knew, no one cared. Now, you have both made her into wonderful fiction and for many thousands of people she is real. At last, she exists, her name can be spoken and the world knows it. We have you to thank for that.'

'But I have done nothing,' Kristina replied, looking to her husband.

'We have all done it,' Charlotte continued, 'we have all created her, we have all helped to kill her.

But now, her life or death is yours to decide. Good luck with her,' Charlotte said, the wine and nostalgia taking over as Imogen gripped her hand.

'You have a lovely evening,' said Imogen, drawing her friend away with her.

'You too,' said Anton.

'Don't worry,' Imogen said, winking at the young couple, 'we will.'

Seona brought the lash across the fat man's buttocks as he thrust into the tethered Librarian. He was enjoying himself and would soon be finished, dawn would break and a new day would start.

The heels were killing her and she was hungry. The constant travel was wearing her down and the company of the Librarian and her entourage was becoming tedious. Yes, they'd seen some nice places, had some wild nights and days here and there, but she was getting jaded. Even the thought of Blair, poor old decent ham-fisted totally predictable and oh-so-solemn Blair was enough to incite some flicker of excitement in her of late.

The Librarian's cries brought her back, and she looked down to see the man madly caressing her silk stocking-hems, his bloated torso bending in a vain effort to get his face near her behind as he continued the relentless burying of his manhood.

She brought the lash up behind her head and stepped back, putting as much as she could into the blow – the narrow leather bands whistled through the air and cracked onto his arse-flesh, eliciting a roar from him as he jerked away and deeper into the kneeling woman, his moans coinciding with hers as he responded with a series of shuddering thrusts. But still, as he resumed fucking at a slower pace, she realised that he hadn't come. She started to raise the lash again, then halted the motion – his pampered pale behind wouldn't take much more.

The article in the newspaper had been brief but shocking. *Sensational Debut.* A fantastic story about a legendary character, a female who made and broke governments, dynasties, and all at the hand of a mere stripling, a totally unknown Czech author.

Seona dropped the lash and left the Librarian to finish him off herself.

It was time for her to go home.

Also available from Nexus:

SWINGING

By Peter Birch

In *Swinging*, Nexus takes the theme of swinging sex a step further than usual, mixing up not only partners, but the sexes too. There's lots of variety between the eight stories, but all have one thing in common: girls are as likely to be with girls as they are with boys, as boys are with boys, in a no-holds-barred feast of uninhibited erotic story telling.

Authors include Monica Belle, with her boisterous tales of misbehaviour with lorry drivers, Zak Jane Kier with a story of what can happen with games of chance, and Paul Scott with all his usual enthusiasm for smutty suburban sex.

Available on ebook now

Also available from Nexus:

THE ACADEMY

By Arabella Knight

Miranda is a spoilt brat. Nothing Aunt Emma does seems to have any effect on her. There's only one thing to do: send the girl to the Academy, an educational establishment with a difference.

Under the steely direction of Mrs Boydd-Black, wayward young women like Miranda are taught how to behave correctly – and severe penalties await those who disobey…

Available on ebook now